The Extraordinary Untrue Life of

MIRAH DE ROTHSCHILD

VIVIEN HART

Copyright (c) 2024 Vivien Hart

All rights reserved. This book or any portion thereof may not be reproduced or used in any manner whatsoever without the express written permission of the publisher except for the use of brief quotations.

This is a work of fiction, and all depictions of historical figures are intended as fictional, for the purpose of entertainment only.

First Printing 2024

ISBN 9798882595325

For my son, Julian. My brave little warrior.
For my wife, Nirvana. For helping to edit, and always cheering me on.
And for my grandparents, Nellie and John. Told you I'd publish books for a living one day!

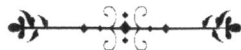

Rothschild, to come to the: *To brag and pretend to be rich.*
Victorian slang (supposedly...)

1

Mirah

The music hall never suffered a shortage of strange faces. There were rough-handed dockworkers who spent their wages in gin, a hardy, rambunctious bunch. Hardier and more rambunctious still were the painted dollymops on their arms, out of place in the colourful silks they had doubtless haggled for at Spitalfields with mercenary ferocity. A seaman complained to me once that they'd bite your hand off if you so much as brushed their shoulder without paying for the pleasure. He sported a nasty scratch to prove it, and I hadn't pitied him one bit. Didn't help that he stunk of fish from the boots up. I wouldn't want him 'brushing my shoulder', either.

Sometimes it was migrants, recently in off the boats, come only for a stiff drink, or a roof, or an hour in the warmth. Sometimes well-bred gentlemen, making the risky foray into Limehouse for a glimpse of bare calf. You could spot those sorts a mile out - too spruce, too eager, flashing their coins with the witless air of one destined to be mugged on the way home.

I was well-acquainted with all these different characters, could tell them apart at a glance.

That was why the woman sitting in the front row stuck out like a sore thumb.

She wore only black, an intricately beaded capelet around her shoulders. A veil covered her face, held there by a small hat, tipped fashionably over her forehead. She sat stiffly, as though in pain, gloved hands relentlessly twisting and untwisting a piece of paper in her lap.

Despite the veil and the darkness of the auditorium, the strange woman's eyes bore into me so intensely there could be no mistake she was staring. Being watched was the point in a place like this, but the veiled woman wasn't watching. She was *staring,* and it made my skin prickle. All through my dirty little limerick she stared, and as I sang, voice half mangled beneath the jaunty piano tune, I tried valiantly not to stare back.

What business could a woman like that have in a place like this? My imagination spun with theories, each more deliciously lurid than the last. She was here because she hoped to catch her husband in the audience, debasing himself. She was here because she admired pretty women as a man would, but couldn't risk openly lusting after her own sex. Or she was simply here because she'd gotten very lost indeed.

Not a moment too soon the last long note of the song rang out, the dusty velvet curtain creeping sluggishly across the stage. I disappeared behind it with a flourish to the scattered applause and jeers of a handful of patrons, for once immeasurably grateful to be backstage.

The music hall lived a thousand different lives before this one. A gin palace, a brothel. The ornate interior of the former lent it a veneer of elegance, if one didn't look too closely at the gold rubbing off, and the mirrored walls and colourful globe lamps of the latter lured many a man in on the promise of exotic delights. The tall ceiling served well, too, allowing for the instalment of a gallery. Wooden columns painted deep plum, 'like a real theatre', Oliver said. Before these different incarnations it had been a humble warehouse, used to store whatever cargo came in off the nearby docks. It was an unassuming, empty shell, which over the years became corrupted. A fitting, four-walled portrait of life in Limehouse.

Shaking off the feeling left by the mystery woman in the audience, I headed straight for the dressing room, a closet shared by all the performers that boasted a single mirror and toilette table squeezed between rails of costumes. Cora was already there preparing to go on next, draped in a vibrant fuchsia saree, embroidered along the hem with a hundred pinchbeck sequins that rustled as she twisted on the stool to look at me.

"Difficult crowd?"

Cora and I were as close as two people could be in a music hall, yet I knew barely anything about her. It was how we did things, here. No one asked anyone anything about themselves they didn't offer up freely. She once divulged to me that 'Cora' was, unsurprisingly, not the name her North Indian parents had given her, but never gave me the satisfaction of knowing the name they had.

"Barely a crowd at all," I said, fumbling with my earrings. "Like performin' to a cemetery."

"That why you're white as a ghost?"

I averted my eyes, painfully aware of Cora's on me in the mirror. It took all my resolve not to snap at her. There was only so much staring a girl could take, and I'd more than had my fill for one night. "I'm feelin' unwell. That's all."

"Poor dear. Was it them oysters Oliver brought? They kept Sabrina hostage in the privy all night, poor thing. Glad I didn't touch 'em."

"Maybe. I don't know."

"I'd stay and cosset you if it would do any good, but I have to work." She gestured to a bottle and half-empty glass on the table. "Get some gin down you. Cure for anythin'." With that she rose from the stool, pecked my cheek, and hurried off towards the stage, the bells around her ankles tinkling.

I listened until her footfalls faded and the music started up again before sinking forwards onto my elbows on the toilette table, head in my hands. Perhaps I'd imagined the staring woman. It wouldn't come as a great shock if I was losing my mind. Sleep was hard to come by lately, between the racket of the streets and the sound of Caleb's hacking cough growing more and more pronounced each night. Caleb hadn't admitted to being sick yet. I wouldn't be shocked if he was on his deathbed before uttering the suspicion that he had a touch of something nasty. I didn't need him to admit it. I heard it all night, a hollow bark wrenched up out of the deepest part of his chest, painful to listen to. It kept me tossing and turning on my straw mattress into the small hours, every cough a pin to the temples.

It wasn't beyond the pale to hallucinate on so little rest. Maybe Cora was right, and gin was the cure. It would certainly put me to sleep.

"Mirah?"

I jolted upright, spinning around on the stool. Oliver was leaning in the doorway of the dressing room, bowler hat sitting crooked on his golden-mopped head. His cologne was so strong I could taste it on the roof of my mouth.

"Oliver. I was just about to come lookin' for you..."

"No need. Cora caught me on her way past, told me you're unwell."

"Unwell? Nah." I affected a smile, glad of the theatre rouge on my cheeks for masking my pallor. "Just tired. Been workin' every night for a month, and my brother's sick..."

"No rest for the wicked, they say."

"Who'd want to rest, when they could be here?" I paused. "It's that time of the week, isn't it?"

Oliver's eyes narrowed. "Aye." He produced a coin purse from his pocket, counted out a sum, and held out his hand towards me like a trapper beckoning a hungry stray dog. I practically leapt to take what was offered, face falling as the pitiful stack of coins was tipped into my palm.

"That's it?"

"It's been a quiet week," Oliver said. "We're all fighting for scraps here, Mirah. You know how it works. We split it all equally."

"All but the work. You aren't the one up there every night with old men leerin' at you."

"No," Oliver agreed. "I get that elsewhere."

I couldn't argue that. Oliver managed much of what happened in the music hall, but he paid his way mostly as a renter over in Piccadilly Circus, entertaining men for a shilling a turn. I didn't envy him. I had experience with the profession myself. Everyone and their mother knew what 'actress' really meant this side of London.

"This won't even cover coal," I mumbled, moving the pennies about in my hand, as if by doing so they might mate and reproduce. "It's gettin' colder. My brother needs a fire and a doctor."

Oliver rested the back of his head against the doorframe, nudging his bowler hat even further forwards. He sighed, dipping his hand into the purse again. "Here," he said, tossing me sixpence. "That's as much as I can spare. I've no desire to see you in the gutter, Mirah. The gents like you. You've got good legs."

"I'm pleased my legs can move you to charity." I smiled weakly. "Thank you, Oliver..."

"Just keep turning up and singing your parts. Got you in mind for a breeches role next. Sailor suit and cap, singing a naval tune, all innuendo and the like."

I made a mock salute. "I'll be first on deck."

"Good girl." Oliver pocketed the coin purse, eyeing me up and down. "Hurry out of your costume, now. Those dresses are expensive, I don't want 'em creased. Oh, and there's a woman outside wantin' to meet you."

I froze in the process of unbuttoning my bodice. "A woman?"

"Proper fancy lookin'. No wagtail, that's for sure. A lady o' means."

"Is she wearin' black?"

Oliver tilted his head. "You know her?"

"No. She was watchin' me on stage."

"Maybe you have an admirer. I'll let her know you'll be with her shortly."

I thanked him, and then he was gone, whistling a tune as he went. I changed out of the stage gown, placing it back where it belonged. Putting on my own red poplin dress was the reverse transformation of a butterfly back into a drab caterpillar. Catching a glimpse of myself in the mirror as I collected my things, I saw how pale and drawn I looked. Perhaps I ought to have taken a lesson from the staring woman and donned a veil of my own. Or maybe I should have just eaten the spoiled oysters and stayed at home.

2

Mirah

My nerves were a tangled ball of yarn walking into the hallway to meet my guest, but when I got a look at the woman, I was relieved to find her just as anxious. The stranger still wore her veil – perhaps to hide her terror, since Limehouse's reputation preceded it – but she was pacing now, back and forth, gloved hands still twisting the piece of paper she'd been toying with in her seat. She stopped when she noticed me. For a few deeply uncomfortable seconds neither of us spoke as I weighed how to address her. Finally, I curtsied.

"Ma'am."

The woman recoiled. "There's really no need for that."

"Forgive me." I rose. "I didn't mean to offend you."

"You didn't." The woman's voice did not match her stature. It was tricky getting the measure of her from the stage, but up close she was slight, a blackbird feather at risk of being carried away by a strong gust of wind. She was nothing like me. I stood nearly six feet tall, something some men complained intimidated them. I always did like that.

"I was told you wished to meet me," I said, after another drawn out silence.

"Yes. Your show was wonderful. You have a sublime singing voice."

"Inherited it from my ma. She was an opera girl in her youth."

"I'm sure she's very proud of you."

"She died when I was ten."

Though I couldn't see the woman's face it was immediately clear she was embarrassed. Her fists tightened on the paper. "I'm sorry, I should not have assumed..."

"You couldn't have known. It's no matter."

"It was still impolite. If it is not too bold of me to ask, what happened to her?"

"Limehouse."

"Limehouse? I'm afraid I don't quite follow."

"Limehouse killed her." I shrugged. "The water, or the air, or the rats. Not certain which. She caught a sickness and was gone within three days. Very quick, mind."

"That is positively awful. Forgive me for prying."

"Forgiven. What can I do for you, Miss?"

The stranger was quiet for a moment. When she spoke again her voice was smaller. "I have a proposition for you."

So that was it, then. My second theory proved true. This woman was the inverted sort and had taken a shine to me and my long legs. It had never happened before, but Oliver would be pleased it wasn't only the gents who appreciated them.

"I'm open to hearin' whatever proposition you wish to make," I said, bringing one hand to rest lightly on the woman's forearm. I traced the delicate black beading on the sleeve of her gown with my fingertips, marvelling at it. The beads were real jet, not the tawdry painted glass that adorned my own costumes. "My time's valuable, but we can discuss a price. I understand a woman like yourself might not carry coins, but perhaps you have a token you could bestow me. A piece of jewellery, maybe..." My eyes found the glint of a gold brooch, hidden beneath the hem of the woman's capelet. Something like that would fetch a handsome price at a jerryshop. I could hire three different doctors for Caleb with that sort of money.

Understanding landed slowly on the stranger. She jerked away, breath hitching into an indignant squeak. "It is not like *that!* I am *not*...that is not what I'm here for!"

I retracted my hand at once. "I must've misunderstood."

"You most certainly did!" With a single angry flick of her hand, the woman lifted the veil from her face to show her outrage in full.

She was startlingly pretty, like one of the dolls I'd coveted in shop windows as a child but could never afford. Her face was a soft oval, her eyes dark and long lashed, crowned with thin black eyebrows that sat very neat and straight on her forehead. Her lips were pink, her cheeks too, and I didn't suppose a woman so well-bred designed to use rouge, so the flush had to be natural, utterly charming in its authenticity. Her hair was sleek and black as ink, a great monument of coiled tresses wrapped around each other like snakes, lifted high to expose a long, pale neck. I couldn't help staring.

"If you're going to insult me," the woman said breathlessly, "I will leave."

"It wasn't an insult. There's nothing insultin' about desire."

The woman turned pinker still. "It's not appropriate."

"Perhaps not. What's your proposition, then? Are you a patron of the arts, come to scout me for the opera your husband is fundin'?"

"I've no husband, and no opera. What I do have is a brother."

"I suffer the same affliction myself. Mine's a bore. Very stern, too observant. Could've made a rabbi of him if he had the inclination." I frowned. "Are you propositionin' me on your brother's behalf, then? That's a new one! You two must be very close."

"They're very nice. You must look a real lady in them."

I scoffed. "Now it's you insultin' me."

The woman whirled to face me. "I meant no such thing! I ask because – well, never mind. You wish to hear my proposition?"

"I'm positively wastin' away with curiosity."

She took a few deep breaths and began to pace as she had in the hallway. "Where to start."

"The beginnin', perhaps."

"Very well." She smoothed out the skirts of her gown and raised her chin as though to deliver a monologue, and I had the novel sensation of being in the audience for once, watching the tragic Shakespearean heroine plead her case. "My father is a wealthy man. Very wealthy. He made our fortune in moustache wax."

"Moustache wax? Really?"

"Are you familiar with Acker's Patented Moustache Colourant and Wax?"

"I don't think I'm really the target clientele," I said. "You couldn't come up with a name that was less of a mouthful?"

"I didn't choose the name!" the woman snapped. "Father did. Acker was my mother's maiden name. Only right that he used it, since it was her money that launched the enterprise."

"Acker wasn't the part I had a dispute with."

"Well, that's how we made our money. It is my brother Ernest who puts it all at risk. He has never contributed to the business but spends the allowance Father grants him freely. He passes all his time at his gentlemen's clubs, he gambles, he drinks, he – *whores*." She lowered herself to a whisper on the word, as if she feared offending my delicate sensibilities. "He is a bad man, and as it stands, will inherit almost everything when Father passes. Time is running out. My father is sick. When he dies Ernest will ruin us within a year. I am confident of it."

"Your father not leavin' you anythin' of his moustache wax empire?"

"Nothing I consider of real value. Jewellery, furniture, paintings. The bulk of the fortune was invested into real estate, and I cannot inherit that unless Ernest is written out of the will. If he inherits the properties he'll sell them off and fritter the money away."

"So where do I enter into this?" It was marvellous to me that this trembling wisp of a woman had concocted a solution to her problem, one which required her to go slinking around the darkest parts of London unaccompanied. She may have been small, but I couldn't call her a coward by any stretch.

"I need you to seduce him."

"Your brother?"

"Yes. Seduce him, make him love you, convince him to marry you. Then I will reveal it all to my father, who disdains scandal above all else, and he will cut Ernest off with a shilling. I'll inherit instead of him, and the family fortune will not be squandered away in some gin shop or brothel!"

"Squandered on women like me, you mean."

The woman came up short, red-faced again. This time I was neither charmed nor moved by her embarrassment. The woman had to be joking. What she was asking was no small favour – to seduce and ruin a man was one thing, but marry him? To expect me to willingly shackle myself to a man she herself just called a wretch? Marriage was a chain not easily broken, and it was always the woman who came out worse off.

"I understand it is crass," the woman said. "But you would be perfect for the position."

"Position!" I laughed. "As though you're hirin' a housemaid and not a sister-in-law! You haven't even told me your name!"

"Eloise," the woman answered. "Eloise Byron. No relation to the notorious poet," she added, swiftly.

"And your brother's name is Ernest? *Earnest* Byron?" I laughed harder. "There's two words in the English language that've never been bedfellows before!"

"I tell you we're of no relation!"

"Whatever you say. No wonder your brother's a scoundrel. Well, Miss Byron-of-no-relation, I'm sorry you haven't had any luck findin' a suitable unsuitable bride for him, but I don't believe you'll have much more with me. I've no desire to be married."

"It wouldn't be a real marriage," Eloise said. "You would wed under a false name, so it would not be legally binding. Not to mention I would pay you. I am willing to offer as much as ten percent of my estate. That's more than enough money to keep you comfortable for the rest of your days."

I wasn't convinced I hadn't gone mad after all. Perhaps I was imagining all of this, just as I thought I'd imagined Eloise to begin with.

"How many other girls have you asked?"

"Seven."

"And why'd they turn you down?"

"They didn't," Eloise said. "I turned them down after speaking with them. I found them all lacking."

"Lackin' what?"

"What it would take to win my brother's affections."

"Good legs?"

"The manners, the decorum. You would have to present yourself as a lady."

"You might want to look someplace other than Limehouse."

"I would help with the act," Eloise said. "Buy you dresses, jewels. Have you taught everything required to fool him. He would not willingly marry a..." She tapered off, her brain working hard to choose her words. I decided to be merciful and do it for her.

"An actress."

"Precisely, yes. He must think you are from a good family." Eloise twisted the paper again. Watching her doing it was starting to send me loopy, and I'd a good mind to snatch it from her. "Forgive me, Miss...?"

"Zelikovich," I said. "Mirah Zelikovich."

"Is that Russian?"

"It's my name, that's all I know."

"Your accent was different on stage. It sounded French, not...."

"The Gutter?" I smirked. "I'm good at accents. That's what happens when you live everywhere as a child."

"You're Jewish, though?"

"Taxonomically."

"I don't understand."

"I am," I said, with a wave of my hand. "But not half as observant as my brother would like."

"I see. You really won't consider my proposition?"

"I'm sorry. I don't wanna be caught up in this. Don't you realise how it would look if we were caught? You might suffer in society, but for me it would be Newgate! Besides, folks think bad enough of Jews as it is." I often kept to myself for that very reason, but I'd heard the insults levied against my brother for going about with his skullcap on. "Can you imagine the papers? A schemin' Jewess conspirin' to trick a wealthy Anglican gentleman out of his inheritance? I'm afraid you'll have to look elsewhere for your girl, Miss Byron. I don't fancy being in the employ of a madwoman, and that's what you are if you think this plot could work."

Eloise bit her lower lip hard enough that I was tempted to warn her against wounding her pretty mouth, but she did not push or protest as I expected. She nodded, pulling her veil back over her face and barring me from was doubtful. There were six years between Caleb and I, and my hair was yellow next to his coal black, our curls the only thing we shared. Regardless, as a small child I'd been just as invested in this cross-country manhunt as Ma, convinced on the promise of bonbons and ponies that we had to find him and make him love us.

The man's last known whereabouts were London, and as always, we'd followed, settling in a leaky building in Limehouse. Many nights Ma would go out in her one fine evening gown and attempt to make an entrance at whatever social function he was attending, calling herself his wife. 'Mrs Hughes', she said, insisting Caleb take the name for himself. She never returned successful, but occasionally brought home a souvenir – sometimes a handful of sugared almonds wrapped in a handkerchief for Caleb and me, sometimes a black-eye or split lip.

She was so hopelessly naïve, so pathetic in her passions, that I'd vowed I'd never be like her. I'd followed her onto the stage, yes, but I'd sworn off the charms of men for life. It was easily done when they had so few of them.

In short, I might well have been the best candidate for Eloise Bryon's scheme she'd find this side of London. I wondered what it would be like to walk in her world the way Ma said I was owed, to waltz in grand ballrooms and ride in tandem carriages with liveried grooms. The streets of Mayfair were well lit and clean, dazzling stages illuminated with colour and elegance. Limehouse was a pit of human misery, a dark whirlpool that sucked down all who resided there and spat out their bones. Suffering was everywhere, mixed into the mortar of the buildings, soaked into the wood of the docks with the smell of the Thames. It was in the alleyways and the gin shops, in the warehouses and tenements, in the gaunt, hungry faces of the people who called it home. I knew it was in my own face too, hardened traces lurking under my pearl powder. It was in Caleb's face as well, but he bore it like a battle standard. He was convinced the world would change for the better. I often joked he'd have been happier in the Paris Commune than Limehouse. He had a confrontational fire in his blood that had never been granted purpose to blaze into an inferno, forcing him to permanently smoulder. I called it his French streak.

It was still raining as I made my way through the streets towards our building, a damp, unpleasant drizzle hanging in the air and turning my hair into a mane. It was always difficult to see the sky through the London smog, thick and foul and at times curiously yellow. It didn't abate even by night, and if the moon were full and beautiful above, I wouldn't have known. The only light in Limehouse come nightfall was cast by the few lanterns hanging outside businesses, the occasional candle in a window. It wasn't a savoury enough place to be granted the benefit of street lighting, save a few gaslamps spaced sixty feet apart from each other, tiny beacons for a lost traveller to aim for. Drunk gin palace patrons turned to stumbling moths once the sun set.

I slipped nimble footed along the docks, past the hydraulic cranes that sat dormant by the basin. They were giant, sleeping monsters, jutting hard and sharp against the night sky, cold metal bones somehow even blacker than the darkness enveloping them. The waves of the Thames lapped softly against the docks, a gentle hissing interrupted by the occasional slap of water hitting brick or wood.

The building we lived in was a narrow, top-heavy thing, crammed between two others and close enough to the basin that we were often kept awake by squabbling gulls. It was always noisy even in the dead of night, the sounds of our neighbours seeping through the paper-thin walls. A coughing fit from one, a baby crying from another. Shouting, wailing, and the yapping dog in the flat beneath ours that Caleb swore a dozen times he would throttle. I didn't imagine Miss Eloise Bryon drifted off to sleep to the same tune in whichever pristine part of London she called home.

Our flat was on the third floor with only a single garret room above, rented out by a lone dockworker who crashed about upstairs at odd hours. Beneath us was a young Irish family of five, owners of the dog, and beneath the family of five an elderly Chinese couple who sat up late into the night making matchboxes. All of us, however different, united by a shared hatred of our accommodation.

A familiar light filtered out onto the floor of the hallway beneath the door of our flat, and as I let myself in I braced myself for the usual scolding. I made it all of three steps before my brother's voice reached me from the tiny dinner table.

"You're late."

"I know." I shed my tasselled shawl, hanging it on the hook by the door where Caleb's coat and cap were already waiting in silent judgement. I'd a mind to take the shawl up again the moment I removed it. It was cold in the flat, the range in the fireplace having cooled since being used to cook. "It's difficult, you know, walkin' back in the dark."

"If you'd been here on time you wouldn't have been walking in the dark," Caleb countered. "I had to start without you."

"A cryin' shame," I said. He was seated at the table, the light from the two candles placed there gilding his dark curls where they fell into his face, which was so stern and impassive even the Shabbos candlelight did it no favours. The smell of dinner made my stomach rumble. Friday night necessitated the best meal of the week, and even if I didn't care for the ritual of it all, it *was* a crying shame that I should be late and the food cold by the time I reached home. "Did you save me anythin'?"

"Of course." Caleb's brows furrowed. "You missed the blessings."

"The Almighty'll understand, I'm sure. He could try employin' some patience, for once."

Caleb let out a disapproving huff, silently sliding a plate towards me as I joined him at the table. Fish, fried on a bed of rice, both of which could be bought cheaply in Limehouse.

"How was your day?" I asked, draining what was left of the wine in our silver-plated kiddush cup, the one remotely valuable possession Ma left us. Caleb snatched it back.

"Fine. I've been given a new manuscript to translate."

"Is it long?"

"Seventy pages or some."

"That'll pay well."

"You'd hope, wouldn't you?" Caleb pushed what remained on his plate around with his fork. "I've had to lower my rates to get work."

That didn't bode well for the coming winter. While I made my money on the stage Caleb earned his with the pen, translating various documents into French. It was menus most of the time, English proprietors of atrocious French-pretender restaurants and cafes who wished their menus to appear authentic. They never had a half clue what they actually said, and more times than I could count I'd begged Caleb to write something outrageously funny. But that would have required my brother having a sense of humour, and was therefore about as likely as a second parting of the Red Sea.

"We'll find a way to get by," I said. "We always do, don't we?"

"How are things at the theatre?"

He always called it a theatre rather than a music hall. It was less seedy, implied a level of acclaim it could never dream of. I wagered it was easier for him to picture me singing in a glorious opera than reciting uncouth limericks in nought but my underpinnings. Often I wondered if he knew what else I sometimes did to secure the rent. He couldn't have been totally oblivious when I disappeared to the Holborn casinos, or fell out of a hansom cab coming home from Cremorne Gardens at the breaking of dawn's back. If he suspected anything he never alluded to it. I was glad. It would have been unbearably awkward for us both.

"Quiet," I said. "It's been quiet a good while now."

"Ah." Caleb drummed his fingers against the tabletop. "Things will pick up."

I nodded. I was aware we were both lying to each other. Caleb knew it as surely as I did. It had become as much of a ritual as the sabbath blessings, lately.

The silence jolted abruptly into a harsh, painful sounding cough as Caleb suddenly hunched over in his chair. I rose, rushing around to him. He shooed me away.

"Let me alone," he wheezed, between barks. "I'm fine."

"You're ill."

"It's only a chill."

"Then let me light the fire," I begged. "We've a little coal. You need to be warm."

"I don't need a fire. I'll be fine once I'm in bed, underneath my quilt."

I had doubts aplenty, but I didn't voice them. It would have been wasted breath. Caleb possessed a remarkable ability to tune out anything he didn't want to hear. He was sick. He didn't need to say it, and I didn't need to be a doctor to know it.

"You should do that, then," I said weakly. "It's gettin' late."

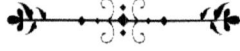

I didn't sleep, lying awake on my straw-stuffed mattress listening to Caleb's lungs rage against him. We shared a room, an issue of great contention, with two single beds on metal frames, separated by a calico curtain that could be drawn between them to give the illusion of privacy. There was no such thing. Caleb could bury himself beneath his sheets and try to muffle his coughing in his pillow all he liked, but I heard every hitching breath, every squeak at the back of his throat. So clear I could almost feel it myself. It was worse tonight, I was sure. Worse than last night, which itself was worse than the night before. From a tickle at the end of summer to this now that frost hung in the air.

I wracked my brain for ways to pay a doctor. Selling my hair was an option. Society ladies were scrambling for hairpieces as fashion demanded more and more of it be piled upon their heads, and my natural ringlets and deep golden colour were sought after. It would fetch a pretty penny, but even then I wasn't sure it'd cover a doctor's fees. There would be the expense of medicine too, and I'd need more coal for the fire to keep him warm as he recovered. My hair was only gold in colour, not worth.

I turned over on my side, slinging one arm over the edge of the bed and pawing around for my clothes. Unlike Caleb, who folded everything with military precision, I was in the habit of discarding my clothes wherever I shed them – a practice picked up from the music hall, where I had to change my skin with a moment's notice. I located my bodice in the dark, feeling out the holes I'd cut into the lining to hide things. My fingertips brushed what I was searching for: the dog-eared, tightly folded slip of paper Miss Eloise Byron gave me. I couldn't make out the address in the pitch black, but I held it anyway, clutching it to my chest with both hands and staring up at the ceiling.

Eloise's idea was ludicrous. It couldn't possibly work, and the danger was great. She could be lying, for a start. Planning to point the finger at me once she had what she wanted. Even if she wasn't, I'd face prison if Eloise panicked and revoked her protection. It was a risk. Too much of a risk for me to give it any real consideration.

Caleb coughed again, and the sound twisted in my chest like a knife beneath my ribs.

4
Eloise

It was neither usual nor seemly for a woman of my station to enter through the street-door - but then nothing of this entire unpleasant business was usual or seemly. That didn't mean I had to enjoy feeling like a servant, even though I may as well have been one. I was the most thankless servant of all: a daughter. I worked myself tirelessly as a mule to maintain our place in the world, and never saw a shred of gratitude for it.

Susanna met me at the door, hastily taking my hat and capelet. "Your father has been asking for you, Miss," she said. "He's had another of his rages. The doctor left, saying he won't come again. Claims he's fed up with the abuse."

I sighed, pulling off my gloves one finger at a time and passing them to her. "What happened?" I asked, leading the way into the now deserted kitchen.

"Your father threw a whiskey glass at him, I'm told."

"Did it have any whiskey in it, this time?"

"I wouldn't know, Miss. You'd have to ask Sophie, she's the one who cleaned it up."

"Poor dear. Where is my brother in all of this?"

"He's still not back, Miss."

"It's been three days. He must be curled up in the corner of some gambling house." I shook my head. "Any letters?"

"No, Miss. I went to the boutique earlier and asked, but Signora Moretti says nothing has come for you. It'll be soon, I'm sure. One of the girls you interviewed will agree. It's too good an offer to turn down."

"And too great a risk to take up. I'm beginning to think I was a fool for even contemplating it. I met a young lady tonight who would be perfect, and she rightly told me I was a madwoman."

Susanna tutted. "That was unnecessary."

"But possibly correct. I will see to Father before I retire."

"He's in a foul mood, Miss..."

"I'm the only one who can bear to put up with him," I called back over my shoulder. "He's never half so foul for me!"

It was swelteringly hot inside Father's bedchamber. Day and night a fire burned in the wide marble fireplace, never permitted to cease. Servants were on a constant rotation of checks throughout the night to be sure it did not die. Even the light in the room was warm, gaslamps burning, candles flickering along the mantle. The flames reflected in the polished wood of the armoire, the chest of drawers, the writing bureau he no longer sat at. All the windows were shuttered despite Doctor Hartley's advice to keep them open.

"Close that damn door!" he barked as I entered. "You'll let all the warmth out!"

"It's me, Father."

"Eloise?" A small, soft grunt of acknowledgement. "Where have you been?"

"I went to the theatre." It wasn't a lie, if one stretched the meaning of the word to the point of breaking.

"Alone?"

"I took Susanna with me." I sat down on the edge of the bed, feather mattress dipping beneath me. He was bundled up like a fussy babe, dressed in a cap and a crisp linen nightshirt, a burgundy quilted robe over the top. It was a wonder he hadn't overheated, but perhaps it was his left leg that kept him cool, free of the covers and propped up on a tower of pillows. His gout had flared up with a vengeance, and his loosely bandaged foot peeked out of its dressing, red and swollen as a balloon.

"You should not go out so late," he said. "I missed you here." He turned his head on his pillow to look at me. His face was ashen, and his silver hair, once dark like my own, was plastered to his forehead in sweaty strands. I remembered the days when the respectable Ambrose Byron was plump, with a healthy flush in his cheeks and thick muttonchops. Now he was gaunt, and there was none of the quickness left in his eyes, save for fleeting moments he chose to waste on a cutting remark. His facial hair remained, though it too had turned grey. Often I could scarcely believe I was looking at my father.

"I'm sorry," I said. "I'm here now though, aren't I? Susanna tells me you threw a glass at Doctor Hartley."

"Oh, don't you start on me too! I had every reason. Old quack thinks he can peddle his snake oil to me!"

"Doctor Hartley has been with our family for years, Father," I reminded him. "He delivered both Ernest and me. He's nursed our family through every sickness."

"He's lost his touch!" Father snapped. "Where *is* your brother?"

I squeezed my hands into balls in my lap. "Ernest is busy. He went out three days ago and has not yet returned. No doubt he will stagger home in a deplorable state."

Father chuckled. I had never hated the sound more. "He's a young man of means," he said, lifting one weak hand to wave away my concerns with infuriating nonchalance. "It is what young men of means do. Your Uncle Horace and I were just the same at his age."

"He is a disgrace, Father. He shames us both."

"He'll grow out of it."

"He's nearly thirty," I countered. "When will he grow out of it? Forty? Fifty? When he repents on his deathbed?"

"You concern yourself too much with this, child. So long as he does not permanently stain our name a young man is allowed some questionable freedoms, before marriage. When I pass from this world –"

"Don't talk like that, Father."

"– when I pass from this world," Father continued, "Ernest shall mature upon inheriting my estate. Responsibility, that's what he needs. He lacks it at present, but mark me, he'll come around."

"And if he doesn't?" I challenged. He closed his eyes and did not answer. "Father..."

"I need to rest, dear one. If you are so concerned for your future, perhaps it is time we see about finding you a husband."

"I don't want a husband."

"Then trust in your brother. He loves you."

I wrestled constantly with that notion. As children we were close, but even as a little girl I'd been acutely aware of the difference in our roles. As the longed-for son and heir Ernest had been permitted every liberty. Whenever I misbehaved, stealing from the pantry or playing tricks on the staff, I'd been scolded for my unladylike comportment. Ernest was a rascal, and I was a villain. Somehow that persisted even now, only Ernest was still a rascal and I had graduated to an old nag.

I had no doubt things would be very different if *I* were the one spending night after night hunched around gaming tables, slinking home at dawn too drunk to walk straight. I was a very reasonable person on most fronts, but that Ernest should be granted immunity based solely on a pathetic little worm between his legs set an indignant fire within me that I feared would one day consume me, and possibly the whole house, too.

"You're right, Father," I said, instead of the myriad of other things I wished to say. "You should rest. I'll see to it you aren't disturbed."

"There's a good girl," Father rasped. "You always were so well-behaved, weren't you?"

I wondered if the question was supposed to be rhetorical, for it was difficult to say. He'd not been around much when I was a child, busy with the business, so there was a very real chance he had no idea and wished for me to clarify.

"Always." I pressed a kiss to his clammy forehead, left the bed, and left the room, the skirt of my gown whispering on the floor as I went.

I had barely closed the bedchamber door when one of the maids went hurrying past with a basket of clean laundry, visibly nervous.

"Sophie?" I reached out to catch her arm. "Is something the matter? Is Mrs Sharp in a temper again?"

I detested Mrs Sharp, our strict, hawk-eyed old housekeeper. She had been with us so long that she still saw Ernest and me as children, and treated us thus, taking it upon herself to chide us in our mother's absence. She walked the halls of the house like a spectre, silent but for the tinkling of the silver chatelaine at her waist, heavy with a hundred different keys. I was looking forward to sending the old bat away for good when Father passed. She must have known, for she was tellingly cautious around me of late, the way an ailing king's favourite might attempt to ingratiate themself with his successor.

There was a crash from downstairs, something delicate and porcelain meeting an untimely end. Sophie flinched, and I understood at once.

"My brother is home, then?"

Sophie nodded. "He's drunk," she said, leaning in to murmur it. "And in a rotten mood, at that."

"He must have had bad luck at the card table again," I mused. "You'd think he'd have become accustomed to losing by now. Stay out of his way, I will manage him."

"Thank you, Miss." Sophie approximated a curtsy with some difficulty and rushed off to do her work.

I found Ernest lying on his back in the middle of the vestibule, one arm stretched out on the Persian rug, the other draped over his face as though the gentle, shimmering light from the gaslamps was too bright for his eyes. Shattered pieces of porcelain littered the floor, the sad remnants of the once very pretty vase that sat on the console by the front door. I stopped halfway down the stairs, gripping the polished banister with one hand.

"Ernest."

Ernest's slack body startled into animation. He pushed himself up onto his elbows and twisted to look at me, eyes so red-rimmed that even in the dimly lit vestibule I could tell he hadn't slept beyond the occasional alcohol induced blackout. His dark hair was a limp, greasy mop, and his ordinarily impressive moustache sat askew. He'd always claimed his part in the family business was advertisement. He used Acker*'s* religiously, pinching the ends of his moustache to a razor-point. He said he took advantage of his admittance to the Savile Club – which had taken more than three attempts – to extol the virtues of our product, convincing his friends to convince their friends that they and their whiskers were in dire need of it. He did nothing else. Nothing practical. Only advertising, and given the state of his moustache at present, he wasn't even doing that well.

Father always said Ernest cut a striking figure. Striking was certainly a word for it. He was a poor imitation of Ambrose in his youth. A lithograph printed again and again until the ink was thin and it barely resembled the image on the original plate.

"Eloise." He spread out his arms grandly. "I'm home."

"I can smell that."

"I'm impressed, from so on high." Ernest squinted at me on my perch. "Always putting yourself on a pedestal, both figuratively and literally."

"It's easily done when sober enough to stay upright. Where have you been? Father was asking for you."

"Father's always asking for something."

"You didn't answer my question."

Ernest shrugged. "Been here, there, everywhere. There's a lot to do in London, f'those of us who aren't complete prudes. Embroidered any nice pillows in my absence?"

I did not dignify him with an answer. I so hated this – the constant, biting back-and-forth that now underpinned our every interaction. At least when we were children we talked without feeling the need to land a blow between every breath.

"You should have been here," I said. "He's very sick, Ernest."

"S'been sick for years," Ernest slurred, averting his gaze. "He's a professional. The man could win ribbons."

"His gout has flared up again."

"Ugh, *stop*. I feel ill enough as it is without having to picture that."

"One day he'll die."

"I don't believe that's a trait unique to him."

"Him much sooner than us."

"Yes, and how you love to keep reminding me of it! What do you want me to do, Eloise? Would you have me enter medicine?"

"I would have you *be here*!" I snapped back, finally sweeping down the last few stairs and moving to loom over him. "You are his heir. When he dies, everything we have goes to you, and..."

"And?" Ernest arched one eyebrow. "Go on. Say it. I know you've been positively dying to."

I hesitated. "I..."

"Say it."

"I don't think you can be trusted to make wise financial decisions."

"There it is." Ernest collapsed back down onto the rug, arms raised to deliver a slow, out-of-rhythm applause. "Finally, you say it aloud. Let me guess, y'think *you* should be the one to inherit the family fortune?"

"I would be a better fit," I said. "I could oversee our finances with our accountant and ensure we did not run ourselves into ruin."

"Ensure *I* did not run us into ruin," Ernest corrected. "You want him to change 'Byron and Son' to 'Byron and Daughter' before he kicks it?"

I chose to ignore him. Never had I been granted an opportunity to truly plead my case. I could not rein in my tongue now. "I would give you a healthy allowance. That way you could continue to live as you please and spend yourself into a stupor... within reason, of course."

"Of course." Ernest let his arms flop down to his sides, tilting his head to look at me. "Why does it concern you so?"

I wanted to scream at him. Was every man in my life to ask me that?

Why did it concern me so! It was my future, my whole life, being juggled precariously in the hands of a fool. *Why did it concern me so!*

"It's our family's legacy," I said. "Does that mean nothing to you? Not to mention the staff. If you were to squander our fortune we would have to make economies and let many of them go. It is not just our lives impacted by this, Ernest."

"The staff?" Ernest scoffed. "What are you, a Communist? That happened fast, I was only gone a day."

"It's been three days!"

"Really?"

I raised my hands, then lowered them again, soothing myself with fantasies of throttling him. "I merely think we have a responsibility to the people we employ. Think of the importance of our reputation. Not that you have ever cared for that, after what you did at Mother's funeral..."

"Oh stop it," Ernest begged, forcing himself to sit up. His face was sickly, almost green in the cheeks. "Y'can leave off on playing the saint, Eloise. We both know why you've made this your cause. You don't want to get married."

Cold dread descended over me, and I stepped back, hands retreating to my chest to clutch anxiously at the fabric of my bodice. "Don't be ridiculous. You know I speak sense."

"You speak the desperate drivel of a woman who does not want her encroaching spinsterhood interrupted by marital duties." Ernest groaned as he pushed himself up off the floor, swaying until he found his balance. Suddenly I remembered he was much taller than I. "If you are going to insult me by saying I'm not fit to be Father's heir, then at least have the decency to be honest about why."

"Does it matter if that's true?" I whispered. "It doesn't make any of the other things I said false."

"No," Ernest agreed. "But you see, I don't care. 'Bout any of it, least of all your aversion to marriage. In fact, I think you've been alone too long."

"Ernest..."

"I think perhaps it's time I found you a husband. You evidently need something to ease that restless feminine mind. I have several friends from my circle who I'm certain Father would accept for you."

I shook my head doggedly. "Not one of those louses!"

"Then don't suggest I hand over my purse-strings to you ever again." Ernest's tone hardened, and I could do nothing but retreat. I'd spoken my piece and my brother had cut it down.

"You should clean up that vase," I said, through gritted teeth. "Sophie has had enough work to do tonight as it is."

With that I turned on my heel, storming up the stairs. I did not glance back at him even when he called my name.

"Why can't you just be like Mother?" He shouted after me. "She was never such a harpy!"

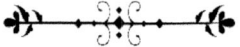

I dearly *wished* I could handle the situation with all the dignity Mother would have. I'd never seen that woman express anger in my whole life. She'd possessed a sage, severe countenance like that of a painting, never showing any displeasure. She must have been angry at times, though. Angry with Ernest and me for our childhood mischief, angry with her distant, uninvolved husband, angry with the world that decreed *that* be her life. She'd been an heiress in her own right when she'd married Father, sole inheritor of the Acker fortune that launched a thousand moustaches. I often suspected she regretted not seizing the freedom that happy fact allowed. Mrs Sharp had been with the family since the early days of Ambrose and Edith's marriage, and stated only that it had been happy at first, and then utterly miserable. Despite all this, Mother never so much as frowned.

Ernest was right when he said I was nothing like her.

I slammed the door behind me when I reached my bedchamber, hard enough to rattle the windows in their casements. I hated Ernest. Hated him. Any sisterly love and affection I once harboured had fizzled into nothing, seafoam hitting the shore. A decline that began that day in Brompton Cemetery.

The man was an imbecile, and the worst kind of imbecile at that – one with power and money. At the rate Ernest was going we would be begging in the gutter within a year of Father's death, bogged down in some quagmire of depravity to scrape out a living from rags and bones. The girl from the music hall came to mind – *Mirah* - all starving and rough-edged, who'd said it was Limehouse that killed her mother. I didn't want to die like that.

But the alternative was to marry. To marry for money and marry fast. To me that felt even more harrowing. It was a death too, and I would sooner throw myself into the Thames than submit to it. A furious storm was breaking within me, so fierce I thought my ribs would hinge open and I would shoot lightning from my chest. I snatched one of the pretty perfume bottles off my toilette table, hurling it at the wall. It burst apart in an explosion of lilac scent and colourful glass.

It wasn't fair. None of it. *I* had been the one to care for Mother and arrange her funeral, and now I was the one caring for Father, wiping his brow and reading at his bedside. *I* was the one overseeing the running of the house, organising the dinners Father still insisted on throwing though he rarely made it downstairs to attend them. I was the one writing Father's letters for him, maintaining our presence in society, combing over the business accounts. Ernest was nowhere, and I was stretching myself thin to be everywhere. It should have been my fortune. I had earned it.

  I threw myself down onto the bed and screamed into my pillow until my throat was hoarse.

5

Eloise

That night I dreamed I was shivering in an alleyway, stomach growling with hunger. I'd still been hungry when I'd risen to a bright, clear autumn day, warm in my vast featherbed. Susanna dressed me in my favourite violet morning gown, taking care to pin my hair neatly. She said nothing of the perfume bottle when she came in to help me prepare for bed the night before, cleaning it up in silence. Susanna was the best maid and companion a young woman could have. She was my confidante in all matters, having entered my family's employment when we were both sixteen. In a way we'd grown up together, more friends than lady and lady's maid.

Ernest was absent from breakfast, likely nursing a splitting headache, and Father had his meals brought to him in his chamber on a silver lap tray, leaving me to enjoy the stillness of the morning alone. Ordinarily I relished the peace, but today I was agitated. For all my despair the evening before I woke with a renewed determination not to let my bad dream come to pass. If Ernest could not be reasoned with, he would have to instead be dealt with. I'd given him the choice, albeit without him knowing, and he had chosen war.

"I plan on paying a visit to the boutique today," I announced to Susanna, standing patiently behind me as I ate. "I need to speak with Signora

Moretti about an important matter." I was careful with my words, for Sophie was present, pouring the tea and spreading preserves onto triangles of toasted bread for me. I didn't doubt that Sophie would agree wholeheartedly with my plan to dethrone Ernest, but she was easily excitable, and it was wiser not to include her.

"Does it concern your new evening gown?" Susanna said. "The one for the opera?"

"Yes." I smiled to myself over the rim of my teacup. "That's the one."

Signora Moretti had been a dancer with the *La Scala* ballet in her youth. Her career was illustrious, but took a mighty toll on her body, and she now got by with an elegant ivory cane in hand, occasionally using it to clip her young apprentices across the back of the head. She took up dressmaking to support herself, and now owned a thriving boutique on Bond Street dubbed, rather unimaginatively, *La Moda Italiana*.

It was not merely her skill with a needle that drew me to her, though. It was her famed discretion. A woman could complain of her husband during a fitting, or a daughter bicker with her mother about the contents of her trousseau, and be confident that whatever was said would never leave the boutique's walls. It was for this purpose that I sought Signora Moretti out.

I could hardly risk any letters of reply coming to the family home while conducting my interviews to find the perfect girl to fool Ernest. Instead I had cleverly employed Signora Moretti as my emissary, receiving and delivering any correspondences of a more delicate nature on my behalf. It was the perfect plan, as Ernest would only ever roll his eyes when I said I was visiting the boutique. It was a busy morning, the streets of Mayfair bustling, and walking with Susanna I made note of everyone I passed. An elderly couple turned their noses up at the newest fashions as they strolled by the shop windows - I heard the husband decry the current women's trends as becoming too tight-fitting for modesty - and a flock of giddy young ladies walked together in gowns of pastel pink, yellow, cream, like a colourful box of Turkish Delight. A mother, barking at her children as a boy in an itchy-looking sailor suit attempted to wedge his licked thumb into the ear of his sister. A young man who looked hopelessly out of his depth, arms stacked with hatboxes as he trailed after a woman who could only be his newly minted wife, already sporting a hat so extravagant half a dozen birds must have died to ornament it.

La Moda Italiana was situated between two competing perfumeries, their windows adorned with rows upon rows of delicate glass vials and bottles. Signora Moretti recommended the perfumeries to her clients alternately, whichever had her favour that week dependent upon arbitrary, constantly changing factors such as whether the owner greeted her in the morning.

The boutique front was painted a deep plum, blessed with a large bay window from which to advertise, the name painted onto it in neat black and gold script. The door, forever swinging open and closed, was tucked into an alcove, the glass panel frosted and gilt at the edges.

It was quiet when I entered, the bell over the door announcing my arrival. A few women browsed the fabrics, discussing styles amongst themselves, but no one paid any heed to Susanna and me. No one save for Signora Moretti, who immediately set down the lace trim she was showing to a customer to greet me. She was always admirably attired from head to toe, demonstrating her wares, and today her dress was a rich emerald. Her hair was braided in a thick coil upon her head, while some flowed freely in ringlets down her back. The quantity and healthy chestnut colour of it convinced me it was a hairpiece, but that was common now, and Signora Moretti wore it well.

"Miss Byron." She bowed her head in lieu of a curtsy. "How lovely to see you. Can I interest you in some of the new silks that have arrived? And there is a printed cotton that would suit your complexion splendidly."

"I would love to see them," I said. "But first, might I discuss something privately with you? An evening gown I wish to have made up for the opera..."

Understanding passed behind Signora Moretti's eyes. "Of course. Come with me." She turned with a great deal of rustling from the dress, leading me through a heavy velvet curtain at the rear of the shop to the private fitting room.

"Letters," I said, the moment we were alone. "Have any letters arrived for me?"

Signora Moretti shook her head. "I am sorry, but there has been nothing delivered here."

My heart sank.

"You're sure?" Susanna pressed. "Nothing at all?"

"I'm afraid not. I understand this is a disappointment to you, Miss Byron. Why don't I show you those fabrics? That will cheer your spirits."

Unlikely, unless the fabrics were somehow imbued with magical powers that would make Ernest see sense, but I had taken up too much of Signora Moretti's time in my foolish endeavour to refuse.

"That would be lovely," I said. Signora Moretti grinned, pushing the velvet curtain aside and disappearing to fetch her samples. Susanna placed a gentle hand on my arm.

"I'm sorry, Miss. There's still time."

"Barely. Father is getting worse and worse, and now that he will no longer see Doctor Hartley..."

"Will you inherit nothing when he passes?"

"Only my own jewels and dresses." Beyond the velvet veil the bell above the door jingled in the shop front again. "I should not have to suffer fear of poverty because Ernest cannot be reasoned with."

"*Mio Dio!*"

At Signora Moretti's horrified exclamation I drew back the curtain, nearly uttering the English equivalent myself.

Standing there in the boutique, a wolf among a flock of sheep, was the girl from Limehouse. Mirah Zelikovich. In the harsh light of day she looked far worse than I remembered. The gloom of the music hall did the tragic wretch favours, but it was apparent looking at her now that she was poor and hungry, dressed in a rough, green linen dress with a band of brown decorating the hem.

"Dear child, I'm afraid I'm not taking on any more apprentices," Signora Moretti told her, visibly mortified by what had just appeared in her establishment.

"I'm not here lookin' for a job. I was given this address by a lady." Mirah's gaze swept the room until it landed on me, nothing more than a floating head peering behind a curtain. "Miss Byron."

I emerged from my hiding place. "Yes," I said. "Yes, forgive me, Signora Moretti. This is a woman to whom I am giving charity."

The other women browsing in the boutique took the opportunity to leave, muttering to each other, and I could only hope I did not encounter any of them in society any time soon. I turned to Signora Moretti. "Would you lock the door, please? I'll pay well for your time."

Signora Moretti still looked as if she would sooner shoo Mirah out of her shop with a broom, but obliged, locking the front door and closing the shutters over the windows.

Standing only a few feet apart I was able to study the girl closely for the first time. The hem of her dress was not brown with embellishment as I'd first believed, but rather a band of mud and filth from the streets, crusted into the fabric. I wondered what she was stepping in that even the dust ruffle sewn to the underside of the skirt could not defend against.

Her hair, like burnished gold, was styled much the same as Signora Moretti's, only it was bedraggled and unwashed, though unmistakably her own. She was skinny and pointy from every angle, with a man's boots on her feet. And yet, through it all, the same beauty I'd first noticed in the music hall shone out. Her eyes were clever and bright, her bone structure almost noble. There was a handsome curve to her nose and a bow to her lips, and her eyelashes were thick and enviably long. She could have been a muse to the Pre-Raphaelites after a bath and brush. I could work with that. Ernest quite liked art, when sober enough to view it without seeing double.

"Miss Zelikovich. I didn't think I'd ever see you again."

Mirah averted her eyes. "I didn't think you would, either. I've considered your offer, though."

"And?"

"I've decided to accept."

My breath hitched. "Thank you! Thank you so much –"

"I have conditions," Mirah cut in, utterly unflinching. "I want it in writin' that you've hired me. That way you won't be able to finger me for a crook if things go bad. I won't take the fall for it alone, if it fails."

I swallowed thickly. "That is reasonable."

"Good. And I want some payment up front."

"How much?"

Mirah hesitated. She glanced down at her feet, and her too-big boots, shuffling on the wooden floor. "I don't know. However much it takes to hire a doctor. A *good* doctor, not some quack."

"Are you sick?"

She shook her head. "My brother."

"Oh. I'll bring a doctor to you. Give me the address, and I'll see it done."

"Really?"

"Yes. My family doctor, Doctor Hartley... he'll look the other way, I know it. He's been with us for years and has no excess of fondness for my father or brother, but he's always been a friend to me. He'll say nothing."

Mirah frowned. "I'll have to convince my brother to let him examine him. He's stubborn as an ox. How'll I explain you both?"

"Wealthy women perform charity all the time."

"You like to make us your little projects, you mean, so you can sleep easier and attend church with a clear conscience."

I bridled at her ungratefulness. "Think what you like of it, the offer is there. Do you accept?"

"What other choice do I have?" Mirah held out one hand expectantly. "I need a pencil and paper."

I nudged Susanna meaningfully and she scrambled to offer both to the woman, who took them and began to scrawl her address.

"Remember what else I said," Mirah added, as she handed the paper back. "I want our agreement in writin'."

"I'll get it done," I vowed. "How old are you?"

"Twenty," she said. Three years younger than me, yet she looked a good deal older. What a life she must have led, to be rendered so weary and fierce in the bud of her youth. "You done questionin' me for now?"

"Yes," I said. "I will be in contact soon."

With that Mirah nodded, marching back towards the door, which Signora Moretti raced to open for her. The bell rang out once again, the door closed behind her, and Signora Moretti blew a gusty sigh of relief.

"That is the girl you've chosen for your brother?" she cried, whirling to face me. "Forgive me, Miss, but that is..."

"Lunacy?"

"Ill-advised," Signora Moretti said, raising her hands in supplication. "A girl like that, straight from the gutter! You can't possibly hope to pass her off as a lady."

"She's a fine actress. I think she can do it."

"And she's pretty," Susanna agreed with a nod. "Beneath the grime, at least."

Very pretty, I noted. A little too pretty. I shook the notion away. "Ernest will take to her, I'm positive."

"And if he doesn't?" Signora Moretti asked.

I laughed, devoid of any real mirth. "She is the only one who accepted. As she so poetically put it herself - what other choice do I have?"

6

Mirah

No matter how long you lived in Limehouse you never got used to the stink – fish guts and vomit and whatever washed up from the Thames. Sometimes the reek was from the tanner's pits south of the river in Bermondsey, carried over on the wind. You could taste it, a bitter tang that clung to the roof of your mouth and made your throat sore. By midday, when Eloise Byron and her genteel doctor had agreed to meet me, the waterfront was teeming, all the smells simmering to their most potent.

The docks were busy. A dozen women sat laughing and bantering as they mended fishing nets, bargemen balanced on the beams of their vessels like cats. A group of dockworkers were clustered in the doorway of an anchor forge, hazy silhouettes behind a cloud of tobacco smoke from their clay pipes. They jeered as people went by, voices drowned out by the intermittent ding of hammers striking iron within the forge, like the ticking of a clock. It made me acutely aware of the time.

I began to wonder if Eloise had lost her way - or more likely lost her nerve. One whiff of Limehouse from the open window of her fine carriage would be enough to send a woman like that running. But she'd been here once before when she'd sought me out at the music hall. Perhaps she was braver than she appeared.

Another five minutes passed, and I was readying to leave when a veiled, black-clad figure appeared from within the crowd. She was arm in arm with a well-dressed older man carrying a brown leather Gladstone bag that immediately advertised his profession.

"Miss Zelikovich." Eloise nodded politely, though I couldn't make out her face. "This is Doctor Hartley. He's been my family's physician since before I was born."

"You're late," I replied, glancing at the doctor. "She told you everythin', then?"

"She has told me enough," Doctor Hartley said. He exuded a calm, diplomatic air that I reckoned was good in a doctor.

"And what do you make of it?"

"Nothing," he said. "I'll have no part in it besides this, but neither will I do anything to hinder it. Now, your brother. I'm told he's the patient?"

I nodded. "He's a difficult one. Don't take no for an answer."

Doctor Hartley huffed a laugh. "Believe me, I am familiar with difficult patients." He shot a meaningful look at Eloise, gesturing forwards with a swing of his bag. "Lead the way please Miss Zelikovich."

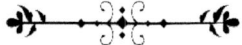

The walk to the tenement building was unpleasant. A thick drizzle started up, cold and damp but without enough heart to be called rain. Eloise walked practically on tiptoe the entire way, using one hand to bunch her skirt up to her ankles and the other to press a delicately embroidered kerchief over her nose. She'd been forced to pull back her veil to see where she was going, her expression was so aghast I might have recommended her for a role in a comedy.

"Are we nearly there?"

"Almost," I confirmed. "What, not enjoyin' your promenade through Limehouse?"

"How do you live here?" Eloise asked, wincing as we passed a crying child and its glaring mother. "It is so..."

"You think anyone chooses this life, Miss Byron?"

"I suppose not."

"There's no supposin' about it."

"This is why I cannot allow my brother to ruin me," Eloise said, still walking as if trying not to step on glass. "You must understand that more than anyone."

I scoffed. "Course you see the way things are here and your first concern is ensurin' it doesn't happen to you. Here. This is the place."

"*This?*"

"Were you expectin' Kensington Palace Gardens?"

I unlocked the door and led both lady and doctor inside, the stairs creaking and dipping as always, causing Eloise to utter many amusing sounds of concern.

"There's a leak," she said, on the top landing.

"There's leaks everywhere," I replied, fumbling for my keys again. "Don't try to count 'em, you'll be here forever." The door opened, whining on its hinges. I poked my head into the flat. "Caleb? Are you busy?"

"I'm always busy," Caleb called from the dining table, which doubled as his office desk by day. I gestured for Eloise and Doctor Hartley to follow.

Caleb sat with his back to us, simple blue skullcap resting precariously on his curls, for he stubbornly refused the use of a grip or pin to fix it to his head. Pages of the manuscript he'd been employed to translate piled up either side of him, the table littered with tallow candles. Their smoky flames did little to bolster the grim grey light filtering into the room from the one unwashed window. The smell of the burning fat was a stink too far for Eloise, who gagged audibly into her kerchief. The sound made Caleb set down his dip pen and turn in his seat. He stood abruptly when he saw our guests, chair screeching on the floor.

"Mirah!"

"This is Miss Byron," I introduced, "and her physician, Doctor Hartley. She's performin' charity here in Limehouse out of the goodness of her ladylike heart. The doc's here to examine that cough of yours."

Caleb flushed. "I don't have a cough."

"Give it about thirty seconds," I said to Doctor Hartley. "My brother's a bad liar. Sit down Caleb, let him see you."

Caleb hesitated to obey, which wasn't new, though he was too flummoxed to be his usual indignant self. His skullcap finally abandoned ship, attempting to escape his head. He caught it clumsily in both hands. "I wasn't expecting us to have visitors," he said, eyes flashing from the doctor to Eloise. "Madam, would you like a chair?"

"I'm content to stand, thank you."

"I could put on some tea?"

"There's no need."

Caleb opened his mouth again, no doubt to offer something else that Eloise would be too afraid to accept, but broke off into another violent coughing fit.

"See?" I said, striding over to place my hands on Caleb's shoulders and force him back into his seat. "It's been gettin' worse and worse."

"That is a nasty cough you have, sir," Doctor Hartley agreed, setting his bag on the desk to open it. "Let's have a quick listen to your chest, shall we? It'll be best if you open your shirt."

Caleb turned redder than a cooked lobster. "There is a lady present!"

"Only one? Charmin'. See how gentlemanly my brother is, Miss Byron? I'll show you where we sleep. She's real interested in improvin' conditions in Limehouse. Aren't you, Miss?"

"Oh. Of course, yes. That's why I'm here."

"Such a charitable soul."

I hooked my arm through Eloise's much to her surprise, pulling her in the direction of the bedchamber. If Eloise meant to complain about the rough-handling she forgot the instant she laid eyes upon the room. Our two shabby beds, the bare walls, the single rattling window that was always shuttered to keep in what pitiful warmth there was. The same grey light that strained Caleb's eyes in the main room shone dully through the broken slats of the shutters, the shadows striping the back wall like the bars of a cage.

"This is where you sleep? Both of you?" Eloise's voice was soft, all the squeamishness of our walk through Limehouse subdued into something that made me squirm with discomfort. Pity.

"We're lucky, really," I said. "I know a lot of families livin' out of one room, some with half a dozen little ones. Even havin' a bedchamber feels a luxury."

"But you *both* sleep in here?"

"We slept separately for a while," I explained. "But it got too cold in the winter. It's better this way, and look," I reached to pull the curtain partition across the room to demonstrate. "We have privacy."

"Dear God," Eloise breathed, scrunching her embroidered kerchief up between her gloved hands. "This is abysmal. No wonder your brother is sick."

As if to punctuate her statement Caleb began coughing again from the main room, the sound jarring us out of the awkward silence that trailed after her words. I tied the curtain back in its proper place and left the room, Eloise following, having since abandoned her quest not to let her skirt touch the floor.

Caleb was buttoning up his shirt as we entered, Doctor Hartley busy packing away an absurd contraption with a brass horn at one end and two curved prongs at the other. In my mind it more closely resembled a medieval torture device than an instrument of medicine, but the only doctors I'd ever met only fit the word in the loosest sense, ill-equipped and always peddling something.

"I've listened to his chest," Hartley said, closing his bag with a loud snap. "Your brother suffers with asthma, Miss Zelikovich."

"Asthma? What does that? Can it be cured?"

"Not cured, but managed. He has weak lungs. They may have always been that way from birth, or they might have become so over the years. I suggest a treatment of potash and tobacco, inhaled regularly, but particularly during the onset of an attack. Mostly he needs clean, fresh air and proper rest. His environment is killing him."

I almost laughed, both at the cruel irony that the conditions of Limehouse should strike our family for a second time and at Doctor Hartley's suggestion. He may as well have prescribed a tincture of pure gold. It'd be about as easy to come by.

"Don't worry about me, Mirah," Caleb said. "I'll manage." There was resignation in his eyes, and I was furious with him for it. I wanted to slap him hard across the face and shake a fight into him. He couldn't leave me. He was my big brother, the only person left to me in this world. If he died the selfish bastard would take the dregs of my heart with him.

"We should leave," Eloise said, after a beat of silence. "Miss Zelikovich, will you walk us out?"

I nodded, completely numb.

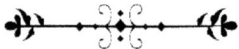

Neither of us spoke as we made the walk back through the streets of Limehouse to where Eloise and Doctor Hartley's carriage was waiting – a hansom cab, rather than Eloise's own – and it wasn't until the doctor was already inside that I finally broke, reaching for Eloise's hand, bare skin touching the soft kid-leather of her gloves.

"You have to do somethin'," I said. "Please. Not for me, I don't care about me. Caleb can't die." It was humiliating to beg, but I doubted I'd ever have access to someone wealthy enough to do something about our circumstances ever again.

"Don't worry," Eloise said, climbing up into the carriage with me still clutching her hand so tightly my arm was stretched to its fullest, shoulder aching with the strain. To my surprise, her fingers squeezed mine. "Meet me at *La Moda Italiana* tomorrow at noon. We'll discuss everything, including your accommodation."

"You're goin' to help us?"

"We're going to help each other."

7
Mirah

"You *must* stop moving. Have you never stood for a fitting, child?"

"Not like this," I said, rubbing the side of my wrist, where a misplaced pin to the cuff of the gown had pricked me. The dress Signora Moretti was fitting me for was like nothing I'd ever worn before. Cream silk with accents of forget-me-not blue on the wide pagoda sleeves, the bodice closed with buttons of mother-of-pearl. The square neckline was made modest with lace trim, and a sweeping train ran from the bustle, a peacock's tail fanning out on the floor behind me. The costumes at the music hall were shoddy imitations of the fashions ladies like Eloise wore on the daily, cut from cheaper fabrics, harsher dyes. I'd never envisioned owning such a gown myself. Now I was getting a whole wardrobe made to my measurements.

There was no time to wait on having them all made, of course, and the one I modelled had been Signora Moretti's own, now being modified to fit as Eloise circled us giving occasional instruction. Watching her buzzing around like a fly was beginning to irritate.

"Am I up to your standards yet?" I asked, dryly. The raised fitting platform I stood on was like a theatre stage in miniature, only I was expected to remain impossibly still rather than perform. It didn't come naturally to me, my limbs wanting to move, my hands itching to do something.

"You look beautiful," Eloise said. "The dress, I mean. It looks beautiful on you. Signora Moretti has a talent, does she not?"

"Talent and a rough hand," I muttered. "How many dresses will I be gettin'?"

"As many as needed. You must look the part if Ernest is to believe you are a lady of means."

"Ain't it a bit counterproductive, spendin' so much on my wardrobe?"

"Not at all. I have a line of credit here, and at the end of it all, it is an investment. If this succeeds, my inheritance will be many times more than the expense of the dresses."

"And if it doesn't?"

Eloise didn't answer, instead humming to herself and reaching forwards to fix the tasselled trim on the apron of the skirt. "I said we'd discuss your accommodation. Your home in Limehouse will not do for the ruse at all. If you were to be seen there it would give us away or start rumours that you have an opium habit. Neither are desirable."

"So where'll I live?"

"I've acquired an apartment for you in Mayfair, in a reputable building on Park Street."

I nearly fell from the fitting platform. "Mayfair?"

"Of course," Eloise said. "You must have a respectable residence for the plan to work, and it will help to be within walking distance of my home at Berkeley Square."

"Berkeley Square?" I echoed. I was starting to feel like a parrot. "No wonder you want to cut your brother out of the will."

"I'll hire you a maid, too. My girl Susanna has a younger sister. I'll inform her of our agreement, and she will serve you as you require."

I wasn't sure how I felt about that. The notion of having someone serve me bordered on perverse, but I couldn't deny it would be a treat not to have to clean the hearth, or sweep the floor, or haggle for a good price for fish. I wasn't about to spit in the face of Eloise's generosity, and surely Susanna's younger sister would prefer working for me than some old toad with wandering hands, or a bitter wife who ran her house like Millbank prison.

"What about my brother?"

"He can live with you," Eloise said. "I thought this arrangement might suit us both. Your brother will find things cleaner in Mayfair than Limehouse."

That statement was high up in the running for most obvious observation in human history, but I refrained from saying as such. "What'll I tell him about how I got there?" I asked instead.

Eloise shrugged. "You are a clever woman, I'm sure you'll think of something suitable. Tell him whatever story you like, aside from the truth. Which reminds me, we must consider your story for my brother. You must have an identity, a past. Something to make your character real and draw him to you."

"I could be an Austrian countess," I suggested, twirling on the platform and sending my skirts spinning gracefully. Signora Moretti cursed.

"Do you speak the language?" Eloise asked.

"I speak a little Yiddish, and my brother says it's basically the same."

"Not in polite society it isn't. And a *little* isn't enough."

"Don't want a countess from the *shtetl*?" I teased. Eloise ignored me.

"You're not far mistaken about adopting a foreign guise," she said. "That will explain why Ernest has not met you before, if you are visiting from abroad...." She began to pace, mind working so furiously that I could easily picture steam coming out her ears. "What other languages do you speak?"

"English and French, fluently. A tiny bit of Spanish, and enough Italian to know Signora Moretti has been swearin' at me under her breath this entire fittin'." The woman in question uttered an acknowledging grunt, pinning more fabric to the dress to extend the hem. I felt sometimes as though I didn't have a single *mother tongue*. Like everything else about me I was an amalgamation of different words from different languages, a life made up of patchwork. Languages were handed down like old clothes in my family. Ma spoke Yiddish and French, but she'd had Caleb taught French and English, and in turn I'd learned enough of all three.

"French is the obvious choice, then," Eloise said.

Listening to her listing off potential aliases and obscure towns in Southern France, my concentration drifted. I could do nothing but stare at my reflection in the full-length, three panelled mirror of the fitting room. I didn't know myself at all in the dress, and the matching Medici style hat, bedecked with blue silk ribbon and cream ostrich feathers, so elegant and refined. I was a stranger, a woman I might pickpocket in an underground station, or watch enviously from the other side of the street.

My face was the same, though. Despite it all I could see my ma in the mirror, and my brother, too. The same dark eyes.

"I want to be a Rothschild. One of the French cousins."

Eloise stopped mid-ramble. "A de Rothschild? Why?"

"No point hidin' the fact I'm Jewish. Wouldn't know the first thing to do if I got invited to church."

"Believe me, Ernest will not be inviting you to church. And I thought you said you were not particularly observant?"

"From what I hear neither are half of the Rothschilds. I'm Mirah de Rothschild, a distant, far-removed cousin from across the channel."

Eloise pursed her lips. "That might work. The best lies are born in half-truths, after all." She nodded, to herself rather than to me. "Very well. Mirah de Rothschild it is. We will do some research into the family tree and find you suitable parents. We shouldn't encounter any of the English

Rothschilds, I don't imagine. My family is wealthy, but we're nowhere near being part of the Prince of Wales's set, for all Father would wish it."

Eloise's words came as a relief. I didn't know the law too well, but lying to royalty had to be some kind of treason, and I didn't fancy dancing a gallows jig for so petty a cause as hers. I'd heard plenty of the decadent parties hosted by and for the fast and intimate friends of the Prince and Princess of Wales at Marlborough House. Some whispered the prince had established his own court in direct defiance of his mother's. I wouldn't blame him. I'd seen the wedding photographs of him and the Princess of Wales, with his mother sat directly between them in full mourning garb. Families were messy, complicated things regardless of whether you were rags or royalty, it seemed.

"I think a matching *casaque* paletot for this dress," Eloise said as an aside to Signora Moretti. She turned back to me. "Now. We will orchestrate the meeting between you and Ernest for two days' time. You must be clean and presentable, and school your accent into something more..."

"Palatable?"

"Yes. Can do you that?"

"Of course I can."

"Good. I will entice Ernest to join me on a walk in Hyde Park in the morning, and you will meet us there, as though you did not expect to see us. I will invent some old acquaintance between us."

"Why the park?" I asked, bemused. "Can't you just invite me to dinner, or to take tea at your home? Ain't that what you ladies do?"

"Yes," Eloise said, slowly. "But it is not as simple as that, with Ernest. He will never pursue a woman he thinks I am angling towards him as a good match. He lives to displease me. If I were to invite you it would appear too blatant. It must be a delightful happenstance that puts you in his path."

I shook my head. "He sounds like a chore."

"He is."

"Do I have to do anythin' else on this walk? Juggle, sing, dance like a bear?"

"No," Eloise said. "In fact, it's best you say as little as possible. We can't afford him questioning you on your parentage. Play the timid maiden who does not wish to speak to a strange man. It will charm him and keep you safe from a slip of the tongue."

"Fine," I said. "I'll be meek as a kitten."

"Good. And remember, no one must know of this. Nobody can find out until it is the right moment to reveal it. Timing is the difference between ruin and success, in this matter. If it should come out when I intend it, it will be seen as a clever lark that exposes my brother for the reckless fool he is. If it should come out when still in its infancy, I will be seen as a grasping schemer. The line is delicate."

"I'll remember," I said. "Now, tell me. Can I take this thing off before she turns me into a pin cushion?"

Signora Moretti cursed again.

8

Eloise

It was a bright, brilliant day in Hyde Park. Winter was well on her way, the sky a crisp clear blue and the grass a carpet of still crystal, adorned here and there with frozen spiderwebs, like lace doilies. I took great care to keep to the gravel pathways, bundled up in my paletot and walking with my arm tucked into Ernest's. He was a heavy, drifting weight at my side, top hat sitting lopsided upon his head, and he stank of gin, sweating it out of every pore. It had taken the combined efforts of both me and Susanna to rouse him from his stupor, and then a shot of sherry and a raw egg to get him out of the house, albeit still bleary-eyed. It occurred to me often that my brother lacked the constitution required of his lifestyle. Had I ever deigned to sink to his level I would have borne it in a far hardier manner.

"Why in God's name did you insist upon this?" he finally asked as we picked our way along the bank of the Serpentine. Perhaps the wind blowing off the water had shocked him into sobriety for the first time in days.

"I'm worried for you," I said. "It isn't good to stay out all night and to sleep away the day. I thought a brisk morning walk would help."

"I feel more wretched than ever."

"That means it is working. The cold is purging the foul toxins from your body."

"And all of the warmth."

"But think how refreshed you will be when we return home!"

Ernest grumbled something under his breath. "Are you doing this because you're still cross at me, for that unpleasantness in the vestibule? It isn't fair to punish me for things I said under the drink."

"I don't want us to be unhappy with each other. You're my brother, and as such, I am bound to you."

"Like a shackle," Ernest said. "You should really consider taking a lover, Eloise. It would do you wonders to be less tightly wound, and then maybe I would be free of your henpecking. You could henpeck someone else – some even find that erotic."

It took herculean restraint not to push him down the muddy embankment straight into the Serpentine for the comment. "I know things have been unpleasant between us since the funeral," I said, "but I would like to put it behind us. I thought a walk today might go some way to mending the rift."

"Yes, dragging me from my warm bed to brave the elements when I feel sick as a dog is endearing me to you more and more."

"Please don't be vicious about it. I swear, the way you behave I sometimes think you are Uncle Horace's son, not Father's."

"Don't insult Mother like that," Ernest muttered. "She would have sooner had a viper in her bed than Uncle Horace."

He wasn't wrong on that front. Uncle Horace, who died a year past, had not really been our uncle at all. He had been Father's closest friend from childhood, the two of them even embarking upon the Grand Tour together in their youth. They had been as good as brothers, but Mother had hated him, taking herself away to her private parlour whenever he called and refusing to sit with us at dinner if he was present. Uncle Horace had been fun. He had travelled often, unlike Father and Mother, who were insufferably tied to

England and never cared for adventure, Father citing a distaste for anything foreign or interesting, from the food to the fashions.

Uncle Horace made up for this single-handedly, always bearing presents for Ernest and me from some far-flung corner of the world. I had a painted wooden bird from Portugal that still sat on one of my shelves even now, and a shawl of Maltese lace that I'd had turned into a pair of fingerless gloves when I outgrew it. I'd adored Uncle Horace when I'd been a girl, begging him to take me with him on his travels, though I was never allowed. Now that I was a woman, I understood why Mother disliked him so.

He was a bad influence. Father transformed into a witless boy in his presence, and Uncle Horace drank too much and gambled too freely, placing bets on horses based on how much he liked their names. It was no wonder I was not permitted to accompany him as a girl. Who knew what debauchery I'd have been exposed to.

I'd never known how Father could be such an open hypocrite, claiming to detest scandal and yet befriending the living embodiment of it. Uncle Horace was a bad habit he could not dispel himself of. It had taken death for him to finally manage it.

"It's a beautiful day," I said, wanting to think of something else.

"It's too bright."

"You ought to have brought your spectacles, then. The ones with the blue-tinted lenses. You said they help with the brightness."

"I broke them."

"How?"

"I must have slept on them, somewhere."

I resisted the urge to roll my eyes, instead offering him my parasol, still folded. "Here."

"I'm not carrying that like a woman!"

"You'll look gentlemanly, carrying it for me," I protested. "Wouldn't that make a nice change?"

Ernest tensed his jaw, snatching it from me and struggling to open it out. "Blasted thing," he muttered. "There is a whole bouquet of flowers mounted on it! How am I to work it when it requires pruning just to open?"

"It's easy, look. Let me."

As we fumbled together to open the damned thing, I spied a figure coming towards us through the morning mist, clad in a cream and blue gown and sporting a matching hat atop her golden curls. Mirah, not walking the path like a lady, but stomping through the frozen grass and leaving a stark trail through the virgin frost. Before I could signal to her the young woman was raising one hand to wave, using the other to hike up her skirt so high I caught a flash of her blue-stockinged calves. I could have fainted at the sight.

"Miss Byron, is that you?"

Ernest narrowly avoided hitting me in the face with the parasol as he finally got it to work, shoving it back into my hands when he realised we had company.

"Oh – yes." I scrambled to compose myself. "How lovely to see you!"

"Indeed. I almost can't believe it!" Mirah closed the distance between us to embrace me, kissing each of my cheeks in turn. The blush that rose in them was embarrassing, my face growing so hot that I half expected steam to start rising off me.

Mirah leaned back to look at me, and I had to admit, she was a fine actress, for there was nary a trace of the girl from Limehouse in her expression. Or her accent, for that matter. She spoke as a lady would, crisp English with a subtle but charming French lilt. "How long has it been?"

"A few years, I'd think."

"I'm sorry, do we know you?" Ernest asked, voice cool with disinterest.

I laughed breathlessly. "Forgive me, yes, how foolish of me. Ernest, this is Miss de Rothschild. Miss de Rothschild, this is my brother, Ernest."

Mirah scoffed. "How many times have I told you to simply call me Mirah? A pleasure to meet you, Sir. If you are anything like your sister I'm sure we will be fast friends."

Ernest raised his eyebrows, now significantly more curious. "De Rothschild? As in – the Rothschild banking family?"

"What other famous Rothschilds are there?" Mirah said, innocently. "I am visiting from France."

"We met a few years ago when she made a flying visit to London," I explained, hastily. "We got along so well that we vowed to keep in touch."

"Yes, you must forgive me for not writing to tell you of my plans. It was all rather spontaneous, I must admit."

Ernest smirked. "I have always found spontaneity to be an admirable trait in a woman."

"Yes, I suspect you are fond of women prone to making thoughtless decisions."

Ernest's brows came together, the look of a man who couldn't tell if he was being mocked. "What brings you to England?" he asked. "Hunting for a wealthy husband? You've come in the wrong season, in that case. And unchaperoned."

Mirah turned her eyes on him, cutting, precise. "I am chaperoned. My maid has only stepped out of sight for a moment to relieve herself. And why would I have need of a wealthy husband? My family has more than enough money."

"I did not mean to imply –"

"And yet you did. Are you in the habit of asking impertinent questions to women you have just met, Mr Byron?"

Ernest stammered, mouth opening and closing like a fish out of water. "I was only curious..."

"If you must know, my mother thought it would be wise for me to leave France for a while, after the war with Prussia and all the trouble with the *Commune de Paris*. You might have simply left your question at 'what brings you to England?'." She narrowed her eyes to inspect him. "Then again, you look as though you've spent the last week imbibing, so perhaps your lack of manners is only the result of your excesses."

Inwardly, I cursed. Being challenged by a woman was the last thing that would appeal to Ernest. This was not the 'meek as a kitten' Mirah promised, and if it was, I dreaded to imagine what 'bold' looked like. Now that I considered it, though, 'meek' was not a word I would commonly associate with kittens. Boundless energy, unquenchable curiosity, and indiscriminate use of claws were all more fitting. I had no one to blame but myself if this went badly. I ought to have known better than to hire a Limehouse ladybird for the part. Mirah's prettiness had blinded me.

As predicted Ernest turned crimson to the tips of his ears, flush with rage, or embarrassment, or a fatal combination of both.

"Why don't we keep walking?" I suggested lightly, hoping to lead him away before the situation devolved past salvaging. Ernest didn't budge when I tugged his arm, planted on the path like a tree.

"You have a sharp tongue, Miss de Rothschild."

"A sharp mind, too," Mirah said. "Which is more than can be said for many."

"Let's definitely keep walking." I was all but dragging Ernest now. "It was lovely to see you again, Miss de Rothschild..."

If Mirah understood the hint to back away, she stubbornly ignored it, drifting along beside us with all the comfortable ease of a dandelion seed in a warm breeze. I had to admit, she carried herself the way I imagined a Rothschild heiress might.

"My mind is sharp," Ernest protested.

"Even dulled by the drink?"

"It is *always* sharp. Test me!"

I looked to him in dismay. "Ernest?"

"Test me," he said again, practically begging.

"Are you sure you want that?" Mirah tilted her head towards him, eyelashes lowered. With every word her breath fled her mouth in a soft wisp of fog, and in the cold her lips appeared exceptionally red, as did the bloom in the apples of her cheeks. I nearly tripped over my own feet staring at her.

"Yes," Ernest said, bestowing his answer with more gravity than he usually did anything that actually required it.

"Fine. A riddle, then, until next we meet. 'When set loose, I fly away. Never so cursed as when I go astray'. Run that through your mind, Sir, and give me an answer when we see each other again."

"So we will?" Ernest said. "See each other again?"

Mirah shrugged. "London is a big city, but society is very small. Now if you'd excuse me, I have an appointment to keep with my dressmaker. Goodbye, Mr Byron. Eloise." She curtsied surprisingly well, then took off with impressive speed, leaving us behind in moments.

Staring after her, I was utterly aghast. None of that had transpired the way we planned. Mirah was supposed to wait for us on a bench with a book – something frivolous and not too thought provoking – and, upon introductions, present as timid and bashful. Rather than allow Ernest to kiss her hand, Mirah had instead opted to try to bite his off. It was a disaster.

"What an unusual woman," Ernest stated, staring after her.

"Yes, she is," I said, breathless. "I apologise, she is not usually so..."

"Fascinating."

I stopped before denouncing her further. Ernest was still watching the path ahead, though by now Mirah was nothing more than a white-and-blue dot in the distance.

"You like her?" I asked.

"It's hard to say." Ernest cleared his throat, tearing his gaze from the retreating figure at last. "She is bold as brass and clearly has no care for a man's ego. Still, it's rather difficult not to like her, isn't it? She's refreshing."

"She is..." I could hardly believe it. After the insults and indifference Mirah hurled at him, Ernest was smitten with her? Perhaps I ought to have trusted Mirah more. After all, a woman like *that* would surely know what appealed to a man more than I would. I didn't have the faintest clue what men liked, nor any desire to learn. Mirah saw men all the time, was *with* men all the time...

I shook the thought away, not wishing to imagine Mirah in anyone's bed. It was improper, unhelpful, and I did not care for how it preoccupied me so.

"Well, stay away from her," I said finally, fixing Ernest with a hard stare.

"Stay away? Why on earth would I do that?"

"She's my friend," I said. "*Mine*. I know what you're like. You're a scoundrel. But she's not for you. Let me have one thing for myself, Ernest. Just one thing."

Ernest paused, then smiled, and it was as false as I predicted. "Of course, sister dear." He bowed his head contritely. "I would never think to poach a friend from your side."

I was counting on that being a lie.

9
Mirah

The marzipan was tooth-rottingly sweet. Reaching into the box for another piece, I marvelled yet again at the absurdity of my situation.

The apartment in Mayfair was nothing short of a palace, *en miniature*. The walls were covered with colourful striped paper, and heavy chandeliers hung from the moulded ceilings, sparkling with countless droplets of cut crystal. The floors were polished herringbone, and sunlight poured into the apartment through large windows, framed with heavy velvet drapes and valances. Even with the chill of the encroaching winter I kept the windows of the drawing room open when Caleb wasn't around, enamoured by the novelty of the fresh, clean air. The smells of London were there as always, but fainter, muted by the earthy scent of grass and trees from Hyde Park. Far more pleasant than fish guts and stale piss, that was certain.

When Eloise had first shown me around the place she'd seemed embarrassed by its size, as though expecting me to declare she ought to have done better, and it made me wonder what Eloise's own home must be like. It had to rival Versailles for her to find this tiny manor house wanting for anything.

It'd been simpler than I expected convincing Caleb to join me in

Mayfair. I'd told him I'd landed a role as a mezzo-soprano at a very respectable opera house, and that the part came with comfortable pay and use of the apartment. He'd swallowed the lie with painful ease, as sick of Limehouse as I was, for all his airs of piety. I knew I'd never be in any danger of him discovering I was *not*, in fact, a mezzo-soprano at a very respectable opera house, because Caleb wouldn't set foot in an opera house if his life depended on it.

I popped my marzipan into my mouth whole as I flipped the page of the journal in my lap. I was reclined on the plush chaise longue in the drawing room in a silk dressing gown, diligently looking over what Eloise had called my 'research'.

There was an irony in the fact I'd spent much of my life wondering as to the identity of my father, only to have one assigned to me for the purpose of the ruse. I was now the daughter of Salomon James de Rothschild, second son of James Mayer de Rothschild, of the Paris-based Rothschild faction. Salomon was conveniently dead, having departed this mortal coil young at only nine-and-twenty from 'excitement gambling on the stock market'. He'd married his second cousin, and fathered no sons, but one daughter. The wife retired from society after his death, and the daughter was still a child. It was ideal, for there would be no one immediate to discredit me.

Less so was the timing. He'd died only eight years ago, which didn't add up with my age at all. Even if I'd been conceived on his wedding night it would make me only ten. Eloise assured me that many of her set would know very little about the short life of Salomon James de Rothschild, and he was the only candidate that wouldn't put me at risk of exposure, or too far away from the Rothschild fortune to be of interest.

It was now my duty to memorise all the facts of Salomon's life, from his date of birth – the thirtieth of March – to his travels in the United States and Canada on behalf of the family. That wasn't all I'd been set to memorise, either.

With a grand dinner at Eloise's home looming on the horizon, the hostess herself had provided me a detailed list of every guest expected to be there, which I'd been tasked with memorising in time for the meal. I had to admire Eloise's thoroughness.

The doorbell rang, a jarring, metallic clanging that sent me bolt upright on the chaise, my box of marzipan pieces flying across the room and Eloise's journal sliding off my lap. I stood just as Tabitha – my new maid – entered the drawing room.

"Are you all right, Miss?" she asked, toying with the frill of her pinafore as if it bothered her. She was young, only ten-and-six, short and plump and very pretty. It was her first foray into domestic service, according to Eloise, her silence on the matter of myself bought with the promise of Eloise securing her a position in a respectable household once it was all done.

"Yes," I said, hurriedly smoothing out my dress. "Would you answer that?"

"I already did, Miss."

"Oh. Who is it?"

"Mr Byron, Miss. Here to see you."

My face dropped; Tabitha's turned white with fear. "I'm sorry, Miss, was I not to answer to him? I can send him away, tell him you're indisposed..."

"No, no. I can see him. I –"

"Mirah?" Caleb, shouting from his bedchamber where he had set up a writing desk, launched my heart up into my mouth. I swore loudly, shooing Tabitha in the direction of the vestibule.

"Distract Mr Byron, tell him I'll be with him momentarily! I'll handle my brother."

Tabitha scurried away to do as she was told as I rushed in the opposite direction, down the hallway to Caleb's bedchamber. I did the only thing that came to mind - snatched the key from the other side of the door to lock it tight.

"Mirah?" Caleb said, behind the door.

"Yes?"

"I heard something crash. Are you alright?"

"I drifted off to sleep and dropped my book. Don't trouble yourself."

The chamber doorknob turned, then rattled. "Did you lock the door?"

"No."

"It won't open." Caleb shook it frantically, voice rising with alarm. "Mirah –"

"No idea what's wrong. I didn't touch it. Perhaps the lock is jammed?"

"I heard it slam!"

"Maybe we have a ghost!"

"If this is your idea of a jest..."

"It ain't. I'll fetch Tabitha to see if we can get it open. Stay put!"

"I don't have any other choice!"

I hitched up the skirt of my dress and dashed back down the hall, skidding to a halt in the vestibule with just enough time to neaten my hair in the wall mirror before Tabitha opened the door and presented Ernest Byron.

He was well dressed as ever, silver-tipped cane in one hand and silk top hat in the other, though he nearly dropped both when he got a look at me. I had to be a state, flush-faced and loose-haired, wearing only a nightgown and robe. He fumbled with the brim of his hat, remembering himself suddenly and dropping into a short bow.

"Miss de Rothschild. Forgive me. I did not mean to intrude..."

"We both know that's a lie," I stated, more bluntly than I intended. "What can I do for you, Mr Byron?"

"Ernest, please."

"That hardly feels appropriate."

"You did not give me the impression you cared all that much for what is appropriate," Ernest said. I had to concede I probably wasn't doing any better at giving that impression in my state of undress. "I wanted to tell you that I figured out your riddle."

"You did?"

"Well, I'd wager I did." Ernest puffed up his chest proudly. If everything Eloise told me about his gambling luck was true, I didn't think he should be wagering on anything. "A dream."

"What?"

"The answer. It's 'a dream'. 'When set loose I fly away, never so cursed as when I go astray'. A dream, as in, an aspiration. They fade so easily, and it is a tragedy."

I gawped at him. He was so satisfied with himself I had to press my mouth firmly shut to keep from laughing. It was hopeless. My cheeks puffed up like a frog's gullet, air escaping between my pursed lips in an inelegant *ppppppt*.

Ernest's brows creased. "What? What's so amusing?"

"A fart," I blurted. "It's – a fart. The answer to the riddle. Flatulence."

Ernest stared, so visibly taken aback that I was briefly concerned his face would freeze in a look of surprise, and he'd return to his sister resembling a ghost. He was handsome, I had to give him that. The same glossy dark hair as Eloise. Naturally arching eyebrows and a jawline I could cut my finger on. Pretty, in an odd way, with girlish eyes and a lovely rosiness to his complexion.

"A *fart?*" he said at last, with such strong emphasis on the word that I fancied anyone walking past on the street outside would hear. Perhaps he thought he'd misheard.

"Tasteless, I know." I shrugged. "I didn't think you'd ever get it."

"It's – tasteless, indeed!" Ernest shook his head. His perfectly waxed moustache curled with his lips as he smiled and then, rather unexpectedly – he laughed. "I would never have expected a lady to come up with something so crass!"

"I didn't come up with it. I heard it from someone else."

"Who on earth are you getting such inappropriate jokes from? You cannot tell me the Rothschilds are all so crude!"

"Well, they spend a lot of time around the Prince of Wales," I reasoned, before catching myself. "No – no, it wasn't from my family. It was from... a servant. My footman."

Caleb chose that very moment to start hammering on his chamber door with such force it could be heard from the vestibule, a thunderous pounding like someone laying siege to a castle with a battering ram. "Mirah!"

"That's him," I said. "His family have been in the service of mine for many years, and so I cannot find it in my heart to send him away. It isn't his fault he's eccentric, he is afflicted by a tragic condition."

"What's wrong with him?"

"His father was an artist."

"Ah." Ernest nodded seriously. "How charitable of you to keep him on."

"Charity is a very Jewish trait, Sir. It is not as it is in the Christian sense; charity is our obligation, not something done to keep out of the downstairs fire." It was helpful to have a brother who was always spouting his beliefs and dropping pennies we couldn't spare into the little tin *tzedakah* box on the mantle.

"How fascinating."

"I'm glad you think so. Your visit was very pleasant. I would invite you inside, but I have only my maid and footman to vouch for me, and I don't think it would be wise. I must be mindful of my reputation."

"Indeed." Ernest bowed low, rose, and set his top hat back on his head. "It was a delight to see you again, Miss de Rothschild."

He spoke as if it were merely a merry happenstance, a chance meeting in the street, and not that he'd come uninvited to my home. How *had* he gotten the address? Eloise wouldn't have given it to him, would she? And risk me being caught off guard after she'd gone to such lengths to plan every detail?

"And you," I said. "Good day, Mr Byron." I moved to close the door, but he threw out one hand to stop it.

"Wait!" His voice rang with desperation. "Forgive me, but – will you be at the dinner my sister is throwing this Thursday evening?"

"Do you not look at the guest list?"

"I leave all that silly stuff up to her," Ernest said. "She always invites ridiculous people, anyway."

"And you're asking if I was invited?"

His cheeks reddened. "I wasn't suggesting you are – I mean. Please come. I would like that."

"You're inviting me without asking your sister?"

"I am the man of the house, with my father indisposed. If I say you are invited, you are invited. Besides, is Eloise not a friend of yours?"

I wouldn't trust Eloise as far as I could throw her. For the purposes of this ruse, however, we were the fondest of bosom friends. I smiled. "Yes. A most dear friend. If you're sure it would not inconvenience her..."

"It wouldn't."

"Then I'll be there."

Ernest grinned. "Excellent. Splendid. We've never had anyone as interesting as a Rothschild to dinner!"

"Is that the only reason you asked?"

"No! No, of course not, I..." Ernest swatted the air, face still burning red. "I am only making an observation. Good day, Miss de Rothschild. I will send along an invitation card."

Caleb began beating the door again. I bid Ernest the swiftest of farewells, slamming the door on his still beaming face, and sprinted back down the hallway to my brother's bedchamber. I fumbled with the key in the lock – it clicked, loudly, and Caleb tumbled out of the room, so wild-eyed and unkempt anyone would have thought he'd been imprisoned for five years, and not merely locked in his chamber for five minutes.

"What happened?" he demanded.

"The key was stiff in the lock," I said. "Must've gotten stuck, somehow."

"How did it *lock itself?*"

"Who knows!" I threw up my hands. "You're always sayin' God works in mysterious ways!"

10

Mirah

Getting ready for dinner felt much like getting ready for a show, right up until the carriage arrived to whisk me away.

I dashed back and forth in the drawing room, fiddling with my earrings as Tabitha searched for the fur-trimmed dolman Eloise had added to my now impressively vast wardrobe, and felt unsettlingly like Ma the whole time. She'd had neither a fur-trimmed dolman nor a maid to search for it for her, but I harboured a hazy girlhood memory of sitting in the middle of a large bed we all shared, watching her dress to go out. I couldn't have said where in the world the bed was, but I remembered blue sky outside, softening into dusk, and heat that made my nightgown stick to me. Probably not England. Spain. Italy. Somewhere oranges grew, I knew. I could smell them now, mingled with Ma's perfume. She'd dressed in the finest things she owned, which were not even half as fine as the things I wore, and ordered Caleb to watch me in her absence.

Caleb had apparently taken that instruction to heart and never stopped, for he'd been sitting with an open book in his lap for most of the evening, and as I passed back and forth from my bedchamber to the drawing room, I noticed he hadn't turned a page in over ten minutes. Clearly he wasn't reading as avidly as he'd have me believe. I suspected he was far more interested in what I was doing. He had a desk and lamp in his chamber, and the lighting in there would be better than in the drawing room, lit mostly by glass sconces on the walls. There was no reason for him to be in the room other than to pry.

"Enjoyin' your book?" I asked, adjusting my necklace in the overmantel mirror. In the reflection I saw Caleb's eyes flash up from the page.

"It's riveting."

"It's upside-down is what it is."

Caleb moved frantically to turn it; there was no need. It was the correct way up, but it proved my theory that he hadn't been paying the least attention to it. He scowled, then closed the book so hard he was lucky he didn't squash his fingers in it. "Where are you going?"

There it was, finally. The real reason he'd been sitting there like a disapproving governess the entire time I was getting ready.

"Dinner."

"Where?"

"Someone's home."

"Who's?"

I rolled my eyes. "One of the opera's wealthiest benefactors," I said, somewhat alarmed by how easy it was to lie. "The main cast have to make an appearance, show our gratitude."

Caleb's face scrunched up, and his fists with it. "Ah. Mirah... you know I don't approve of..." He winced as if the words were physically painful to get out, broken pieces of porcelain in his throat. "I won't... stop you. Just know that you are worth more than that."

I flushed, understanding suddenly what he thought was going on. He didn't believe me about the opera. Or he did, but under wildly different circumstances to the ones I'd laid out. He thought I was someone's mistress, my fine clothes and our lavish apartment paid for in flesh at the whim of a wealthy gentleman. I couldn't even be offended. It would have made more sense than what was actually happening. I wondered if it would make things better or worse if I told him it was a woman paying our way. I mustered as much false indignation to my face as possible. "It ain't what you assume. I got the role on my own merit." That wasn't a lie, really. I *was* playing a role, and I'd earned it. The only difference was my stage was the streets of Mayfair rather than a theatre.

"Ain't it?" I knew I was in trouble when Caleb's accent slipped like that. He'd been tutored in Queen's English as a boy, and always took pains to speak it that way, but for all his efforts, the East End had weaselled its way into his accent, nonetheless. When he spoke like me I knew he was too worried or angry to keep up pretences.

He set his book aside and stood, stepping towards me with an almost pleading air. "Then where did you get this jewellery, this dress, the *furs?* Who's payin' for that carriage waitin' outside? I'm not tryin' to preach morals to you, Mirah. I'm scared. It's a dangerous game you play, and a precarious position to be in."

"Who's payin' for my clothes and carriage ain't your concern. Go back to your book, Caleb. Stop workin' yourself up or you'll set yourself off coughing again, you heard the doctor." I adjusted the apron of my dress, avoiding his gaze, though it burned into me. "I'll be home late. Have a good evenin'."

With that I glided from the room into the vestibule, thanking Tabitha as she emerged from the bedchamber with my dolman and draped it over my shoulders. Caleb watched me go, muttering to himself in French.

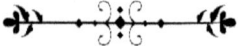

The house was every bit as grand as I'd envisioned. Perhaps not Versailles, but the closest to it I was ever likely to see in my lifetime. It was a towering white-faced townhouse, four stories high, with Grecian pillars holding up a portico above a blue-painted door, all shiny and smart with its brass lion knocker. As my carriage drew to a stop in front of it, I did my level best to bottle my nerves before they could escape, thanking the groom who opened the door and helped me down onto the cobbled street. It was so much cleaner than Limehouse.

For a moment I simply stood there as the groom lingered behind me, waiting for me to ring the bell. The smell of food wafted up from the basement kitchen – accessed down a set of spiralling wrought iron stairs to the left – making my too-often-empty stomach growl. It made me fear I'd give myself away instantly, years of painful hunger driving me to gorge myself as if it were my last meal. Ladies, I supposed, would be far more finicky and wasteful.

I'd lost track of how many times this evening I'd begun to think this was a foolish idea. Not only foolish, but dangerous. I wasn't walking into dinner, but a den of wolves. The smart part of me wanted to climb straight back into the carriage and flee.

"Miss?" the groom ventured, voice wavering with nerves. "Are you well?"

I turned to look at him. Could he see I was frightened? I forced a smile. "Quite well, thank you."

There was no going back, I realised. As soon as I'd taken any form of payment from Eloise Byron – the doctor's fees, the dresses, the apartment, even the damn *marzipan* – I'd been trapped. To balk now would be shirking my end of the deal, and I didn't doubt Eloise had sharp teeth behind those pretty lips, like any good she-wolf. She hadn't even given me the signed agreement I'd insisted upon, yet. If I failed her, she could go running to the authorities with any story she liked, and between the weeping society lady and the Jewess from Limehouse it was a fool's bet who they'd believe.

There was nothing for it but to follow it to its natural conclusion, whatever that was.

With a deep breath I stepped up to the front door, heels of my shoes clicking on the tiled steps, and gave the bell pull a hard tug. It rang out inside the house and a few seconds later the door opened to reveal Eloise's maid, Susanna, hair slightly askew beneath her white cap.

"Miss de Rothschild," she said, urging me inside. "Forgive me, we're rushing to prepare everything."

"Am I on time?"

"You're early," Susanna said, closing the door behind her. "Miss Byron saw to it that it would be that way. Your invitation says half an hour earlier than the others. This way, come. Mr Byron and the rest of the household cannot see you." She ushered me along down the hallway past the stairs, glancing back over her shoulder to check we weren't being watched. "Miss Byron has her own parlour for her private use. She's awaiting you in there."

She rapped her knuckles against the door and hurried away to continue with the dinner preparations, leaving me alone in the empty hall. My heart pounded in my chest, wondering what I'd do if Ernest came around the corner and saw me – but before I had to fret too deeply on that scenario, the parlour door opened, a pale hand shooting out to pull me into the room.

"You're here," Eloise breathed. "Thank God! I was worried you'd be late and get here the same time as everyone else!"

She was dressed so gloriously that for a moment I couldn't respond.

Her gown was rich wine red, with black tassels mounted upon the shoulders like military epaulettes and the same fringing along the hem of her overskirt. Jet buttons ran up the front of her bodice, the neckline of which was cut in a low square, and her hair was up, only a few glossy ebony tresses hanging loose over one shoulder, curled into perfect ringlets and brushing her collarbone. Everything appeared bizarrely stark in the dim lighting, the hollow of her throat a pit of inviting shadow. A simple black velvet ribbon was tied around her neck, the bow left to dangle all the way down over her bustle.

When I didn't reply, Eloise's brows pulled together in a serious frown.

"Whatever is the matter?"

"Nothin'," I said, wiping my hands on the front of my dress. They were suddenly very clammy. "I'm a little nervous, that's all."

"Did you do the reading I gave you?"

"Yes. A fortunate thing my brother taught me how."

"How to what?"

"To read. Not everyone in Limehouse can, you know."

Eloise blanched. "I didn't consider that..."

"Didn't expect you would." I glanced around, taking in the room that was apparently only Eloise's, the same size as the entire flat Caleb and I had shared in Limehouse. The furnishings were all soft plum velvet, the walls plastered with lilac and white striped paper and dozens of gold frames housing artfully arranged sprays of pressed flowers. Had Eloise pressed them herself? No, she surely had someone to do that sort of thing for her. She could probably afford a live-in servant whose job it was to exclusively press flowers.

"Well?" Eloise prompted. "Who is going to be in attendance tonight?"

The guest list she had provided me consisted entirely of pompous society friends – or acquaintances, since the sort of things she'd written about them didn't convince me she considered any of them friends.

First there was Pauline Beauchamp – pronounced the English way,

'Beecham', of course. From what Eloise wrote, Pauline had the wealth of an emperor, the fashion sense of a princess, and the brains of a chicken. She had no less than *nine* dogs, at least three of which accompanied her to every event she attended.

Then there was her husband, Henry. A gangling, awkward man who Eloise described as 'blatantly homosexual', an open secret that Pauline was apparently too preoccupied with her canine entourage to notice. Attending with the couple would be the strikingly handsome Leopold Brandt, a wealthy German ale merchant who lived with them, and who Mr Beauchamp followed around like one of the aforementioned puppies. Pauline had apparently been quoted as calling him 'quite lovely', and somehow did not question their unusual living arrangements.

Along with this trio came Helena Hall, with a reputation for glamour and hysterics. Helena was apparently prone to attaching herself anyone she considered a person of influence. A human leech, though devoid any of the medicinal benefits of her zoological counterpart. She was just the sort of guest we wanted, Eloise said, because she'd believe me without question, and belief was like fire: it only needed to catch flame to a few to spread to the many.

I listed these facts aloud like another stage monologue, hands folded neatly over my stomach. Eloise listened intently, occasionally nodding.

"Very good," she said finally, her whole body sagging with palpable relief. "I was worried you wouldn't have paid attention to any of it!"

"I'm an actress," I reminded her. "I know how to memorise lines."

"Yes, yes, of course. What of Mr Cardoza?"

Ah. Him.

Gideon Cardoza, the family's solicitor, was the one dinner guest I was most wary of. There hadn't been much written about him other than that he was blunt and clever, and, unhelpfully, that Eloise thought we'd have 'much in common' for the simple fact that he was also Jewish. My knowledge was lacking, but I had an unsettling feeling a Jewish solicitor in high society might have come dangerously close to meeting *actual* Rothschilds, though Eloise's notes made no mention of it. I did know, however, that the gulf between a Jew like Gideon Cardoza and myself was nearly as vast as that between Eloise and me. His family had been here for generations; he was an English gentleman before all else.

"He an... amiable fellow?" I asked.

"It depends on what mood you find him in," Eloise said. "He has a razor for a tongue, but he can be interesting company."

In my experience interesting company was not usually a compliment. Far more often it was a warning, the sort of term Cora might use to describe a handsy, intoxicated gentleman at the bar before she handed him off to me. I dearly hoped Mr Cardoza didn't prove to be *that* sort of interesting company. I could picture him now, a greying, bitter old man, aged by mountains of paperwork and disillusioned with the legal system.

"I'm sure I can manage him," I said. I'd managed many a man like that, in my time.

"Excellent. Let's go along, then. Ernest will be with us shortly, I'm sure. As soon as he's done preening..." Eloise gestured towards the door. "You read my notes on him too, I hope?"

"Yes."

I'd read them three times to imprint them on my brain. Ernest Byron, spoiled only son. He liked horses – betting on them, anyway – was overly invested in his appearance, and squandered a small fortune on hats, leaving them in carriages or gin palaces as prolifically as most people left calling cards. He pretended to like absinthe but hated liquorice since childhood. He was bad at cards and good at checkers and had fenced at school, always losing. He'd loved reading before his descent into depravity, and had a great fear of dogs on account of having been bitten by a great aunt's ugly Cavalier King Charles as a child, which necessitated him being seated as far from Pauline Beauchamp as possible.

It was curious that Eloise could recount so much about her brother in minute detail and yet feel no qualms about her plan. How hard her heart must have been to recall stories of him as a child, and still have grown so hateful towards him as a man that she wanted to see him ruined. It was a keen reminder that behind Eloise's smiling eyes and lyrical voice was a society woman, with a personality as cut-throat as any Limehouse robber.

It reminded me of something else, too. "I want our signed agreement," I said. "Like you promised."

Eloise observed me thoughtfully for a long moment, and I thought she was about to refuse. Finally, though, she whisked around and glided over to a small, lacquered black bureau by the window. "I'm a woman of my word," she said, taking a tiny key from somewhere in her dress and opening a drawer. "Here."

I took the envelope she offered, tearing it open to read the contents. It was exactly as I'd asked – a statement of intention, detailing our business together. Eloise's signature took up a preposterous amount of space on the page, all looping and dramatic. It suited her.

"Thank you," I said, tucking it into my bodice.

"I'd say you're welcome, but you didn't give me much choice on the matter. Come, then. Let's go to dinner." Eloise raised her chin proudly and headed for the door.

"He came to visit me, you know," I said, following her. "Ernest."

Eloise froze, hand resting on the doorknob. "What? When?"

"A few days ago."

"At the Mayfair apartment?"

"Where else? Haven't stepped foot in the music hall since we made our agreement, and I sure as hell wouldn't go back to Limehouse for any other reason."

"How did he get the address?" Eloise demanded. She left the door to grip my arm, fingers squeezing my bicep so tightly her nails dug into me. "Did he say?"

I shook my head.

"Damn it!" Eloise released me suddenly, and for all it pinched, I found myself oddly disappointed when her hand was gone from my arm. "Did he give any indication he did not believe you?"

"No," I said. "He believed everythin', I think. We only talked at the door, and he invited me to this dinner. I didn't tell him you already had. He mostly came to tell me he'd worked out the answer to my riddle."

"The one about *flatulence?*"

I laughed. Of course Eloise figured it out. Clearly the wits in this family had been unevenly distributed. "He got it wrong," I reported.

"I don't care!" Eloise snapped. "You should have told me about this the moment he left your apartment!"

"I thought perhaps you'd told him where to find me."

"And have him spring a visit on you with no warning? As though I would be fool enough to risk such a thing!"

I'd been right about that, then. That would be a dangerous game, even more dangerous than the one we were already playing. "Maybe he knows."

"No, I don't think so. My brother doesn't have the patience or self-restraint to keep a secret, especially if revealing it would cause me grief. If he knew he'd have told all of London by now." She pursed her lips. "Unless he plans to reveal it at dinner tonight, of course."

My blood froze in my veins. "Think I should leave?"

Eloise shook her head. "It's too late for that. We need to see this through to the bitter end." Bitterness being the more likely outcome, I thought. With that she left the room, dress train sweeping behind her, and signalled me to follow. I was helpless to do anything else, though my heart was now beating so hard in my chest I worried it would break through my ribs and escape me. I wanted to argue, but the words died on my lips as we reached the end of the hallway.

Ernest was standing there in his perfectly tailored dinner suit. His eyebrows raised when he saw me. "Miss de Rothschild." He dropped into a hurried bow. "You're early."

"I like to be punctual," I stated, amazed I was able to speak so calmly.

"Another admirable trait." Ernest smiled, and it was so pathetic that I found it nigh on impossible to believe he knew the truth. Ernest Byron did not strike me as a particularly talented actor, and his luck at cards only strengthened my belief. He finally remembered his formalities, straightening up and directing me towards the drawing room. "Wonderful that you're here. Please, go on through." He glanced at his sister. "Eloise."

"Ernest."

The air in the house felt much colder than when I'd arrived.

11

Mirah

I made several laps around the drawing room as we waited for the rest of the guests to trickle in, both hands clasped in front of me. Eloise made it clear in her notes that it was customary for the guests to congregate in the drawing room for an aperitif before dinner, to make idle chatter about what I could only assume were banal society matters. Each lady was to be accompanied to the table by a gentleman, who would be obliged to see her 'safely seated' before finding his own place. It made me question what would constitute 'unsafely' seated. I didn't expect we were to encounter any wild animals or enemy soldiers on our trek from the drawing room to the dinner table. The closest I'd ever come to such pomp and ceremony was Caleb insisting we sit at the table for Shabbos dinner every Friday, and I'd have taken a fit of apoplexy if he ever pulled my chair out for me.

The drawing room was as finely decorated as every other inch of the house. A large carved fireplace, gold overmantel mirror reaching high to the ceiling. A pair of mahogany divans with matching armchairs took centre stage, upholstered in wine red fabric and buried beneath a dozen tasselled pillows, and by the window stood a beautiful grand piano. Its wooden case was so polished and shiny I wondered if anyone ever actually played it – was it

Eloise's? It had to be. It couldn't be Ernest's. Eloise looked like she'd play the piano. Those long, graceful fingers of hers were perfect. I could picture them gliding smoothly over the ivories. Soft, with just enough pressure to elicit a pleasant tone, music so sweet that imagining it reverberating through me made my stomach squirm. I wasn't sure I was even imagining her playing the piano anymore. I rushed the thought away, frantically seeking something else in the room to occupy me.

There were a dozen stern-faced portraits dotted along the walls, watching me with such severe expressions that I thought maybe they saw me for the imposter I was. These had to be Eloise's ancestors, a fine pedigree of countless wealthy snobs dating back centuries. I could see some of her in their faces. The large, dark eyes. The dainty nose and deadly poise.

The largest portrait was of two small children, painted side by side in front of a beautiful young woman. It was so happy and peaceful that at first I struggled to understand what I was seeing: Eloise and Ernest, fresh-faced, innocent babes. They looked so comfortable standing together that it made me unexpectedly sad. Eloise had one chubby hand outstretched to grip Ernest's sleeve, both smiling. Their mother wasn't, though. She was elegant, very much like her daughter, but there was sorrow in her eyes that bled through the paint. One pale hand rested gently on Ernest's shoulder, a dazzling pearl and amethyst ring glittering on her finger, painted with such care to detail that I assumed it had to be some sort of heirloom.

The doorbell rang before I could conjure up any sort of conversation, and moments later Susanna announced the arrival of the Beauchamps and Mr Brandt.

Pauline was the first into the room, a chariot driver pulled by three yapping balls of fur that I scarcely recognised as dogs. I'd seen plenty of dogs in Limehouse, scabby mongrels scratching their hinds bare. These dogs were nothing like that. They were small, with big, bulging eyes and stumpy legs lost beneath a veritable cloud of fluff. And they were dressed in hats and costumes – that *definitely* distinguished them.

"Oh, Mr Byron! Eloise! How lovely to see you both!" Pauline cried, handing off the dogs' leads to the man behind that I could only assume was Henry Beauchamp. He was gangling, with soft, cherubic curls of golden hair and fluffy sideburns, and eyed the three dogs nervously as they began straining at the leash to reach Pauline. Over their ceaseless yapping it was difficult to hear anything at all.

"It's a delight to see you again, Mrs Beauchamp," Eloise said, loudly, accepting an enthusiastic embrace from Pauline with a smile so tight I had to smirk.

"Yes," Ernest said, taking a cautious step away from the dogs. "It is always nice to have you here. Henry."

"Ernest." Henry nodded. "I hope you're well?"

"Very."

It was a shouting match over the dogs, until at last Pauline knelt in front of them. They flung themselves at her, scrambling over the heap of her skirts, pink tongues lashing her hands and face. "Oh, my darlings. Please be quiet, my darlings. Mama is here, Mama won't leave you all night, she promises..."

I looked on, my dawning sense of horror mingled with the dangerous need to laugh. The dogs settled as though they could understand, just in time for Mr Brandt - who had sensibly been waiting in the hallway for perhaps precisely that - to enter. He was tall and handsome, just as Eloise's notes promised. Chiselled jawline, immaculately dressed. So immaculately that I couldn't help question what on earth about Henry Beauchamp attracted him, if the rumours were true. And from the way they eyed each other, Henry's entire neck reddening as though he'd not arrived in the same carriage as the man, it appeared they were.

Pauline was a burst of colour herself, draped from head-to-toe in peachy-pink, gown embellished with roses in every place it was possible to embellish a dress. The only thing more colourful than her was the dogs. One wore a dark blue bi-corn hat, trimmed with gold, and a matching jacket with epaulettes. Another wore a frothy white dress, the hem of which it repeatedly stepped on in its excitement, and what appeared to be a wig, studded with silver stars. They couldn't possibly be *real* silver, I reasoned. Even someone as disgustingly wealthy as the Beauchamps would recognise how ludicrous that was. Surely.

The third dog, who Pauline was currently peppering with kisses, wore what could only be described as princely regalia, complete with medals and a blue silk sash, which shifted as the dog's tiny body wiggled with delight.

"Mr Brandt." Ernest stuck out one hand in greeting as Leopold skirted around the dogs to greet his hosts. "Welcome."

"It is a pleasure to be here," Leopold said, his English heavily accented. "We brought a gift. Some of my finest ales. We have given them to your housemaid."

"Delightful. We'll serve them after dinner."

Leopold nodded, eyes suddenly cutting to me. "And who is this? Forgive me, I don't believe we've met before, Miss...?"

"This is Miss de Rothschild," Eloise injected, rushing to my side and grasping my arm. "She is visiting from France."

"De Rothschild?" Pauline stood, cradling the princely dog in her arms like a babe. "From the –"

"The banking family, yes." I laughed awkwardly. "I'm not certain why people keep asking me that."

Henry raised his eyebrows. "You never told us you were friends with the Rothschilds, Ernest!"

"She's a recent acquaintance," Ernest said, proudly.

"I've known her for years," Eloise added.

"Well, it is a joy to meet you, Miss de Rothschild! I'm Pauline. This is Napoleon," she gestured to the dog in the bi-corn, "Sisi – for the Austrian Empress," the dog with the stars in its wig, "and Albert. For the Prince Consort of course. God rest of his soul, and God save the Queen."

I nodded gravely. "I'm sure Her Majesty would be deeply moved by the tribute to her husband."

Eloise pinched me hard.

Helena Hall was the next to arrive, all but throwing herself at Eloise to kiss her cheeks in the continental fashion. Her dark purple dinner gown was emblazoned with gold embroidered peacock feathers, and hideously large diamonds adorned her ears. Her necklace, also diamonds, looked heavy enough to ground a ship. It made me worry for the structural integrity of her spine.

"Thank you for the invitation tonight," she said, kissing everyone else in turn until she got to me. "And you must be Miss de Rothschild! Miss Byron told me so much about you at tea. I must say, I have such enormous respect for the Rothschild family."

"How lovely." I stood stiff as a statue as I received the same blessing as the other guests. "I'll be certain to pass on your admiration."

"Oh, please do." Helena leaned back, frighteningly serious. "And I hope we come to be fond friends, you and I. You haven't considered investing in jewellery, have you? My father has a contact with several mines, and he gets the jewels wholesale at very competitive prices. He's looking for distributors to sell them for what they're *really* worth."

"Jewellery?" Pauline cocked her head, bearing an uncanny resemblance to one of her dogs. "I thought your father was in the stock exchange?"

"That was months ago!" Helena waved her hand, gesturing to her very sparkly ears. The diamonds appeared impractically heavy, stretching her earlobes in a way that could not possibly be comfortable. "Now he's in jewellery. He's being very generous, you know? He's giving people who wouldn't ordinarily have the opportunity the chance to start their own business – like women!" She turned beaming to me again. "Wouldn't you like to be a woman of independent means? Not that there is any shame relying on your family, of course."

"Ah..."

"You can work as much or as little as you like! It's entirely at your convenience!"

I was relieved when the bell in the vestibule rang again, for it distracted everyone from the look of panic I felt crossing my face.

"That must be Mr Cardoza," Ernest said.

The feeling of relief dissipated like smoke. Mr Cardoza, the notoriously sharp family solicitor. There was no time to prepare myself, for mere seconds later Susanna was guiding a gentleman into the drawing room. My mouth dropped open.

Either this man was not Mr Cardoza, or my imagining of him had served me wrong. This gentleman was young, no older than Caleb, and strikingly pleasant to look at. He was clean-shaven, his hair a glossy chestnut brown, swept back with a lemon-scented pomatum I could smell from across the room. His clothes were exquisitely tailored, all jet but for the splash of blue silk at his throat. His shoes were either brand new or diligently shined each day, and a silver watch chain ran from the button of his waistcoat to his pocket, just as brightly polished.

"Gideon," Ernest said. "Good of you to join us."

"I am on time," Gideon replied, apparently sensing a note of displeasure in Ernest's voice. He whipped his watch from his pocket, casting a discerning eye upon it. "Precisely two minutes early, in fact."

Immediately I had the dreadful sense Gideon Cardoza would not be as easily fooled as the others. His eyes swept to me. They were bottle green, and perilously clever. "I don't know you."

I fumbled into a curtsy. "Mirah de Rothschild," I said. "Of the –"

"Rothschild banking family, yes. I haven't been living in a cave in the Alps with my fingers in my ears. I'm quite familiar with the Rothschilds."

Just *how* familiar was the question. My tongue was lead-heavy in my mouth. "A delight to meet you, Mr Cardoza. I'm told you're a solicitor for the Byrons?"

"I'm *the* solicitor for the Byrons." Gideon held out his hand towards me, and it took me far too long to realise I was supposed to extend my own to him. He bent and kissed it politely, now close enough to examine me. "I'm sure we'll be swift friends, Miss de Rothschild."

12

Eloise

I never noticed how long the dinner table was until now, sitting at one end watching Mirah mentally reciting the order of the silverware to herself. I had planned the seating arrangements as thoroughly as one would a battle plan. It was unsociable for husband and wife to be seated together, and so I spared Mirah as much danger as possible in placing her close to Ernest – who as host dominated the head of the table – but beside Henry Beauchamp, whom I was positive posed no threat to us, and who had accompanied in Helena Hall, now on his other side. Opposite Mirah was Leopold, who had escorted in Pauline, now beside him, her dogs tethered to the chair leg. Next to Pauline sat Gideon, on whose arm I had entered. It was painfully precise.

As hostess I was obliged to head the other end of the table, forced to stare my brother down over a long expanse of glittering crystal and fine china, opposing generals in a war he did not even know we were waging. If it were not considered distasteful, and if it would not have prevented me keeping a close eye on Mirah, I would have placed a large bouquet of flowers as the centrepiece purely so I did not have to see Ernest.

"I hear a medical school for women has opened recently in London,"

Leopold said, leaning to one side as Susanna placed individual soup tureens upon the table in front of each guest. "How wonderfully modern that is. In Germany a woman must be fortunate enough to be the wife or daughter of a professor if she wishes for a university education. Or go to Switzerland."

"Switzerland is lovely," Henry put in, mildly.

"I don't see the point of it, myself," Ernest said.

Henry blinked. "Of Switzerland?"

"Of the women's medical school. Medicine is a ghastly profession for a woman to enter into."

"Why?" Mirah asked. "Do you think we've no stomach for blood?"

"Well, do you not fear a woman might faint at the sight?"

"Why would we? We see a lot more blood than most men."

Henry inhaled some of his wine, spluttering loudly.

"Oh dear," Helena said. "Poor Mr Beauchamp appears to be choking."

"I'm fine!" Henry cried, setting his glass down and thumping his chest with one fist. "Truly! I'm fine."

Ernest was red as a cooked lobster, staring at Mirah. "I didn't mean to offend you," he said, adding, almost worriedly, "you don't mean to become a lady doctor yourself, do you?"

"Don't trouble yourself about that," Mirah said, eyeing the food as Susanna lifted the lid off one of the soup bowls, releasing a wisp of delicious smelling steam. I wondered if Mirah had ever seen so much food on one dinner table before. The thought that she hadn't made me shift in my seat, bizarrely uncomfortable. What sort of things did eat in Limehouse? I pictured tasteless grey slop, and fish more bone than flesh, sharp scales that cut the roof of one's mouth. I pictured hard heels of bread, and dog passed off as mutton – a horror story I once heard and had no desire to verify. It made my stomach turn.

"Miss de Rothschild, surely you don't intend to eat the oysters?" Gideon Cardoza's voice brought me hurtling back to the present. Mirah was leaning forward, frozen in the act of reaching for the platter of oysters Sophie had just placed down. "Do the French Rothschilds not keep the laws of *kashrut* like their English cousins?"

Mirah's hand retreated at once. "Of course we do. I was reaching for the wine."

"It is Mr Byron's duty to serve your drinks at the table. He seems to be chomping at the bit to fulfil it."

"Yes. Forgive me." Mirah laughed weakly. "I'm so hungry that I've forgotten myself." She turned her attention to the soup being ladled into her bowl by Susanna, one hand hovering carefully over the arsenal of different spoons laid out on the tablecloth. Her eyes flickered briefly to mine as her fingers brushed one, and I nodded subtly. That was, thank God, the soup spoon.

"I can't say I blame you, Miss de Rothschild," Helena Hall chipped in. "This all smells divine!"

We survived the first few courses without incident. Oysters, onion soup and beef bouillon gave way to fried whitebait served with a Greek salad, and chicken fricassee upon a bed of rice. The fourth course was a choice between mutton on the bone, drenched in mint gravy, and grilled trout slathered in lemon butter. As more wine flowed and silverware scraped against china, I was pleased to see Mirah use the correct utensils for everything, keeping her conversation light and perfectly vague.

That was, of course, until Helena Hall had to go and open her mouth.

"You simply must tell us more about your family, Miss de Rothschild!"

Mirah paused, a piece of mutton halfway to her lips. "My family?" She set down her fork and smiled, though her gaze flashed to me again. "Surely you all know plenty about my family already? They are quite famous, as you all keep reminding me. I wouldn't want to bore you."

"We don't know as much as we'd like," Helena pressed. "But I was ever so disappointed to hear your cousin was defeated in the election. Such a shame."

"He's ever so disappointed himself," Mirah said. I didn't doubt she was correct. Lionel de Rothschild had been first elected to the House of Commons in forty-seven, and spent the next decade trying to take his seat. Since succeeding the man had been re-elected and defeated enough times that it was like watching a tennis match, but now, at his age, I fancied he was done playing.

"Is it true your English cousins are friends to the Prince of Wales?" Henry asked.

Mirah gave an obliging nod. "Oh, yes. Very good friends." That at least was something else easily verifiable. It caused quite the clamour when six years earlier the prince made his attachment to the family public, travelling to Buckinghamshire to stay at Mentmore, the Rothschild mansion said to boast no less than six-and-twenty bedchambers and an enormous glass-roofed grand hall.

"I can't imagine," Henry said, awed. "Friends with royalty. You'd be privy to all manner of scandalous stories. I hear the prince is a shameless hedonist!"

"Don't talk like that at the dinner table, Henry," Pauline scolded, too busy feeding one of her dogs a scrap of meat beneath the table to look at her husband as she addressed him. "It's tantamount to treason."

"Why are you not staying with your English cousins at Piccadilly House?" Gideon raised his wine glass to his lips, gaze fixed on Mirah so intently I was half expecting him to burn a hole through her skull. "It is odd that you came all the way from France and are not residing with them. A young woman, all alone. I cannot imagine why."

"Ah. Well, I confess, I promised my mother I would not..." Mirah looked down, pushing her food around on her plate. "She does not approve of how freely my English cousins associate with gentiles. After an aunt of mine married out of the faith the thought of me residing with them horrifies her. She'd hate to think of me dining here tonight. I don't share her opinion, but so long as it cannot get back to her that I am living with my English cousins, she can believe whatever she likes about the company I keep."

Inwardly I applauded the quick-thinking. Perhaps she had anticipated the subject coming up and prepared accordingly. Or maybe she was thinking of her brother, by her own account an unsociable sort.

"Then why did she allow you to come to London in the first place?" Gideon asked.

"She thought it was best," Mirah said. "After the war with Prussia, and the whole debacle with the Paris Commune."

"She sends you late. Why not when all of that was underway?"

"She had no urge to part with me with the country in such turmoil."

"It seems rather counterproductive to instead send you away now."

"This is an impertinent line of questioning, Mr Cardoza," Ernest interrupted, his sternness taking me by surprise. Doubtless he was remembering how thoroughly Mirah had scolded him for his own prying when they'd met in Hyde Park. "Can you not see you are making my guest uncomfortable?"

Gideon dipped his head. "Forgive me, Miss de Rothschild. Sometimes I am too inquisitive for my own good. There is a certain impertinence that comes with my profession. I was a barrister previously, and so am oft too accustomed to cross-examining people. Good at it, too, I am told."

Mirah's throat moved as she swallowed hard. Her smile was strained. "Forgiven, naturally."

There was a tense lapse in conversation for a few moments, before Pauline perked up with a little sound of delight. "Oh! Did anyone else hear? The Kennel Club is publishing the first volume of its Stud Book next month!"

I had never been so happy to talk about dogs.

The conversation about the Kennel Club went on far longer than reasonably acceptable, so long that I would have ordinarily steered the topic elsewhere three generations of pedigree ago. Tonight, though, it felt the safest subject in the world.

As Pauline jabbered on about her desire to breed her dogs – a prospect which did not appear to thrill Henry, who polished off two glasses of wine in one course – I noticed Mirah and Ernest conversing amongst themselves at the other end of the table. It was subtle, the occasional whispered remark that caused one or the other to smile or laugh. Mirah played her part effortlessly, Ernest's eyes never straying from her.

I wasn't sure why it irked me so. It was all part of the plan, was it not? And yet I caught myself gripping my cutlery so tightly that when I released it, the side of my thumbs were left with an imprint of the floral embellishment on the handles.

We were all but finished with the fourth course when Helena Hall let out a small sound of surprise. The rest of the table went very quiet. I glanced up from my plate – when had I stopped watching Mirah and Ernest? - and realised what caused the sudden silence.

Susanna had appeared to remove the plates of those finished with their meal, but Mirah was not among them. Instead she had picked up the bone of the mutton to strip it clean, doing so with the sort of intense precision that I could only imagine came from years of abject hunger. Her dark eyes flashed up to meet those of the other guests, and before anyone could say anything, she dropped the bone, turning first scarlet, then white with horror.

"I apologise," she said, shooting me a pleading look. "I just..."

"Is that how they do it in France?" Helena asked, wide-eyed.

Mirah hesitated for less than a heartbeat before nodding. "Oh, yes. This is how we do things *a la parisien,* these days. It is supposed to be a great compliment to the host that a guest does not wish to waste a single morsel. I forget that English society is a little more... formal."

A few thoughtful hums passed around the table. Helena Hall was the first to lunge for her own mutton, snatching the plate back from Susanna to do so. Henry followed suit, and Pauline, until everyone – Ernest included – was doing the same, a pack of ravenous animals laying waste to the scraps. It was deranged. I took a very large swig of wine, and joined in.

Only Mr Cardoza abstained.

13

Eloise

Never in my life had I been more grateful to leave a dinner table. When Susanna and Sophie took away the delicate Russian coffee cups of the last course, I could have fallen out of my chair from relief. The battle wasn't won yet, though. A digestif was to follow in the drawing room, and there would be more dangerous conversation to dodge.

As we all filed out of the dining room in the same order we'd entered I caught myself watching the back of Mirah's head intently as she walked beside Ernest, hanging off his arm and laughing at something he'd said. The sound of her laughter was lovely, lyrical, and yet I prickled with irritation.

"Is something troubling you, Miss Byron?" Gideon asked, drawing my attention.

"Of course not. Why?"

"You are frowning."

I immediately made to soften my face, shocked and embarrassed that I showed anything in my expression at all. I'd always imagined I had a better face for cards than Ernest.

"Perhaps a touch of indigestion?" Gideon suggested, and I could not tell if he honestly believed that or was offering me an excuse. I didn't care for the implications of the latter.

We settled on the sofas and armchairs as one of the footmen passed back and forth between us, serving Leopold's ales from a silver tray, and though I succeeded in planting myself directly across from Mirah, she did not even look at me.

"What shall we do now, then?" Henry asked, hiccupping loudly. His overindulgence at dinner was showing, for he was practically melting out of his armchair. "What do you all say to a game of bridge?"

"Oh, I love bridge," Helena said. "My papa is a bridge champion, do you know?"

"Of course he is," Gideon muttered beside me, just loud enough for me to hear. "What *doesn't* the man do?"

"Miss de Rothschild, do you enjoy bridge?"

Mirah tore her gaze from Ernest momentarily, cheeks pink. "Oh. Not really. How about dominoes? I'm very good at that. I always beat my..." She stopped, flushed, and cleared her throat. "I always beat my cousins, whenever we play."

"Oh, I hate dominoes," Henry complained.

"Henry," Leopold said, "your drink."

Henry sat up swiftly, righting his glass in his hand, which had been tipping precariously far forwards, one of Pauline's dogs lapping at the contents.

"Let's not play any games," Ernest said. It was the furthest thing I'd expected to hear from him, and that might have been shamefully obvious, for I snapped my head around to look at him.

"You don't want to play a game?"

"Well, we shouldn't encourage gambling." Ernest shifted his shoulders. "It is a bad habit."

Anyone who knew my brother would forgive me the sound I made. Had he hit his head on the door frame on his way in and become concussed? I noticed his eyes drift to Mirah at his side, and realised. Our plan was working. He did not want Mirah to think him a man of vice. I wondered how long he could keep up the act. Likely not as long as Mirah could keep up hers.

"Games are dull, anyway," Pauline said, airily. She had taken up the entirety of one of the two sofas herself, flanked either side by the two dogs that were not trying to drink from Henry's glass. "What about music? That piano by the window is beautiful, Miss Byron. Do you play?"

I'd been so focused on Ernest and Mirah that I'd all but forgotten I was in the room, not a passive observer but the hostess. Pauline's words dragged me back to earth and made my stomach sink.

"Oh. The piano?"

"Yes, she plays," Ernest said. "Very well, I might add."

"Goodness, then you simply must play for us, Miss Byron!"

I knew I was turning red. I felt it, hot up the back of my neck and creeping into my ears. "I don't really do so any more..."

"Don't be foolish, Eloise," Ernest said. "You are talented. Go on. Play for our guests."

"Ernest, please."

"Everyone is waiting."

I wanted to leap from my armchair and strangle him, but the whole room was watching, even Mirah, her dark eyes transfiguring me to stone. I wished they really could petrify me, for at least then I would have a good reason not to play. Instead, I forced a smile and stood.

"Very well. Just one song..."

Pauline squealed with delight, so shrill that the two dogs either side of her pricked their ears to attention.

My heart was racing as I took a seat on the piano stool, lifting the fallboard and staring at the keys. I hadn't touched them in years, and was afraid of what might happen when I did. Memories were soaked into the mahogany wood of the case, staining the ivories, and I dreaded putting my fingertips to them, should those memories come flooding into me. I hated Ernest for pushing me to this. He knew very well why I did not.

I expelled a soft breath through my nose and began to play.

I was eight years old again, squeezed onto the end of the bench with Mother and Ernest, watching her hands move gracefully over the keys, my own so much clumsier as they played a chord, then another, and another, just the way she'd shown. Her voice was in my ears, gentle and loving and full of praise. Then Ernest had his turn at the other end of the keyboard. I remembered lessons on breezy summer afternoons, carols on Christmas Eve. I remembered Ernest and I sneaking down from the nursery whenever our parents entertained, watching through the crack in the door as Mother played for all their guests. Most of all I remembered how she had only ever looked happy when she was playing. So happy she hadn't even shirked from Father's hand on her back.

By the time I was done playing the song, finishing to a smattering of applause, my vision swam with tears. I was glad I was far enough across the room for no one to notice. I hadn't even realised I was playing, lost somewhere in the past, hands guided by memory and instinct.

"Lovely!" Helena cried, shooting up to give a standing ovation. The sudden movement sent Pauline's dogs into a frenzy. The two on the sofa sprung up and started yapping, which in turn caused the one sniffing around Henry's legs – Albert? – to leap onto the low occasional table closest to Ernest, who flew to his feet, nearly upending his ale all over Mirah.

"Stay away!"

"Oh, he doesn't mean any harm," Pauline said, rising to collect Albert. "My poor darlings. They're very sensitive, and loud noises often alarm them."

"We know," Henry mumbled, taking a large swig of his drink and scrunching up his nose as he got a mouthful of dog-slobber.

Mirah reached out one hand to touch Ernest's arm. He was still standing, gripping his glass so tightly it was a wonder it did not shatter in his hand. "It's all right," she said, softly. "It can't hurt you."

Ernest swallowed hard, dropping hesitantly back onto the sofa. I was rather pleased the dogs had their little outburst, for it served him right for making me play.

"Well, that was eventful," Leopold said, when calm was finally restored. "You play splendidly, Miss Byron!"

"Indeed," Gideon agreed. "What of you, Miss de Rothschild? A Rothschild daughter must be very accomplished."

Mirah stiffened. "I don't really like to play."

She didn't know how, I realised, struck by a sudden desire to teach her. Not that it would do her any good now. Gideon persisted. "Neither does our hostess," he said, "but she was gracious enough to oblige."

"I'm really not very good," Mirah insisted, gripping her glass tightly. "But I could sing."

Sing. Of course. I'd entirely forgotten the talent she inherited from her mother. I'd only heard her reciting uncouth limericks, but even then there was no denying her voice was most agreeable.

"Please sing for us," Helena begged. "Perhaps Miss Byron could play the accompaniment?"

Mirah looked at me. My mouth was too dry to respond, but I nodded.

"Alright," Mirah said, making her way towards me. "Do you know Cherubino's Aria, Miss Byron? *Voi Che Sapete*?"

I nodded again.

"If you would, then."

It took me two false starts to recall the piece – an embarrassment, for what lady did not know Mozart? - but once I began in earnest, Mirah straightened back her shoulders and started to sing.

Her voice was angelic. There was no other word for it, cloying and cliché as it was. I barely glanced at the keys as I played, held captive by Mirah's grace. The music poured out of her, as if she were not a singer at all, but a conduit for something greater. Each note, each lyrical rise and fall, made something in me tremble. I might have hit a dozen wrong notes without even registering it. My chest swelled with the strangest sense of pride. I wished to turn to everyone else in the room and announce that I knew her better than any of them, that perhaps this song was meant for me, a secret shared between us.

But I couldn't, because I didn't. And it wasn't.

When I turned my head to look back at the others, Ernest was staring at her too.

14

Mirah

The last note of the song was still ringing in my ears, but the room was dead silent. Then the applause broke over me in a wave. Even Pauline stood, though it started her dogs up barking again. I was shaking to the tips of my fingers, legs weak as reeds. I'd never performed to a room like that before. It was different in the music hall. No one visited those establishments to see an opera, or to truly listen to a singer. They came to drink, and laugh, and leer. Sometimes they came purely to solicit a girl to do other things with her mouth.

Here in Eloise's drawing room I was more than just a pair of good legs in clocked stockings who happened to sing well. I was an accomplished lady, with talent and skill to be admired. Was this how Ma felt when she performed on real stages in real opera houses, before some wealthy man got my brother on her? The thought made something twinge in my chest, a dull ache beneath my ribs.

Henry clapped. "Bravo! You could be on the stage!"

"That's hardly an appropriate thing to say to a lady, Mr Beauchamp," Helena interjected. "Everyone knows what *opera girl* truly means. You should not insult Miss de Rothschild with such vile insinuations!"

The pride I'd felt was sucked straight out of me, bitterness taking its place. It wouldn't do me any favours to forget what I was, mistake myself for something better.

"Well, it will be difficult to follow such talent," Leopold said. "Does anyone else wish to showcase their musical ability? Mr Cardoza?"

"I'd sooner pull out my own teeth, thank you," Gideon replied.

Helena, however, thrust her ale glass into Leopold's hand, adjusting her heavy diamond necklace and marching determinedly towards the piano. "Oh, go on, if you all insist. Papa says I have ever such a lovely voice!"

Either Helena Hall's dear papa was lying to her, or the man's hearing was beginning to fail. A cat with its tail in a thumbscrew would have sounded sweeter. Pauline's dogs, howling along, carried the tune better.

It was a miracle I showed nothing in my face throughout the performance, and I thought perhaps I ought to give God a second chance for granting me the composure. Caleb would certainly approve of that, even if he did think I was busy making the beast with two backs with some pompous gentleman to pay our way. Maybe if I only ventured to utter the Shema now and then he'd stop sticking his nose in my private affairs.

"That was very nice, Helena," Pauline said, as Miss Hall returned to her seat. Henry, who now may as well have been on the floor for how much he was sliding out of his chair, opened his mouth to say something, but a stern look from Mr Brandt clamped it shut again.

"Thank you," Helena said. "I will be performing at a soiree my papa is hosting in a few weeks," she added. "He'll be discussing the merits of the exciting business opportunity he's offering. It will be very exclusive, but I'm certain I could secure you all invitations."

A ripple of uncertain hums and overly polite excuses made the rounds through the room, from all except myself and Gideon, who rolled his eyes.

The clock on the mantle striking midnight made everyone in the drawing room jump. Panic rushed over me, recalling a fairytale Caleb once read me where a servant girl attending a royal ball in splendour must be gone before the stroke of midnight, lest the spell break. For a terrible moment I was that girl, half expecting my pretty silks to wither into rags, my face and hands to stain with ash. But that wasn't how the world really worked, and the childish fear passed as swiftly as it came over me.

"Goodness, I had no idea that was the time," Henry said, making to stand and swaying precariously as he did. "We'd best make our way home."

I was the last of the guests to leave, lingering in the vestibule as Eloise and Ernest bid everyone goodnight.

"It was delightful to meet you, Miss de Rothschild," Gideon said, adjusting the lapels of his coat. "When next we meet you simply must tell me more of your English cousins. I expect the menus at their dinners are sublime." His eyes twinkled.

That was when I realised I'd walked into a trap.

Eloise insisted on seeing me home in her carriage, but I barely registered her words. I was positive I was going to be sick, and as Eloise bundled me into the carriage I leaned over and popped open the window, determined that if I was going to vomit it would not be all over this rich woman's shoes.

I was shaking so much I didn't even acknowledge Ernest, standing on the doorstep to wave me off. He'd tried to beg the honour of helping me up into the cab, but Eloise shooed him away and slammed the door before he could get a word in. As we started off down the street the cool air in my face helped, even with the bouncing of the wheels. I pressed my head against the cold glass, every rumble vibrating in my skull. I hoped it would shake my brain into mush and spare me having to tell Eloise what a mess I'd made of everything.

"You did splendidly tonight," she said, satisfaction evident in her tone. She was seated on the bench opposite me, smiling broadly. "There were a few – hiccups, shall we say, but you navigated them like a true lady! And your quick-thinking, with the bone at dinner... just wonderful. You should be very proud of yourself; it was a fine performance!"

"No it wasn't," I said, lifting my head. "I completely fucked it."

"What do you mean?"

"Mr Cardoza. He knows."

Eloise's mouth fell open. "How? How could he possibly –"

"He tricked me. At dinner." I dropped my gaze as I mumbled the words. I didn't like being the bearer of bad news, and I didn't want to see Eloise's face when she realised how thoroughly I'd doomed us.

"I don't understand..."

"He asked me if I kept to the laws of *Kashrut*, 'like my English cousins'."

"And?"

"And I don't think the English Rothschilds keep kosher. Or if they do, it's very loosely." I sighed. "My brother complained about it. He read somethin' about how because they're throwin' all their fancy dinners for royalty, they're assimilatin', eatin' whatever their guests eat. Even turtle soup! Mr Cardoza knows it. He was tryin' to catch me out. He succeeded."

"Surely you can't be certain of that..."

"Even so, I still fucked it. I forgot all about it and mixed meat and dairy at dinner. That ain't allowed. That he didn't say anythin' about my choice of dish only proves it. I fucked it!"

"Could you please stop saying you *fucked it*?"

"Sorry." I leaned back against the seat, utterly defeated, and brought one hand up to wrangle the decorative comb out of my hair. "I've ruined us. My brother would say it served me right."

"You haven't ruined anything yet," Eloise said, firmly. "Mr Cardoza said nothing of it."

"But he will."

"Unless we motivate him not to."

"How do you hope to do that?"

"Believe me, there are ways to convince a man to hold his tongue." Her eyes twinkled in the lamplight, half mischief, half secrets, and I got the sense there was a great deal she was keeping from me. I didn't like that. We were both liars, yes, but I'd been more comfortable when I thought we were liars together, sharing in the same scandalous, perilous untruth. That she might have other secrets made me uneasy. I didn't know why. Of course she had other secrets. Everyone did, especially ladies, and why should I be privy to them? She barely knew me.

We passed the rest of the ride in silence, Eloise leaning to open the carriage door for me when we drew to a stop outside my building. I still wasn't used to the sight, all clean, pale stone and wrought iron balconettes, lamps lining the pristinely swept street. There were no urchins begging at the roadside, no pure-collectors digging through the gutters, and the night was still, missing the Limehouse lullaby of brawling and retching and angry seagulls. In a way I missed those sounds. It was a bit *too* quiet in Mayfair.

"Come inside with me," I blurted. I didn't know where the invitation came from, but it was out of my mouth before I could stop it. Eloise froze.

"Come inside?"

I nodded. "Yes. For a nightcap."

"Ah. Well." Eloise cleared her throat. The door was hanging wide open, a draught creeping into the cab, but we were still seated. "I don't know if that is a good idea. I should be home soon, else Ernest will wonder where I am..."

"He knows you're accompanyin' me home," I said. "We're friends, aren't we?"

Eloise stared at me, lips parted as if she wanted to speak, but couldn't.

"For this ruse?" I clarified.

"Oh. Yes, we are..."

"Friends invite their friends in for nightcaps. It's only polite."

"Miss, is everything well?"

Our heads swivelled in unison to the open door, where the groom who'd been riding on the back of the carriage was now standing, concerned.

"Everything is perfectly fine," Eloise assured him. She glanced back at me, and finally smiled. "Keep the carriage parked here, if you would. I'll be joining Miss de Rothschild for a quick nightcap."

It was risky business inviting Eloise Byron into the apartment when Caleb would be there, but once I'd asked and she'd accepted I could hardly rescind the offer, especially when she was the one paying the rent. I told myself that so long as we were quiet, we wouldn't have any problem; Caleb's cough was easing up since moving to Mayfair, and he slept more deeply for it. He probably had a whole year of sleep to catch up on.

Tabitha met us at the door, having apparently opted to stay awake to see me in, which made me feel unbearably guilty. The gaslamps were still burning in the drawing room to welcome me home. I kicked off my silk pumps as we entered, sending them flying much further than I'd anticipated.

"Whiskey?" I offered, tossing my earrings onto the closest table, a dainty little octagonal thing I thought could serve no greater purpose than holding a single candle or fancy vase. Eloise sat down on the sofa opposite, doing so much more primly than I, knees together and hands folded in her lap.

"Whiskey?" she said. "That's a little strong, don't you think?"

That was precisely the point. I wanted to be drunk. So drunk I didn't have to think about Gideon Cardoza at dinner, or the fact that Ernest had somehow gotten hold of my address. "It's only a glass," I said. "I don't fancy wine, and openin' a bottle of champagne will be noisy. My brother is asleep just down the hall."

"I'd quite forgotten about him."

"If only I could be so lucky."

Eloise's lips curled into a smile. "I won't argue your opinion. You know how I feel on the subject of brothers."

"Only too well. How you feel on the subject of brothers is payin' my way." I moved to head to the kitchen, but Tabitha cut me off.

"I'll fetch it, Miss," she said. "You sit down."

I would have refused, but my feet were sore from the uncomfortable new shoes, the sofa beckoning to me. She was gone before I could make any protest, and so I sat. "He doesn't seem so awful, y'know? Ernest, I mean."

"You've only known him a short while. You'll learn."

"Don't misunderstand me, he's an imbecile, but he doesn't strike me as cruel."

Eloise pursed her lips for a second, and I was worried she was about to get up and leave. Tabitha reappeared with the drinks just in time.

"Thank you," I said, taking both glasses from the tray and thrusting one towards Eloise. "You ought to go to bed now, Tabitha. You shouldn't have waited up for me."

"You're my mistress, Miss," Tabitha said. "It's my duty. It wouldn't do for you to come back to a dark house and have to get a drink for yourself, would it?"

I frowned. "I've come back to worse. I'm capable of lightin' some lamps and fetchin' a bottle for myself. Don't stay awake on my account in future."

Tabitha appeared to want to argue, and though I disagreed with her completely on the matter, I half wished she would, just so I didn't feel so much like one of Eloise's ridiculous friends, ordering someone around. Instead she merely nodded, gave a curtsy, and left. I really wished she wouldn't curtsy.

"You need to become more comfortable having somebody serve you," Eloise said, bringing her glass to her lips. "Even at dinner tonight you kept reaching to do things for yourself. It is an obvious tell."

"I don't think that'll be easy for me," I said. I stretched out on the divan, resting my feet on one of the scrolled arms. "I've had to fend for myself most of my life, and when I was too young to fend for myself, Caleb was fendin' for me."

"Where was your mother?"

"I told you, she died when I was ten."

"But before then?"

"She did her best." I took a swig from my glass, a trail of fire trickling down my throat into my stomach. It settled there pleasantly, warming my insides. "I had a strange childhood. Don't even know what country I was born in."

"How is that possible?"

"I never thought to ask her, though I think I was born in France. We were there the longest, before England. We moved around so often I never really knew where we were. How do you think I know so many languages, despite growin' up so poor?" I smirked down into my drink, amber in the firelight. "I'm a child of the continent!"

"Why did you move so often?"

"Chasin' my pa. Or the man she'd have me think was my pa, anyway. I don't believe for one quick second he was actually the man who did it." I shrugged. "He was some wealthy gentleman, see. Ma had it in her head she was his lawful wife, though she never produced anythin' to prove it. She thought she could make him love her – us. All three of us. She dragged us halfway 'round the world followin' him. Maybe I'm not so different to all your lot after all. I probably did the Grand Tour three times over as a babe!" I laughed and drained my glass.

"I'm sorry," Eloise said, softly. "That sounds so..."

"Don't pity me over it, please. I hate that."

"But it is deplorable, what that man did."

"What did he do?"

"He abandoned your poor mother!"

"Did he?" I raised one eyebrow. "How would I know? I know only what Ma told me, and she wasn't there half the time. Who's to say what the truth is. Doesn't matter anyway, does it? Chasin' a rich man across the globe didn't get her anywhere but dead." I reached out and set my empty glass down on the table with an air of finality.

I could tell Eloise wanted to say sorry again, as if the word meant anything. I'd made my point, though, because she took an impressive gulp of her own drink instead, making a face as she did.

"I know what it's like," she said, finally, bringing one fist to her chest to quell the flames from the liquor. "To lose a mother."

Though tense from recounting my own story, I softened minutely. I should have guessed that, from the sad painting on the wall and the fact no mother was ever mentioned in this wild inheritance scheme of hers.

"When?" I asked.

"About five years ago, now."

"How?"

"A sickness. Not like your mother, though. It was something that grew in her, Doctor Hartley said. He tried to cut it out, but... it grew back." Eloise clasped both hands around her glass, fingers interlaced. "Father took it very hard. Things were difficult between them, but he loved her very much. I think that's when he stopped trusting Doctor Hartley."

"And your brother?"

"Ernest took it hard, too, but he dealt with it in his own way."

There was something in her tone that made me want to press further. It wasn't quite bitter, but I sensed a great deal more beneath her words that she left unsaid. Or maybe that was just the whiskey, whispering nonsense into my brain.

"Maybe I should go and get the bottle," I said, when I noticed Eloise's eyes glazing over. "We can drink until we both forget."

Eloise laughed. "I wouldn't turn down one more glass."

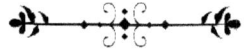

I couldn't say how many more glasses we had between us, because I wasn't pouring them by any traditional measurements. All I knew was that I was delightfully warm all over, tingling from toes to fingertips, and somehow progressed from sitting to hanging upside-down off the sofa with my legs in the air, stockings on full display.

Other than my unorthodox position, I didn't think I was so egregiously drunk. Eloise was far worse. At some point she'd moved from perching daintily on the edge of the sofa to sitting on the floor, her skirts fanned out around her. Some of her hair had fallen from its arrangement, long dark strands that she kept having to blow out of her face.

"Ernest continues acting as though he's the head of the household," she said, muttering it around the rim of her glass. She'd been on the topic for some time now, showing no sign of relenting. "But *I'm* the one who runs it. I'm as good as Father's secretary, not that Father would ever acknowledge that. I write his letters, arrange all his appointments, yet still he keeps the drawers of his bureau locked and doesn't allow me into his meetings with his accountant, or Mr Cardoza..." She scoffed. "You'd think he'd trust me more."

"Speakin' of Mr Cardoza, how you plannin' on keepin' him quiet?"

"Oh, I have some idea. Do you recall what he said, about having been a barrister?" She pointed to an imaginary wig on her head. "He was well respected, terrifying in the courtroom by all accounts. Then he left the bar suddenly and became a humble family solicitor instead."

"Why?"

"Rumour has it someone blackmailed him into leaving. I wouldn't be surprised if he has a few delectable secrets." She hiccuped.

"So your plan is to blackmail him too?" I didn't like where this was going. Fraud and impersonation of a Rothschild was bad enough. Adding blackmail to our growing list of crimes didn't strike me as wise.

"That makes it sound so crass," Eloise said, tucking her knees up against her chest to rest her chin on them. "I merely plan to remind him that we all have things we'd rather remain private."

"Blackmail, right. How d'you know he's not already told someone what he knows?"

"It's not his way, believe me. The man has a flair for dramatics. He'll wait until I have implicated myself as thoroughly as possible before he tells anyone."

"You think we ought to stop?"

"No. I'll just have to keep implicating myself. Meanwhile, we must work to discover Mr Cardoza's secret."

Eloise Byron was as ruthless as she was ambitious. In a way I respected it, even fearing the consequences. Something of my unease must have shown in my face, because she shuffled closer on her bottom, the deadly serious look in her eyes a comical juxtaposition to how she moved. From upside-down the effect was doubly absurd.

"Do not pain yourself over it," she urged. "Yes, you're a liar, I am a liar, but we're hardly the only ones. Everyone you met at dinner tonight is the same. Helena Hall, for example – what a joke! Her father is renowned for his duplicitous business schemes. I had to steer my own father away from investing in one of his ventures once, though Father insists on keeping the Halls around out of some misplaced sense of guilt for backing out!"

"Her jewellery was impressive."

"I wouldn't be surprised if those ugly things she was wearing all evening are naught but cut glass."

"Really?"

"Really. Her father is so deeply in debt he could be a miner himself."

"And the Beauchamps?"

"Well Pauline is a fool, but an honest one. Her husband and his bit of German sausage are liars, but that's for good reason, so I cannot fault them. Mr Cardoza is no different, save one thing: he's a *good* liar."

"What about you?"

Eloise leaned back, the smile slowly fading from her face. "What do you mean?"

"Are *you* a good liar?" I shifted on the divan, swinging my legs to one side to right myself until I was seated properly. "You must have some secrets other than this one. Everyone does. My brother, for example, puts on that ridiculous accent as if he ain't from the gutter. You should hear him when you rile him up! So, what about you? What's yours?"

I watched the colour creep up Eloise's slender neck, her cheeks glowing crimson as the flush reached her face, already ruddy from the drink. "I don't have any," she said, her blush contradicting her.

"You can't expect me to believe that. Society ladies are full of secrets!"

"What do you know of society ladies? You've met three of them." Her words were sharp, cutting through my humour. I felt certain I had soured our merriment beyond repair.

"I didn't mean –"

"Yes, you did." Eloise gazed up at me from beneath her long black lashes, her demeanour suddenly changing; I felt the difference like the pressure dropping in the air before rain. "You truly want to know my secret?"

"If you'll share it."

"Will you share yours, if I do?"

"Maybe," I said. "If yours is worth it."

Eloise hesitated. I thought perhaps she was going to abruptly sober up and accuse me of trying to pry information out of her, but then she leaned in towards me. Her lips came within an inch of mine, as though to kiss me, but before I could process the unexpected closeness she lurched violently back, leaving me to tumble forward with my lips parted. Eloise jumped to her feet, full skirts nearly knocking over the table with the whiskey on it.

"Forgive me," she said, bringing one hand to her mouth. Her fingers touched her lips as if she expected them to be cut from coming so close to mine. As if my teeth were sharp, the fangs of a feral dog from the streets of Limehouse. I didn't know if she was apologising for the almost-kiss or nearly tipping up the table. If it was the latter she could do whatever she liked - it was technically *her* table - but I sensed it was the former.

"It's all right," I said.

"No. No, it is not." She stepped away, turning in a few frantic, wobbly circles, and then started abruptly towards the door. "Goodnight, Miss Zelikovich."

I shot off after her, lifting my skirt so that I could run. It was far easier to chase after her without my delicate silk pumps, although my stocking-clad feet slid on the hardwood floor. She fled the apartment and down the stairs into the main vestibule, flinging open the front door with such urgency anyone on the street would have thought the house ablaze. Her carriage was still parked outside, the driver jolting awake as she launched herself into the crisp night.

"Eloise! Wait!"

"I must get back."

With that she threw open the carriage door, both of us shocked to discover the groom asleep inside, cap tipped over his face. He shot upright with a loud inhale as if risen from the dead, rolled off the bench with a thud, and scrambled out as Eloise pushed past him into the cab without waiting for him to climb out.

"Tell the driver to go fast," she ordered, voice tart. Watching her trip on the hem of her dress, propping herself up inside the carriage, I realised just how drunk she was. Just how drunk *I* was, my head spinning as I stood at the side of the road.

Eloise didn't look at me as the groom slammed the door shut and jumped up onto the back of the carriage. The driver rubbed the sleep from his eyes and spurred the horses to a canter, the clopping of their hooves echoing on the too-quiet street, and just like that, she was gone.

I watched her carriage until it turned the corner, shivering in the sharp evening chill. My stomach twisted like an old rag, something acidic clawing its way up my throat. I thought it might be my heart escaping, wanting nothing more to do with me. No – not my heart. Definitely not.

I keeled over and decorated the front step with Eloise Byron's fancy dinner.

15

Mirah

My skull had cracked open like an egg, my brains all dribbled out.

At least that's what I thought must have happened, with how badly it hurt. The pain was a lance in my temples, a dull pulsing behind my eyelids that spread through my forehead. I opened my eyes slowly, cringing against the light.

It was morning, and I was sprawled on the drawing room sofa still in my dinner dress with a blanket draped over me. A fire crackled in the hearth, embers spitting up the chimney, and a glass of water was sitting on the octagonal table in place of the whiskey bottle.

"Next time I'll just leave you to die."

I groaned, lifting my head off the pillow. Caleb was sitting in the armchair by the fire, arms crossed like a stern mother, staring right at me.

"Please do, if it'll spare me your judgement."

Caleb scoffed. "Nothin' is going to spare you my judgement. Not after last night. I heard everythin'. Not bloody quiet, are you?"

My heart stilled and I completely forgot I was dying an alcohol induced death, sitting bolt upright. The room spun, and I flung out an arm to brace myself on the sofa, gripping it for dear life as if it would take off galloping from under me like a wild horse. "Everythin'?"

"Everythin'. I know exactly what you and your fancy friend are up to, trickin' her brother. A rich lady come to do charity in Limehouse – I should've known better! *She's* the one payin' our way!"

"Ain't that better than if it was a gentleman?"

"No!" Caleb threw up his hands. "Not when you're committin' fraud! Do you have any idea how much trouble you could get yourself into it? You ain't a Rothschild!"

"I could be for all you know. Ma was never very forthcomin' about our Pa."

"Mirah!"

"I'm sorry, alright?" I shivered in the morning chill, pulling the blanket around myself. "I know it's not good, but what other choice did I have?"

"Any other choice! Literally *any* other choice!"

"You were sick," I countered. "Fixin' to die!"

"I was fine!"

"Like hell you were. I had to hear you hackin' up your lungs every damn night. That didn't sound so fine to me. Eloise said she could help you if I agreed to her plan."

"Eloise?" Caleb's voice dripped with contempt. "That informal with a lady of means now, are you?"

My cheeks burned. I prayed that for all he'd heard, he had no idea just how *informal* things had really gotten between us before Eloise had run off into the night. "She's helpin' us."

"Helpin' to set us up for a long stint in Newgate! Honestly, I always figured you for clever!"

"Now you tell me that," I mumbled. I couldn't look at him. I was used to his chiding, but this was different. Usually when he scolded me for something I was happy doing it anyway, confident in my own convictions. This time I knew he was right. I hated that. "What do you expect me to do about it?"

"Stop," Caleb begged. "Tell her your little deal is off!"

"I can't. I already took things from her. The apartment, the dresses, the *doctor*."

"So?"

"So if I bail out, who's to say she wouldn't go straight to the coppers claimin' I tricked her? Who d'you think they'd listen to, me or her?" I busied myself with smoothing out the wrinkles in my dress. It was useless after sleeping in it. It still smelled of last night's perfume and liquor, faint and sour. "Besides, if this works out it'd be a whole new life for us."

"We don't need a new life."

At that, my head snapped back up. "You're jokin', right? You want to live in that shithole in Limehouse forever?"

"No," Caleb said. "But I want my sister alive and well and not rottin' in a prison cell. That's what's important to me. We don't need to live in luxury. We can find ways to get by, always have."

"Barely."

Tense silence followed my words, all the colour leeching out of Caleb's face.

"You're right," he said, finally. "Barely. But I'm scared for you, Mirah. I watched Ma run herself into the grave chasin' what you're after. I don't wanna' watch you do the same."

"You watched Ma run herself into the grave chasin' a useless man. I'm not like her." Caleb looked as though he had more he wanted to say, but I cut him off, rising to my feet. My stomach growled, turning itself inside-out. "God, I feel sick."

"I'd make some comment about it teachin' you a lesson, but I know that's wasted on you."

"Good that you know that, it'll save us time," I said, dropping back onto the sofa, head in my hands. It felt like it was about to drop right off my shoulders, and hurt so badly I was inclined to let it. "Fetch me a bowl."

"Too much rich food in your stomach makin' you ill?"

"Bowl. Please."

Caleb had apparently been anticipating this, because he produced the porcelain bowl from my washstand immediately, thrusting it beneath my nose.

"Thank you," I mumbled, forcing my chin up slightly to look at him. He was flickering in and out of focus. "And please, let me alone about Miss Byron. I'm too deep in it now to back out, I have to see it through to the end."

Caleb pursed his lips. "Fine. You ain't a little girl any more, I can't stop you. But I'll have nothin' to do with it, you hear?"

A twinge of guilt prickled my insides, an unpleasant companion to the feelings already churning around in there. "That could be a problem," I admitted.

"Why?"

"I might have told Ernest you were my footman."

"*What?*"

I lurched forward and emptied my stomach into the bowl.

Eloise and I had planned to meet that afternoon at Hyde Park to discuss our next move, but I was starting to fear she wouldn't come. I kept running through the night before in my mind, half believing it had been a fever dream. It couldn't have been. I remembered her lips so close to mine I could smell the whiskey on her breath. I couldn't have invented that. My mind wasn't that ambitious.

I huddled deeper into my cashmere paletot, so soft against my skin that I wanted to disappear into it forever rather than sitting here on a cold iron bench waiting for someone who might not show up. I'd offended her real badly last night if I recalled, but I was positive she was the one who had almost kissed me, not the other way around. Even if Eloise was frightfully charming, I wasn't a fool. Girls from Limehouse didn't kiss people like her. I'd never have dared, no matter how deep into my cups I was. Besides, I'd sworn myself off that sort of weakness – didn't rightly matter if it was a man or a woman, affection was a fatal thing. Ma proved that. This was business, and nothing more.

I was considering starting back home when I heard the steady clop of approaching hooves, swivelling my head around to look. It was Eloise, riding side-saddle on a pretty bay pony, accompanied by the same groom that had fallen asleep in the carriage, mounted on another horse a short distance behind her. She was resplendent in a sleek black riding habit, crop in hand and a hat tipped forward on her head, ornamented with a taxidermy songbird. She slowed her mount from a trot to a walk as she grew closer, then stopped, alighting the saddle with a word to the groom not to bother dismounting.

"Miss de Rothschild," she said, coming to join me on the bench. "Good afternoon. Lovely weather we're having, wouldn't you agree?"

I would have agreed, had I not been sitting out in it for the last forty minutes freezing my teats off.

"It was splendid having you to dinner last night," she went on, setting the riding crop down in her lap. The groom had come up alongside Eloise's now riderless horse, taking the reins in hand. "Everyone was delighted to meet you."

Was this all we were to going to do? Sit here talking as though I truly was a Rothschild, and nothing had happened last night but a very civilised dinner party? I didn't know what to say. Finally she stood, smiling so blithely I was convinced she couldn't remember a thing after the second glass of whiskey. "Shall we walk together? My groom will wait here with the horses."

So that was her plan. She wanted us out of earshot.

I nodded, and we took off together up the path side by side. I was distinctly aware that she didn't take my arm, as a good friend might. Maybe she recalled more than she was letting on. I wondered faintly how she wasn't nursing the same skull-splitting headache as me. Unless she was, but was remarkably better at hiding it. She could have been an actress herself, if so.

"I apologise for being late to meet you," she said as we walked, our skirts swishing in perfect harmony. "Father had a spell this morning, and it waylaid me for a while."

"A spell?"

"He grows forgetful, sometimes. Confused. He keeps calling me Edith – my mother's name."

"Oh." I paused. "Eloise, last night..."

"What of it?"

"Are we goin' to talk about it?"

Eloise didn't look at me, chin raised high, still smiling. "There is nothing to talk of. I drank too much, I behaved unlike myself. That is all there is to it."

"Is it?" I didn't think so. Drink couldn't change a person's nature that greatly. Although, I'd kissed a fair few toads under the spell of the green fairy, giving it some thought. Was it possible it really had been nothing but the result of too much whiskey? I couldn't decide if I was relieved or insulted by the idea.

"Yes," Eloise said. "Now let us say nothing more of it. We know what we need to do next, don't we? We have two matters which we must attack with speed and ferocity."

"What do you mean?"

"Mr Cardoza. We must find out what we can about him, so that I may persuade him to keep silent. I'll begin making enquiries. About my brother, too, and how he came by your address. He certainly doesn't appear to suspect anything. He was positively smitten with you."

"That's good," I said, hearing my stilted reply. "How do you propose we find out about Mr Cardoza?"

"I'll ask around in society. That reminds me - you'll have to host a dinner at your lodgings, soon."

I came to an abrupt halt, only catching myself from stumbling at the last second. "What?"

Eloise stopped a few paces ahead, turning to face me. Her expression was terrifyingly serene. "It is necessary."

"I can't," I said. "I don't know how."

"I'll teach you. It is the safest option, believe me. Rather than be at the mercy of someone else's hosting, you will be in your own domain, in control of the menu, the seating. We'll hire a chef for the night. Besides, having people see your fine rooms will further convince them of your identity." She began walking again without waiting for me.

I wanted to say no. To finally put my foot down and tell her enough was enough. I didn't care any more about the luxurious Mayfair apartment and the beautiful dresses. I'd go back to Limehouse, if that's what it came to.

But the memory of Caleb's cough echoed in the back of my mind, along with a hundred nights going to bed with an empty ache in my stomach. No. I couldn't go back there. I wouldn't. I wanted more.

I rushed to catch up. "What about my brother?"

"You'll have to get rid of him for the evening." Eloise shrugged. "That won't be too difficult, will it? Send him to a pub or a music hall. Men love that kind of debauchery."

"Not all men are like Ernest. Caleb is dull as dishwater. He doesn't go anywhere like that."

"You'll think of something."

"Do we have to invite Mr Cardoza?"

"Of course." Eloise finally deigned to look at me again. "If we snubbed him it would be obvious to him that we know he knows, and he might reveal us sooner. It is best to keep him close for now."

I disagreed. Personally I'd have preferred to never see Mr Cardoza again as long as I lived, but evidently I didn't have any choice in the matter. I hated the game this ruse was turning into; I didn't have Eloise's stamina for it.

"Fine," I said, sure to imbue the word with as much anger as possible so she'd know I agreed only under duress. "But I want you to know I hate the whole idea."

Eloise huffed. "You're at perfect liberty to hate it, so long as you don't allow it to hinder your performance. As for how my brother got your address, I'll ask him directly. He's not clever enough to lie..." She twirled her riding crop in her hand thoughtfully, likely imagining using it to beat an answer out of him. "In the meanwhile I'll have dinner invitations made up for you."

"*Excellent,*" I deadpanned, in the refined, lady-like voice I'd adopted for my persona. Eloise threw me a scathing look.

"Do not be wicked," she said. "And do not let yourself succumb to fear."

"You aren't the one pretendin' to be a member of one of the wealthiest families in Europe," I said. "I've every bloody right to be scared!"

Eloise stopped again. "I'm not the one pretending to be a Rothschild, no. But our lives are intertwined now, Miss Zelikovich. Remember that. If this all comes out before it is meant to, I will forfeit my place in society."

"Sounds easily as bad as Newgate prison," I said, with no shortage of sarcasm.

"I know it seems trivial to you, but you don't know how cruel society can be," Eloise argued. "I would end up an outcast, entirely alone and friendless, and with little money if Ernest inherits as he currently stands to. That is not a good fate."

"What's your point to all of this? I already know high society is a den of wolves. I've figured that much out for myself."

"My point is that if it is a den of wolves, we must both be as courageous as lions. It is the only way to survive them." Eloise outstretched one gloved hand to touch my arm, then apparently thought better of it. Colour bloomed in her cheeks, and when our eyes met, I knew it hadn't just been the whiskey, no matter what she claimed.

"Alright," I said. "Let's show Mr Cardoza we have claws."

16

Eloise

When I burst into the house and began immediately pulling off my hat and gloves, I told myself that I was breathless and red-cheeked from the cold, and that there was no other reason for the state in which I found myself. Another voice in my head, beneath the pragmatic one, denounced me for a liar. Mirah Zelikovich was the true culprit, with her tumbling locks of gold and her tongue so sharp it was a wonder my lip wasn't cut from the almost-kiss I longed to forget.

And yet, I wanted to remember it, too. To savour it even. I was furious with myself for wanting that, and furious that the drink had rendered the memory hazy and fragmented. I wanted to go back in time and complete the act. Wanted it whole and full like a hearty meal, and also to destroy the thought of it and never entertain it again.

Getting tripped up by girlish desires I'd long attempted to quash was the last thing I needed at present. It was bad enough to see a pretty girl and want to test the softness of her lips under any circumstances, but this particular pretty girl was of the most unsuitable variety.

For one, she was not from my world. She had grown up hard and fast, that sharp tongue of hers whittled from the rough streets.

The largest concern was the most obvious one: I had hired her to seduce and ruin my brother. There could be no real fondness between us if we were to succeed. Though I adamantly reminded myself of these factors, I couldn't so easily chase the blush from my cheeks, nor stop my heart rioting against me.

"Miss?"

I hadn't even noticed I was pacing the vestibule until Susanna interrupted me. I whirled around to face her with such speed that the few loose tresses of my hair whipped me.

"It is a brisk day," I said, before she could ask. It was clear in her raised eyebrows that she intended to. "Cold. Refreshing to ride in, though."

"I see." Susanna did not lower her eyebrows, but held out her hands towards me. "May I take your cloak, Miss?"

"Oh. Yes. Of course." Swooping it free of my shoulders I caught a strong whiff of Miss Zelikovich's perfume. It was *my* perfume, actually. I had purchased her a bottle of the same brand I wore, bought from one of the competing perfumeries that bookended Signora Mortetti's. Though I had worn it every day for years my nose was suddenly conspiring against me to associate it with that woman. Was there no end to it? "Take it," I all but begged, thrusting the cloak into Susanna's arms.

"Is there anything else I can do for you?" Susanna asked. "Perhaps some hot chocolate to warm you up?"

"Please."

"I'll do that right away, Miss."

I nodded my thanks, only then noticing a familiar coat and bowler hat hanging on the coat-stand by the door. "What is Mr Cardoza doing here?"

"He has an appointment with your father, Miss," Susanna said, folding my riding cloak over her arm. "Usual business, he said. He arrived some forty minutes ago. I expect they'll be done soon."

I should not have let Mr Cardoza's presence unnerve me so. He paid regular visits to my father, relaying details of our legal affairs to him. There was no reason to think this visit any different.

Except, of course, that he might know the truth about Mirah's identity.

What if he was up there telling Father right now? Seeing to it that what little I was set to inherit of my own was struck away from me? I stared up the long staircase with mounting dread, imagining the conversation going on behind my father's locked door. So many of his important conversations happened like that.

All I could do was try not to unravel myself with these thoughts. I couldn't let Mr Cardoza sense my fear – had Mirah and I not only just discussed this in Hyde Park? My own words were empty to me now, hollowed out by the very idea of Mr Cardoza and my father alone together.

"Where is Ernest?" I asked. I would distract my nerves by tackling the second of our problems.

"Out, Miss."

"Already? What is it this time? Have they a dire need for moustache wax at the Savile Club?"

"Shopping, I believe. He said he intended to purchase a gift for Miss de Rothschild."

I tore my gaze from the stairs to look at her. "He's buying her a gift?"

Susanna nodded. "He said he was going to a jeweller on Bond Street. It must be pretty pricey."

Pretty pricey was an understatement. This was a good development. It meant I hadn't been wrong when I'd figured him for smitten. He had to be more taken with her than I'd realised to spend money on her, for Ernest more commonly preferred to spend money on himself. Why was it then that it didn't it *feel* like a good development?

"When he gets in, I need to speak with him," I said. "Somehow he acquired the address for the apartment on Park Street. I have to find out how."

Susanna tightened her arms around my cloak, bowing her head. "Oh..."

"Is something wrong?"

"I'm sorry, Miss. You see, Mr Byron got the address from me."

Susanna's words succeeded in distracting me from Mr Cardoza, albeit in the worst possible way. I reeled back, feeling as though a beloved pet dog I had allowed into my home for years had suddenly bitten me.

"You? *You* told him?"

"I'm sorry, Miss!" Susanna took a pleading step towards me; I moved away until my heels were touching the bottom step of the stairs. "He asked me if I had it. I said no, but he told me he knew I was lying. I didn't know what else to do."

"You should have refused! How could you do this? How could you – betray me, so flagrantly?"

"He's my employer –"

"So am I!"

"I was worried he'd send me away me if I didn't do as he said," Susanna said, clutching my cape so pathetically I wanted to wrench it from her, if that would not entail getting another waft of that perfume, which I was now considering throwing out.

"Well unfortunately for you, it's me you should have been more concerned with!" Rage simmered inside me. It was hurt and anger towards Susanna, yes, but I had to concede some of the fury was turned inwards at myself for allowing a girl from Limehouse with a beautiful voice to undo me so thoroughly. "Go and fetch your belongings. You are dismissed."

At that, Susanna dropped my cape – then scrambled to pick it up again, her mouth hanging open, her eyes practically popping out of their sockets. "Dismissed? Miss, please –"

"You heard me. Go."

"I've been in your service since you were a girl!"

"And now you've betrayed my trust. Leave. And don't think to hold what you know against me; I am still paying for your sister's employment, remember."

Susanna stood there for a moment, lip trembling, a sorry sight that did move me some. I didn't want this to happen. I'd have never wished it. Susanna had been my friend for many years. She accompanied me everywhere it was appropriate for a maidservant to accompany her mistress, and always agreed with my most cutting remarks about others. For a short while I had even harboured feelings for her that toed a line beyond mere friendship. That was the very first time my cheeks had reddened at the thought of another woman, but I'd dutifully forced those feelings back down inside myself until they passed.

I would just have to do the same with Mirah Zelikovich.

"May I stay this last night, Miss?" Susanna asked quietly. "So that I can secure myself lodgings this afternoon?"

"Very well," I muttered. "Speak with Mrs Sharp about your pay."

Susanna nodded. She hung my cloak up on the coat-stand next to Mr Cardoza's coat, gave a wobbly curtsy, and left.

I sank down onto the stairs, already feeling the loss of her, like an organ had been cut out of me. How could she have hurt me this way? It was all Ernest's fault. Everything I'd ever had that was just my own he found a way to take or pollute. Now I had set Mirah up for him to take as well, and even though I planned for it, picturing him draping an expensive necklace around her neck made me want to hurl the first breakable item I could find against the wall. Tears rushed to my eyes – I brought my thumb to my mouth and bit down on it, hard, to keep them at bay.

"What a melodrama that was."

The voice startled me, and I sprang to my feet too fast, Gideon Cardoza catching my elbow before I slipped on the stairs.

"Mr Cardoza," I said, breathless. "How good to see you. About that..."

"It's not my place to get involved," Gideon said. "You were dismissing an unruly maidservant, I take it?"

"Yes..."

"Unpleasant business. Are you alright?"

"A little shaken, that is all. She was in my service for a long time."

"Then she must have done something truly unforgivable for you to send her away."

I swallowed thickly. "How is Father?"

"I am a solicitor, not a doctor, but not particularly well," Gideon said. His brown leather satchel was swinging from his left hand, stuffed fat with papers. I wondered if there would be anything interesting inside. "He was perfectly lucid when I arrived, but he is tired now. I would visit him, were I you."

"What business did you have with him?"

"That is strictly between my client and myself. Although, if he continues to grow less *compos mentis*, your brother may need to be the one making legal decisions for him."

That would be a disaster, for Ernest wasn't likely to disinherit himself. Evidently we would have to act fast. "Ernest would not be very good at that. Perhaps it should be me?"

"That is a matter you will have to take up with your father."

"I will." I paused, and then, feeling brave, added, "Miss de Rothschild is to host a dinner at her lodgings, soon. She's asked that I invite you."

Gideon smiled easily. "Has she now? Well, who would I be to turn down an invitation from a Rothschild? You may tell the esteemed heiress that I will be there. Good day to you, Miss Byron. I do hope your next maid is less insolent than the last." He dipped his head respectfully, and then left me on the stairs, collecting his hat and coat.

Father's bedchamber was so warm that I thought it a wonder the pomade had not melted out of Mr Cardoza's hair. Ordinarily Father spent his days in the dark, reading by candlelight, identifying the time of day by the meals that were delivered to him; he'd even had all the clocks removed, insisting that the ticking upset his gout.

It was odd to see him propped upright in bed, illuminated by the blinding mid-afternoon sun, for the curtains were open so that Mr Cardoza had natural light by which to work. His complexion was sickly, emphasised by the whiteness of the bedsheets, his nightshirt, his cap. He was staring out of the window when I entered, towards the rich greenery of Berkeley Square, though it was too bright outside for him to see anything.

"Edith?" His watery eyes swept to me in the doorway.

"It's me, Father. Eloise."

"Oh. Come closer. You've grown, dear one!"

I approached the bed, perching myself on the edge of the mattress. "How are you feeling? Is there anything I can fetch for you? Tea, or something to eat?"

"No, no, I'm quite alright. You look upset, child. Has something happened?"

"I had to dismiss Susanna," I said. "It's not worth going into why."

"That's a shame. She's such a lovely girl."

"Yes." The word was a sharp stone in my throat. "Did you have a good meeting with Mr Cardoza?"

"Oh yes. You know, that Mr Cardoza is a nice young man. So well-dressed and smart. Good prospects, too, although I don't know what his family are like. He'd make a fine husband. I don't believe he's currently attached..."

"I don't think we'd suit each other, Father." That was a polite way to put it. Strongarmed into marriage with Gideon Cardoza I didn't know which of us would snap first. "Speaking of attachments, Ernest has been taken with a young lady, of late."

"Is she a suitable girl?"

"I wouldn't know." I didn't want to lie to him.

He chuckled. "Well, maybe that's all that boy needs, a good woman to calm him down. It can do wonders for a man to be in love..." His eyelids grew heavy, his head lolling back onto his mountain of pillows and his voice trailing off into a yawn. "Close the curtains, dear..." I didn't even have to. He was asleep in moments, gentle breathing hitching into snores so loud they shook the bed. Had he always snored like that? If so it was no wonder Mother was miserable. She was a saint for not smothering him.

I remained seated on the edge of the bed, trying to decide what it was that I was feeling. I did not like lying to him, but he left me no choice. My eyes swept the room to his bureau, situated against the wall in the direct path of the sun. It was taunting me, inlaid mahogany lit up like a beacon, light bouncing off its polished surface into my face. How was it fair that Mr Cardoza, a man who was neither friend nor relation, had access to things that I did not? I'd toiled thanklessly for this family since Mother's death and was still excluded from affairs of business. For all I knew those locked drawers contained all the details of my inheritance. My future.

I rose from the bed.

Lying to my ailing father was bad enough, but I was about to do much worse. No reasonable person would blame me for it. What was I to think but that my father did not care for me? I wanted to see for myself just how much he cared. To the last shilling.

The drawers were locked. I tried them a few times before plucking a pin from my hair. I'd heard a lock could be persuaded with them, and it sounded easy enough. I stuck the pin into the keyhole and jiggled it around.

And around.

And around.

"Blasted thing!"

There was a brief halting to Father's snores. I froze, holding my breath. After far too long he started up again even louder. I exhaled.

The bureau was still refusing to render up its secrets. Admitting to myself that I was not a master locksmith after all, I tossed the pin aside and grasped the drawer-pull, bracing myself against the bureau to yank it hard. It rattled but didn't give. I tugged harder, fingers hurting, throwing all my weight into my mission.

"What's happening?"

When Father spoke I released the drawer-pull so suddenly I went reeling backwards, only catching myself at the last second. He was sitting upright in bed again, wide-eyed confusion mingled with desperation.

"Edith?"

"No, Father –"

"Edith. My love..." His mouth creased up, and he hunched forwards, hiding his face in his hands. "I'm so sorry, my darling. You were right, you were always right. That boy, that poor boy! What have I done!"

"Father –"

"Edith, forgive me!"

I didn't know what to do. I'd never seen my father cry before, but here he was, sobbing so forcefully I thought all of Mayfair would hear. I rushed over to the bed, touching his shoulder gently.

"I forgive you, Ambrose," I said, hoping that adopting my mother's patient tone would soothe him. "I forgive you."

His weeping trailed off, growing softer, and then he was still and snoring again, as if nothing of any note had happened. My heart was a weight in my chest. I watched him for a few minutes, wondering what world he was in when he spoke to my mother, what sins he believed he needed to atone for. I recalled the man he'd once been, so distant and unknowable, and hated that he was the same even now. Hated that I would never have the chance to know him.

17

Mirah

It took three consecutive days of pleading for Caleb to agree. In the end he only did so to avoid the miserable weather, because when the night of the dinner rolled around it was wet and wretched outside.

"I won't address you as 'ma'am'," he said, adjusting his cravat in the mirror of the vestibule. "All I'll do is help Tabitha carry plates and dishes to the table. I am not a domestic servant."

"No need to be such a snob about it," I said. "Think you're better than Tabitha, do you?"

"That isn't what I mean and you know it. I don't want any part of this ruse."

"You don't need to speak. Just carry things, as you said. You can do that with your mouth shut, can't you?"

It was nothing short of a miracle that I'd convinced him to play the part of a footman, even if only nominally and for a few hours. It must have been more appealing than the alternatives, those being to brave the elements for a smoky pub or lodging house, or to sit in complete silence in his bedchamber and pretend not to exist. He might well have managed the latter, working in solitude as he often did, but I sensed a morbid curiosity existed beneath his veneer of disapproval. I couldn't blame him. Dinner at Eloise's had been something of a spectacle, a glimpse into another world.

Caleb could posture all he liked, but I knew it interested him. He was a contradictory person: he spoke of worker's rights and revolution, but at the same time I fancied he thought himself a cut above most. The paltry - but not insignificant - education he'd received as a young boy was one of the only things that made me believe Ma's assertions about his father. For all my brother claimed to hate the upper class, I was sure he privately considered himself a gentleman's son.

"What if it goes wrong?" he said. A worried crease had formed between his brows, softer than his usual frown. The same question kept me awake all night the evening before, harrying me along all day on the heels of the not-kiss with Eloise. One of us had to be brave though, and it had always been Caleb when I was a little girl. Now it was my turn.

I reached up to fix his skullcap, already slipping off the back of his head. "It won't."

Eloise and Ernest were first to arrive, both dressed so magnificently they looked to be competing. Then came Helena Hall, who Eloise told me had been sitting outside in her carriage when they'd arrived, waiting so as not to appear overly eager. Five minutes after her the Beauchamps and Mr Brandt turned up, and Mr Cardoza another ten minutes after them. He carried a leather satchel that he insisted on keeping when Tabitha took his coat and hat at the door, and his hair was windswept, not flawlessly sleek like last time. For a man who'd been perfectly punctual at the first dinner he appeared visibly irritated by his own lateness when he stepped into the drawing room.

"Forgive my state, Miss de Rothschild," he said, eyeing the aperitifs the rest of the guests had already been served. "I had an appointment with a client in Hammersmith that ran late, and it has taken me an age to get here. I do hate the Underground. It feels so dreadfully unnatural, and finding an empty hansom at Victoria is a nightmare. It's like the last days of Rome."

"You're very much forgiven," I said, smiling in a way that I hoped accurately conveyed a wealthy lady who felt slightly put upon. "Would you mind fetching Mr Cardoza a drink?" I glanced meaningfully at Caleb, standing awkwardly by the door. He didn't suit being a footman, with his sulking posture and permanent scowl.

He went grudgingly to the drinks tray, pouring as I'd instructed, and then returned with a glass, which he thrust towards Mr Cardoza so roughly that the contents sloshed dangerously close to the rim. "Here."

Gideon raised an eyebrow, gaze flashing between Caleb and I. Was he taking stock of our features, able to tell that we were siblings? I'd always thought we looked different, but there was some of Ma in our faces that neither of us could escape, and we had the same dark eyes.

"Thank you," he said at last, accepting the drink.

"It's a *Milano-Torino*," I told him, hoping to divert his thoughts. "A cocktail from Italy. It has Campari and sweet vermouth in it."

"Delicious." He didn't sound convinced.

"I must thank you again for hosting us, Miss de Rothschild," Pauline piped up. She'd claimed an entire sofa for herself and the three dogs that had accompanied her, her husband and Mr Brandt forced to balance precariously on the furthest ends like a pair of gargoyles. The dogs – stepping all over the sofa and knocking off the throw pillows – weren't the same three I'd met at Eloise's house. They were dressed differently, for one thing.

Clearly my staring didn't go unnoticed, because Pauline pulled the one wearing a lush fur mantel and heavy gold chain into her lap with a bright smile, propping it up to wave one of its paws at me like a person. "This is Henry."

"Named for Henry the Eighth," Henry Beauchamp added, his laugh cracking anxiously. "Not me."

That was an easy enough guess. I didn't think Henry Beauchamp was particularly enthusiastic about having one wife, let alone six.

"And these are Charles," Pauline gestured to the one in a ruff the size of a dinner plate, "and Cleopatra," in a very ornate gold headdress and collar.

"They're lovely," I said.

Ernest, who it appeared had been waiting for a gap in the conversation to address me, cleared his throat loudly. "Not as lovely as you, Miss de Rothschild."

"Thank you. It is every woman's dream to be told she is lovelier than a dog."

"I'm sorry, I didn't mean –"

"I know. It is quite alright, Mr Byron. I appreciate the compliment nonetheless."

"Then allow me to make another." He passed his glass to Eloise, who made an indignant sound at being delegated to the duty, and slipped a hand inside his tailcoat. "Here."

I didn't know what to say when presented with the small velvet box. I wasn't used to receiving gifts, and didn't know the appropriate response. Instead of risking saying anything I merely stood there and waited for him to open it. The rest of the room had fallen completely silent, save the heavy panting of one of Pauline's dogs.

"I do hope you like this," Ernest said, raising the lid.

Helena Hall gasped audibly. I was too shocked to make a sound – a good thing, because I could think of only one word that might have left my mouth, and it certainly wasn't Rothschild-appropriate.

The brooch was beautiful. An eagle in flight, exquisitely cut from gold, gripping a cluster of arrows in its talons. Upon three of its feathers the words *Concordia, Integritas, Industria* had been engraved. I knew even less what to say than before. But I did know that an unmarried woman accepting a gift from a gentleman came with loaded implications.

"If you do not care for it, I can return it and select something else," Ernest said, swiftly. I had been quiet too long. I shook my head.

"No. It's lovely, Mr Bryon."

"It is made out to resemble your family crest, you see? The eagle, and the five arrows."

When I looked up at him he was smiling nervously, desperate for my approval, and I suddenly hated myself for deceiving him.

"Thank you," I managed. I had to fight the words out of me. A crest for a family I was not part of. I shuddered to think how much money he'd spent on it, for it had to have been custom made. I'd no clue how I was expected to respond to it. Should I fawn on him for the kindness? Take insult at his boldness? Or else receive it with the cool, polite indifference of a woman who received such things often? Rothschild women probably got gifts like this all the time. Probably had whole drawers overflowing with them.

I glanced at Eloise for help, but even she was lost for words, eyeing the open box as though it wasn't a jewellery box at all, but Pandora's, brimming with all the evils of the world. I would have to fend for myself.

I gathered my scattered thoughts, penned them in like unruly sheep, and smiled. "It is wonderful. I will treasure it always."

Ernest's tentative smile became a grin. "I am glad it pleases you. Please, allow me." He took the brooch from its box, affixing it carefully to the square neckline of my dress. It was an innocent gesture, and yet I held my breath, aware that every set of eyes in the room was upon me. Innocent, yes, but strangely charged, his gaze focused intently on my collarbone.

The brooch securely pinned, he stepped away, and the air rushed back into my lungs.

"Splendid," he announced. "It suits you perfectly."

I had no idea how it could. I stole a glance at Mr Cardoza, and it was clear our thoughts were one and the same: *fraud*.

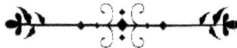

The Italian cocktails went over brilliantly, and we were all two drinks in before Tabitha knocked at the door and announced dinner. As we paired off to enter the dining room, however, Eloise caught my sleeve.

"May I speak with you a moment, Miss de Rothschild?"

"But I am supposed to escort her," Ernest argued. The Beauchamps, Helena Hall and Mr Brandt had already made their way through to find their place-cards. Gideon Cardoza waited in the doorway, satchel in one hand and his other arm folded behind his back.

"I am sure she can survive the arduous journey to her own dinner table, Ernest," Eloise said. "I must borrow her time regarding a feminine matter."

"Like what?"

"If you must know, I'm in urgent need of a sanitary belt and a rag."

Ernest gagged like a duck choking on a large chunk of bread. "Good God, Eloise! We are in polite company!"

"A woman's monthlies do not oft take that into account, brother."

"Fine, fine. Dear Lord." He shuddered, then bowed. "Miss de

Rothschild." As he took his leave he all but shoved Mr Cardoza out of the door with him. "Come on."

"Are you to escort me instead, then?" Gideon joked. Ernest didn't reply.

The wry smile vanished from Eloise's face once we were alone, her hands flying out to grasp my arms. For one exhilarating second I thought she was going to kiss me – for real, this time. I wondered what I'd do if she did, with all her fancy friends in the other room. Then she spoke, and the illusion shattered: "Did you see Mr Cardoza's case?"

"Of course."

"We have to check it."

"Don't be ridiculous," I lowered my voice to a whisper. "He'll see!"

"Not if there is ample distraction. We must, Mirah."

"D'you honestly believe he'd carry around incriminatin' documents about himself?"

"Where else would he keep them?" Eloise challenged. "Locked up at his office, or in his lodgings, when he has already been blackmailed once and locks can be picked? No. He'd keep them on his person." There was an unhinged logic to what she was saying. I was loath to acknowledge it.

"How do you expect us to get hold of them?"

"Simply continue being the charming hostess. I'll find a way. I went to great lengths to orchestrate this opportunity, I won't let it pass."

"You orchestrated this? How did you –"

"I merely recommended Mr Cardoza's services to a dear friend of mine in Hammersmith." Eloise shrugged it off effortlessly. "Mrs Deighton is a very wealthy old widow with a lot of affairs in need of attention. She is also very pushy with the tea and cakes and will not allow you to leave for talking your ear off. I knew she would make him tremendously late, and he would be forced to come straight from his work with the satchel in hand."

"Poor bastard."

"He is our *enemy* Mirah, remember that. And is that your brother, acting as footman?"

"You wouldn't believe how much grovellin' that took," I said, now dreading this meal all the more. Whatever Eloise planned to gain access to Mr Cardoza's satchel, I didn't think it could end in any good way.

18

Mirah

Somehow the first few courses were not a disaster.

I owed that at least in part to Eloise's careful planning of the seating arrangement. I was placed at the head of the table with Ernest closest to me on the right and Mr Cardoza opposite him. I hadn't wanted to sit so near to Mr Cardoza, but Eloise was insistent. These things, she explained, had nothing to do with who someone *wanted* to sit near, even under less perilous circumstances. Placing Gideon anywhere else would have been dangerous – a snub, and an opportunity for him to whisper his suspicions into the ear of another guest. With me at the head of the table and Eloise on his other side there was no one for him to collude with.

Pauline had been assigned the other table head. I didn't think it was usual for a guest to be seated there, but it was the best place for her with her dogs' leads tied to the table legs at her feet. It also put her far away from Ernest, and, more importantly, put Ernest far away from the dogs.

"The food is exquisite, Miss de Rothschild," Henry Beauchamp said, as Caleb went around placing plates in front of everyone. He did so with much more force than necessary, and several times I was convinced he was going to tip haddock souffle directly into the lap of one of my guests. Whether it would have been accidental or intentional was hard to say.

"I'm sure you've noticed by now that tonight's menu is mostly fish-based dishes," I said, offering Henry a careful smile. "The meals are all kosher, you see. I must confess, Mr Cardoza, you embarrassed me somewhat when we dined at the Byron's."

Gideon tilted his head. "Is that so?"

"Yes. I prescribe to the laws of *kashrut* when I am home with my mother, for she is very observant, but I must admit I am more... *permissive* with my dining habits, when out from under her watchful eye. This evening, though, I felt inclined to honour her wishes. A guilty conscience, perhaps." The truth was that Caleb would've raged for forty days and nights if I'd suggested the likes of turtle soup and pork belly grace the dinner table. For all I was prone to riling him, that was a boundary I was unwilling to cross, in part because his temper would be unbearable, but also because some small, highly inconvenient part of me felt a lingering allegiance to the way Ma had raised us.

"I have to say, Mirah is an odd name for a Rothschild," Gideon said. "Last I heard all the Rothschild women appear to take turns with the same four names. Charlotte and Hannah and Louisa and such...."

"Mirah is only one of my names," I stated, with an ease that surprised even me. "My full name is Charlotte Leonora Hannah Evelina Mirah de Rothschild."

"I can see why you chose to shorten it," Henry said.

"Besides, I'm not the only one with a different name," I pressed on when Gideon continued to fix me with that all too knowing look. Neither of us was backing down. "There's my cousins Constance and Anna, here in England."

"Do they have twelve names each, too?"

I didn't know. I sipped my wine to avoid answering.

"How is your work going, Mr Cardoza?" Leopold asked suddenly, gesturing to Gideon's chair. He had put his satchel down on the floor at his feet, dangerously close to Eloise. "A client in Hammersmith, you said?"

"Yes, yes. An old widow." Gideon picked at his meal disdainfully. I couldn't tell if he was displeased with the food or merely stuffed full already from the tea and cake Eloise said Mrs Deighton was so eager to thrust upon guests. "Kindly woman, very talkative."

"I don't understand why anyone would be a solicitor," Henry said. "Don't you miss being a barrister? That sounds so much more exciting."

Gideon glanced up from his plate, his smile thin and forced. "It was my life's passion."

"To be a *solicitor?*"

"To be a barrister."

"Then why would you stop?"

"*Henry,*" Leopold warned. Henry, apparently catching that he was about to launch his own foot into it, promptly closed his mouth.

"I imagine you have some exciting stories from your time at the bar, Mr Cardoza," Pauline said. "What is your opinion on the Tichborne case, earlier this year? I was enraptured by it! Ever such a *cause célèbre!*"

I froze, and prayed I hadn't gone noticeably pale.

The Tichborne case, or, what happens when a butcher in Australia named Thomas Castro or Arthur Orton (unclear which) sees an advertisement in a newspaper offering a reward for information on one Sir Rodger Tichborne, heir to the Tichborne baronetcy, presumed lost in a shipwreck in fifty-four, and decides to put himself forward as the man in question. It had caused a sensation. It was also gut-wrenchingly relevant: Sir Thomas-Arthur-Rodger Whatever His Name Was was now serving a long stint in Newgate for trying his luck.

"That was quite a case," Gideon agreed, setting his fork down. "The fellow was an imposter, of course. The evidence was overwhelming, it is only right that he was convicted. Two seven-year terms is not long enough, in my opinion."

"Fourteen years for seeking a better life seems apt to you?"

My heart dropped. All eyes turned to Caleb. He was standing directly across from Gideon behind Helena Hall with a silver tureen still in hand, gloved fingers gripping the handles fiercely.

Mr Cardoza straightened up in his seat, suddenly far more interested than before. "Fourteen years for causing suffering to a family with his lies."

I tried to convey my alarm to Caleb through frantic eye-contact, but he either didn't catch on or chose to ignore it. Infuriatingly I knew which was more likely. "If the man was a fraud, he was a fraud because he was poor, and wished to improve his life," he said. "He was treated unjustly by the courts, as poor men always are."

"You imagine it is acceptable to trick a grieving family, just because one is poor?"

"Not acceptable, but understandable. There ought to have been leniency."

"Leniency leads a bad example."

"Lady Tichborne accepted the man as her son, despite the evidence against him," Caleb countered. "That should have been enough."

"She was vulnerable. She believed what she wanted to believe. People often do in these cases."

The was a lull in conversation, Pauline's dogs whining. Caleb and Mr Cardoza stared each other down across the table, two cats posturing to fight. I didn't look at Eloise. I couldn't. I knew she'd be shooting lightning bolts at me with her eyes.

Mr Brandt clearing his throat broke the silence. "It's unusual to meet such an outspoken footman."

"Yes," Helena said, with significantly more disgust. She'd been outstandingly quiet so far, sulking over the brooch I'd received from Ernest. "And most inappropriate!"

The eyes that were previously fixed on Caleb swept to me instead. I stammered, overcome with the urge to crawl beneath the table and hide there for the rest of my days, which now appeared significantly fewer in number than when I'd first sat down.

"Yes," I said, recovering myself. "Yes, you're right." I turned to Caleb, striving to appear stern and ladylike. "How dare you speak to my guest that way?"

Caleb wanted to argue. With every fibre of his being he wanted to, ire bubbling away under the surface, a kettle about to reach a boil. I pictured him blowing off a jet of steam so hard his skullcap went shooting off his head.

"I apologise for his insolence, sir," I said to Mr Cardoza.

Gideon waved it off. "Do not, Miss de Rothschild. I appreciate a differing opinion as much as the next man. It is rather refreshing to debate the matter so hotly. Most find me too intimidating to put up any sort of fight."

Everyone returned to their meals, the silence so unnerving that I half expected an accusation against me to come hurling out of it at any minute.

"Don't trouble yourself Miss de Rothschild," Ernest said, just as I was considering climbing out of the closest window. "I recall what you said about the poor man. Did you know Miss de Rothschild has such a charitable heart? She keeps this outspoken fellow on out of saintly goodness. His father was an artist."

There was a ripple of agreeable 'ah's, 'oh's, and 'poor soul's from around the table, the tension lifting. It felt as though a ten-tonne weight was removed from on top of me.

Caleb only glared, approaching with the large silver tureen he'd been holding, and, looking me dead in the eyes, slammed it down onto the table so hard the flatware jumped.

One second everyone was seated around the table enjoying *cod à la bechamel* and *dauphinoise* potatoes. The next, all hell broke loose. Pauline's dogs, who had been whining faintly the entire dinner, bolted, their combined strength pulling Pauline Beauchamp's chair from under her. She tipped back with a squeal of surprise, a flurry of skirts and a flash of undergarments. Henry sprang into action – not to catch his wife, but to give chase to the dogs, as Leopold set about helping Pauline. Helena screamed as 'Charles', in his oversized ruff, jumped into her lap having broken free of his constraints.

The dog named Henry made a mad dash around the dining room, his human counterpart running after him. Leopold, having aided Pauline to her feet, joined the chase, the two weaving circles around the table to catch the fugitive canine.

"Don't hurt him!" Pauline shrieked.

I didn't know whether to help or not. Looking to Eloise for guidance, I noticed she was suddenly gone – no, not gone. She'd dipped beneath the table herself, and fleetingly I thought she was attempting to wrangle one of the dogs, before I realised the truth: she was going through Gideon Cardoza's case.

Mr Cardoza himself was too busy watching the chaos unfold with barely restrained amusement to see her rooting through his satchel right next to him.

"No!" Henry Beauchamp cried, as Henry the dog stopped his erratic freedom run to cock his leg and urinate all over one of the beautiful velvet drapes.

"Don't disturb him while he's relieving himself!" Pauline yelled, when her husband made a grab for him anyway. Pauline snatched Charles from Helena's lap, almost weeping, just as Leopold managed to get control of Henry – both Henrys. Mr Beauchamp looked as if he wanted to die.

I'd completely forgotten about the third dog, Cleopatra, until she popped up between Ernest's legs with her headdress jingling, having managed to drag the whole chair she was still attached to underneath the table with her.

The dog howled. The glass in Ernest's hand went flying.

It was unfortunate, really, that Gideon Cardoza was seated opposite Mr Byron, putting him in the direct line of fire. Very unfortunate, and I didn't laugh at all. Not on the outside anyway.

Caleb had, though. He hadn't even attempted to stifle it.

The claret was so red against Mr Cardoza's light brown waistcoat it looked as if he'd been shot. He wiped at it furiously with a serviette as the dogs were corralled back under the table, Leopold tying no less than three knots in their leads. It was no use, the pretty, scalloped serviette totally inadequate, forcing Mr Cardoza to the scullery in search of a damp cloth. I made Caleb go with him, rather than poor Tabitha, who was shaken by the whole ordeal.

"We will pay for new drapes," Henry said. "Truly, I cannot apologise enough."

"There's no need. These things happen." Not to most people, I fancied, but I was too relieved to feign anger. The scene caused by the dogs diverted attention away from me, as well as provided Eloise the distraction she'd needed to go through Mr Cardoza's things. She was now back in her seat sipping her wine, admirably stone-faced. I couldn't tell if she'd found anything of use.

"This has been a very memorable evening," Ernest said, in what I sensed was an attempt to console me. No doubt he imagined I was putting on a brave face, torn up inside over the ruin of my civilised dinner party as any good lady would be. He smiled at me as he spoke, stiffly waxed moustache stretching with his lips. A single fleck of cheese from the *dauphinoise* potatoes clung to the end of one perfectly formed curl, hanging on for dear life.

I reached out to pick it free. Ernest froze, smile faltering.

"You had food in your moustache," I said, by way of explanation. He merely stared at me, becoming so dangerously red in the face that I worried I'd offended him, a strange emotion welling behind his eyes that I couldn't name.

"Thank you," he said, bordering on breathless. That was when I realised exactly what it was in his eyes: adoration. His eyes were the same deep blue as his sister's. So close I noticed the family resemblance between them for the first time.

I was instantly uncomfortable. I couldn't say why - it was my job to seduce this idiotic dandy of a man, and I'd gotten far more lurid looks from others of his sex. Why was this different? I glanced discreetly at Eloise, a finely dressed blur in the periphery of my vision. Remembering the night we'd taken a nightcap together I felt my own cheeks turn as red as Ernest's.

"Miss de Rothschild." My gaze snapped back to Ernest as he spoke. "Would you care to accompany me on a carriage ride through Hyde Park tomorrow afternoon?"

I knew I was supposed to say 'yes', but I was suddenly writhing with guilt over the way he looked at me. As if I were the first star in the sky on a summer's night. I told myself I was being ridiculous. No man had ever fallen in love over a piece of cheese being plucked out of his moustache.

"Of course, sir. I would be delighted."

"Excellent. I shall pick you up tomorrow at noon. Your footman or maidservant is welcome to accompany you as a chaperone, of course."

I didn't think I'd get Caleb out for a pleasant turn around Hyde Park as my footman if I held him at gunpoint. A flash of alarm passed through me. "I should go and check on Mr Cardoza," I said, rising from my seat. "He and my footman have been gone for a while."

"I'll go, Miss," Tabitha offered.

I raised my hand to instruct her to stay put, for once grateful she insisted on being obedient. What if Mr Cardoza had confronted him in the scullery with what he knew? What if Caleb snapped and beat the man to death with a copper pan over the finer details of the Tichborne case? That was unlikely, Caleb was no brute, but that didn't stop my mind running as wild as one of Pauline's dogs.

I left the dining room hastily, hearing Leopold make a valiant effort to steer the conversation to Rossetti's latest painting as I went.

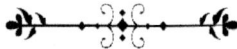

There was no one in the scullery.

Bizarrely there was no one in the kitchen either, save the chef, who'd dozed off in a chair with his head on the large wooden table and a glass of cooking brandy in one hand, which did not bode well for the rest of the meal. Mr Cardoza *had* been there, though – a wet rag left dripping a small puddle over the edge of said table confirmed that. It conjured up the *Mary Celeste*, the brigantine found mysteriously abandoned on the Atlantic two years ago. My brother and the Bryon's solicitor had completely disappeared, leaving behind nothing but a damp cloth.

My first thought was that they'd gone outside to fight. That was how disputes were often settled in Limehouse. Perhaps Caleb had challenged Mr Cardoza to a duel, not that we had any pistols or swords handy. Maybe a couple of paring knives? The image would have been funny if there wasn't a real chance of it happening.

Something hit the ground with a heavy thump.

Whatever it was, it came from behind the closed pantry door. A new fear seized me, an icy hand clenching my heart. Caleb wasn't a brute, no, but that said nothing of Mr Cardoza. What if he'd been blackmailed into leaving the bar over something awful? Was I about to find my brother dead in our pantry? I placed my hand on the latch, heart thudding in my chest, and threw open the door.

Potatoes came rolling out at my feet from the half-empty burlap sack on the floor. My gaze travelled upwards, and halted. My brother and Mr Cardoza were shoved up against the rickety pantry shelves, limbs entangled, Caleb's skullcap sliding off the back of his head. They both stared at me, their breathing so hard and ragged I feared Caleb was in the midst of one of his asthma attacks. It was unusual to fight in a pantry - that was where my mind initially went. It was even more unusual to fight with your trousers unbuttoned.

Oh.

I tried to back out and tripped over a potato.

18

Eloise

They had been gone far too long.

Nearly twenty minutes had elapsed since Mirah ventured to the scullery in search of Mr Cardoza and her brother. Blessedly no one else appeared to have noticed the staggering length of time she'd been absent, swept up in some of the dullest conversation I'd ever had to endure.

Truth was, much of this pageantry was dull to me. The smiles and nods and requirement to feign interest in even the most banal topic. At times I allowed my mind to wander, weaving grand adventures for myself. Swashbuckling on the high seas or chopping a path through deepest jungle. This evening my mind did not drift an inch. I was terrified of what Mirah's long disappearance meant for us.

I stared at the standing clock the entire time Helena Hall droned on, watching the minute hand crawl around the face bit by bit. Beneath the table one of my legs was bouncing, a reflexive movement I had no control over whatsoever. I worried it would set off the dogs again.

"What do you think, Miss Byron?"

I startled out of my thoughts. Pauline Beauchamp was blinking her big soft cow-eyes at me.

"Excuse me," I said, forcing a smile. "I believe I was momentarily distracted. What do I think of what, Mrs Beauchamp?"

"The Chimney Sweepers Act."

"I don't really know enough about it."

"It will require chimney sweeps to be licensed, to prevent children being employed."

"Papa thinks it's a dreadful idea," Helena said. "After all, who *else* is small enough to fit inside a chimney?"

I was rescued from having to answer by the long-awaited return of Miss Zelikovich, shadowed closely by her brother and Mr Cardoza. She and Gideon took their seats, so impassive I wanted to lunge across the table and shake an explanation out of them, simultaneously impressed and frustrated by Miss Zelikovich's acting capabilities. If she was in any way distressed it didn't show, and she slipped back into dinner conversation as easily as one slips into a clean chemise.

It was only her brother, breathing hard as he made the rounds pouring drinks – and doing so without protest – that gave it away. Our plan had not survived the night unscathed.

The rest of the meal passed with a distinct lack of dramatics. Pauline's dogs remained calm and polite for the remainder of the dinner, having the audacity to behave as though they had been that way all evening, and Helena Hall kept her prattling to a minimum, her eyes occasionally lingering on the gold brooch at Mirah's collar.

Digestifs in the drawing room followed dinner, but I abstained, wishing to keep my mind focused. When it came time to leave Ernest and I were the last to make our exit, bidding Mirah farewell at the door.

"Go on out and wait in the carriage," I told Ernest as I pulled on my evening cape. "I must speak with Miss Byron alone again. Another feminine matter."

"I'm going." Ernest donned his hat and fled the vestibule as if it were on fire, climbing into the carriage parked outside. It was raining now, sheeting down, wet cobbles shimmering gold in the street-lighting.

"What happened?" I asked Mirah, whirling on her.

"He knows," she said. "Mr Cardoza. I was right. He confronted me about it."

"And said what, precisely?"

"That it was obvious to anyone with any brains that I ain't a Rothschild. He said if I were I wouldn't be 'floatin' around London unaccompanied'. Said I'd have been sent with a chaperone, or made to go to Frankfurt and pick a cousin to marry."

Mr Cardoza had an infuriatingly strong point. "Did he say anything else?"

"That he isn't plannin' on revealin' us."

"What? *Why?*"

Mirah scoffed. "He's havin' too much fun watchin' it all unfold. Says he don't need to reveal us because I'll piss it up myself before long."

I cursed inwardly.

"You find anythin' in his bag?"

"Nothing of any use. Only papers relating to Mrs Deighton's affairs. Can you believe that old crone is leaving her entire estate to her *cat?*"

"Maybe I should marry the cat and we can make our fortune that way," she muttered. "Be less dangerous than what we're up to now."

"Has anybody ever told you your dry wit is exhausting? Forget the case. What about you? Did you learn anything during your confrontation with him? Something he may have said in the heat of the moment?"

Mirah pursed her lips hard, two pressed rose petals. "No," she said. "Nothin' at all."

Ernest was quiet the entire ride back to Berkeley Square.

Ordinarily I'd have welcomed the respite from his endless jibes and flippant comments. Had his silence been the result of too many Italian cocktails, I would have merely enjoyed the peace, content to watch the raindrops rolling down the carriage window, racing them the way I had as a girl.

I suspected, however, that his uncharacteristically taciturn mood was not brought on by an excess of sweet vermouth.

These suspicions were confirmed when we reached home. Shaking rainwater off his silk topper, my brother turned to me and announced: "I am in love."

I felt his statement as a blow to the stomach, hard enough to wind me. *I am in love.* A myriad of different feelings rushed up within me, racing and snapping at each other like feral dogs to take precedence. The first was triumph, for that was the aim of this ruse, but it was followed swiftly by haughty disbelief. What did my indolent, selfish brother know of love? He'd barely spent a minute alone with Mirah, how could he claim to love her, to even know her? The bold, impossible nature of his declaration was laughable.

On the heels of both feelings came something else. Something sharp and painful that tugged at my insides, a fishhook in the pit of my stomach.

"I know you asked that I leave her be," Ernest said, with a peace-seeking air that did not suit him. "But I cannot help it, Eloise. You must believe me. I did not expect to feel this way, but I am set on it. I am set on *her*."

The fishhook twisted in my gut, curling my innards into a knot. "How can you be sure? How does one know when they're in love?"

Ernest shrugged, laughing a rough, broken laugh. "I cannot say. I only know that I feel a change in my very core, and she is the only explanation for it. She is sharp and witty, but there is a deep tenderness in her, too."

That fishhook was digging deeper into me with every word, now being tugged as though reeled back in on a line. I smiled, and knew it did not reach my eyes, could feel the absence of in my own gaze. "If you really are in love," I said, "I will not keep you from her."

Ernest's smile widened. "Thank you, Eloise. I know things have been troublesome between us, since Mother…"

"Don't. Don't talk about Mother, please." For some reason the mere mention of her had me writhing with shame.

Ernest was quiet again for a moment. "Goodnight then, Sister. Sleep well."

"And you."

I watched him climb the stairs, clinging to the banister, whistling a tune as he went. I couldn't recall when I'd last seen him so happy. Truly happy, not the artifice brought on by wild parties and fast friends. Guilt flared within my chest, a single match struck in the dark pit of my loathing. I smothered the flame at once, heading straight for the drawing room.

"Susanna!" I called, pulling off my lace gloves. "Susanna! Fetch me some hot chocolate, please!" I was all the way to the divan before remembering I had dismissed her, regret crashing over me as I did. I bit back a scream, hurling my balled-up gloves across the room.

"Miss?"

Mrs Sharp poked her head around the doorframe, and briefly I regretted throwing my gloves already, for I would have much preferred to throw them at her. "*What?*"

"Has something happened?"

"I'm perfectly fine," I insisted. My head was both heavy and light at once, and for the first time that evening I realised I was, in fact, rather drunk. "Fetch me hot chocolate."

Mrs Sharp appeared inclined to scold me. I raised my hand to silence her before she could open her mouth. "Fetch it. Please."

Mrs Sharp went off with a huff, leaving me alone with my thoughts. It was fatal. All my traitorous mind wanted to focus on was Mirah Zelikovich, and the not-kiss we'd almost shared in her Park Street lodgings. Envy was burning through me like a deadly fever, so fierce and potent that I wouldn't have been surprised if I truly took ill with it. I wanted to laugh at the irony. I was the one to set this into motion, orchestrated it perfectly so that Ernest would fall in love. And now I wanted her, instead.

That was the reality of it. I could not escape it, try as I might. Her clever wit and beautiful voice had ensnared me. It was typical. Even when he'd done nothing himself, Ernest found a way to render me miserable. I resented him for it. Had he only been more cautious he would not have fallen into my trap, and I would not be forced to endure watching Mirah laugh at his jokes and accept his gifts.

I wished I'd let him ruin himself the day of Mother's funeral. I was too kind, protecting him from Father's wrath. Made the mistake of feeling *sorry* for him. I could have saved myself a world of grief.

It was an age before Mrs Sharp returned, carrying the silver chocolate pot and dainty porcelain cup on a tray. She set it down on the table closest to me, the chatelaine at her waist clinking. Though she said nothing, she hovered, and I sensed she wanted to.

"Whatever it is you mean to say," I muttered, "*say it.*"

"I'm worried about the way things are between you and your brother of late."

"What business is it of yours?"

"Your dear mother entrusted me to watch out for you both. She'd be so upset seeing the two of you now."

"It is Ernest with whom she'd be upset," I argued, bristling. "*He* is the one gambling and whoring his way through London, not I."

"The two of you were inseparable as children."

"People grow apart," I said. "Mother and Father did, though no one has ever had the decency to tell me why."

Her silvery brows creased. "I could not say, Miss."

"Could not, or will not?"

"I swore to your mother I wouldn't. I don't know all the details, anyhow."

"Mother is dead," I pointed out. "Father is halfway to following her. Tell me."

"All I know is that there was some trouble with your Uncle Horace."

Of course there was trouble with Uncle Horace. There had always been trouble with Uncle Horace. How that trouble could have gotten so bad as to doom a marriage, however, was beyond me. I wondered what it was he could have possibly done that was so egregious. Perhaps he insulted Mother and Father failed to defend her. Perhaps he had even attempted to seduce her. No, that did not seem likely; no matter how loyal Father was to Uncle Horace, he would never have stood for that. The mystery was frustrating. Just another secret that Father barred me from.

"You may leave me, Mrs Sharp," I mumbled, reaching for the chocolate pot.

"Very well, Miss. But do remember; your mother and father never made peace, before she passed, God rest her soul. I know your father regrets it."

"What a lovely thing for me to remember."

"All I mean is don't let the matter with your brother end the same way."

"I don't plan to expire any time particularly soon, Mrs Sharp, unless you have slipped something into my chocolate."

"That isn't what I meant. I know you're both still grieving..."

"Please leave," I said. I didn't want to hear it. I couldn't, not in this state of mind.

Mrs Sharp nodded. "Do you require anything else this evening?"

"No, thank you. You may go to bed."

I sat alone in the drawing room once she'd gone, listening to the clock tick and staring at Mother's piano, silently taunting me. What *would* she have thought of me if she was alive? I hoped she'd be proud of me. When she'd become sick I was the one to oversee her medicines and meals, and when she died I had not wasted time weeping. I was the one to dress the house for mourning, to send out black-bordered letters and die-cut memorial cards, to arrange the flowers, the coffin, the service.

Even after she was interred in the family tomb in Brompton Cemetery, I continued my duties while Ernest frittered away his allowance. I'd darned the hole she'd left in the fabric of our family, no matter how thin I had to stretch myself to do so. Besides, she was the one to teach me the importance of independence. Not by anything said or done, but by the sadness I knew lurked behind that passive, ladylike exterior. She was a dam built of cold cream and scented powder, holding back a flood of emotions that could have drowned us all had the walls ever crumbled. Seeing that I'd sworn myself off marriage forever. It was easy, having no natural inclination towards it. I regarded men that others deemed dashing and found nothing to be admired but the women on their arms. It was less easy to defend myself against Ernest's machinations.

Mother should have been pleased I was protecting myself, ensuring I would never need to rely on a man as she had. It just so happened that the man was my brother.

I took a sip of hot chocolate and grimaced. No cinnamon. I missed Susanna.

19

Mirah

It was a bizarre reversal of roles for me to be overwhelmingly and justifiably furious with Caleb. He vexed me endlessly, but it was a brother's prerogative to be a pain in the arse, apparently sometimes to such an extent you decided to get them disinherited and destroy their lives. Caleb criticized and complained, lectured and lamented, and poked his head into my personal affairs at every opportunity. I'd been mad at him since I could form memories. But I'd never been truly *angry*. Not like this.

Even now I didn't know if angry was the word for it. It definitely resembled anger, burning in my chest and filling me with the urge to beat him into next year – the *Hebrew* next year, for in my mind January was far too close for what was warranted. But every time I thought of him in that pantry with Mr Cardoza that hot-coal-feeling was doused by icy dread. It wasn't just anger, it was worry. More than worry, it was stone cold fear.

My brother had spent his entire life being safely and predictably dull. He didn't smoke, couldn't sit through a single act at the theatre, wouldn't gamble, play parlour games, or even read penny dreadfuls. His entire world had always been work and Torah, with the occasional break to peruse *The Jewish Chronicle*. I'd never even seen him look twice at another man, or woman, no matter how scantily clad or alluring. Or maybe he had, and I'd chosen not to notice rather than confront the notion that my brother was a sexual being. No sister wanted to know that, least of all the details.

Regardless, the point was that in all these years Caleb never took any risks beyond those necessary to living in Limehouse. And now, at the worst possible time, he'd decided to launch himself into a passionate affair with the least appropriate person imaginable. A man who could ruin us both with a single word.

Even worse, Caleb apparently didn't see the danger he'd put us in, somehow convinced Mr Cardoza wouldn't reveal me. I was more concerned that Mr Cardoza was playing two steps ahead of us. If his attraction to men was the secret he'd been blackmailed over, had he chosen to implicate my brother to keep Eloise and I from wielding it against him, knowing I'd never risk exposing Caleb? If that was the case, he needn't have bothered. No matter what was at stake I wouldn't have breathed a word about his fondness for his own sex. It didn't feel right threatening to send a man to prison for something he couldn't help. Besides, I'd have been a raging hypocrite, wouldn't I? I was still imagining the tingling of Eloise's lips on my own in my dreams.

I was still imagining it even now, fully awake, waiting outside the Mayfair apartment for Ernest to arrive. It was overcast, chilly, and I buried my hands deep into my dark fur muff. The dress I wore was lavish, mauve satin silk trimmed with dusky pink lace and accents of black. It boasted a matching capelet and a hat bedecked with pink carnations and a plume of ebony feathers. The gold brooch Ernest gifted me was pinned front and centre on the collar of my cape.

Tabitha stood beside me as I waited, unnervingly quiet. She'd been quiet for days now, but I was too scared to ask why. Maybe she was starting to resent me, a Limehouse whore enjoying slap-up meals and pretty clothes while a 'respectable' girl like herself had to beat rugs and polish silverware.

At last Ernest's carriage rounded the corner from Upper Grosvenor Street onto Park Street, rescuing me from Tabitha's unsettling silence. Even at a distance I could tell it was Ernest's carriage, a fancy Landau with the top folded down, pulled by two silver horses. My first impression wasn't awe, as I'm sure he intended, but concern. The sky looked like it was fixing to rain, and I didn't know how fast you could put the cover back up on one of these opulent rich-person carriages. I smiled all the same as it came to a stop in front of the house, Ernest alighting to greet me.

"Miss de Rothschild." He removed his silk topper and bowed. "You look radiant."

The dress *was* beautiful, that was undeniable, but worse still was that I *felt* beautiful in it – a dangerous thing. The outfit was layers upon layers of luxury, right down to the corset cover and chemise, daintily embroidered on the necklines. The corset was faced with peach silk, boasting lace trim and pale blue flossing, and even the waistband of the bustle cage fastened with a mother-of-pearl button. Some of those things weren't completely out of reach of women like myself – you could buy all kinds of colourful clothes for cheap now in the ready-to-wear shops, or haggle for a pretty second-hand chemise at Spitalfields – but I'd have never owned this many fine layers, or dared to wear them all at once on a casual outing. I was a little nesting doll of lies, and yet when I admired my silhouette in the mirror, it suited me. God, it suited me.

"I'm honoured that you agreed to join me this afternoon," Ernest said. "Please, allow me. Your maidservant may sit up front with the driver." He offered his arm, the groom who had been perched on the rear bench appearing before us to open the door.

I reached behind myself to bunch up the waterfall of my skirt as gracefully as I could, discreetly pinning it up with the small brass clip hidden beneath my overskirt. With far less fabric to manoeuvre I climbed up into the carriage with ease, planting myself on the seat. Ernest joined me, taking his place opposite. The door shut, the groom hopped back up behind the rear axle, and we started off.

"The weather is quite brisk today, isn't it?" Ernest said, as we rode through the park. 'Brisk' was an understatement. While it was cold standing outside waiting for him, it was even colder now the carriage was moving. The breeze was sharp, smelling of the mulch and rotting leaves that littered the ground like an ugly brown carpet. Ernest had the misfortune of having taken the seat that was facing forward, and I could barely hear him over the buffeting wind and the creaking of the carriage.

"*C'est une belle journée,*" I said, sarcastically.

"What does that mean?"

"You don't speak French?"

"Languages weren't my strongest suit at school," Ernest admitted, squinting. His eyes were watering, his cheeks stung bright red. "French just sounds like garbled nonsense to me. I mean – not that it is. It is a beautiful language." He cleared his throat. "I'm sorry I was delayed, by the way. I had an appointment with my barber. I must keep my moustache in fine order, given the family business."

"You must be up to date with all the trends in facial hair."

"Oh, I am. Some of them are ghastly. I'm sure you've seen that awful style this year, where men allow themselves to grow lengths upon lengths of wild beard?"

"You don't fancy following the trend yourself?"

Despite the wind-burn, he went very white. "I don't know. Do you think it would suit me? They do say all the intellectuals are growing them, don't they? Darwin has one."

"No, I don't think it would suit you." Best that only one of us was deceptive in our appearance. I tried to picture Caleb sporting an *intellectual* beard, a great thick bush of hair reaching down to his chest like Moses. The image was hilarious.

Ernest fortunately did not catch the implication of my words, instead nodding decisively to himself. "Yes. I thought as such. I much prefer a good moustache."

"A pity I cannot grow one, then." He looked at me, perplexed, and I laughed. "A jest, sir."

"Ah. Yes. A good one. I see you're wearing the brooch."

"Of course." I brought one hand up to brush it, the gold smooth and cold under my fingertips. "It really is lovely. I cannot thank you enough."

"Do you think your family would approve of it?" He was nervous, chewing noticeably on his lip in a way that made him look as if he was trying to eat his own moustache. "Your mother, in particular?"

I forced a laugh. "Why, are you going to send one to her, too?"

"No, no! Not unless you think that would be wise? I merely...want them to like me."

My stomach sank as I understood. I didn't know why. This was what we'd planned. "My English cousins would," I said, eschewing eye contact. "I do not know what my mother's opinion would be." I assuaged my conscience with the fact that wasn't a lie. I *didn't* know what Adele de Rothschild would think of him, nor did I know what my actual mother's thoughts would be. Probably not particularly favourable.

"You said that she is very observant," Ernest said. "And that she would not approve of you socialising so freely with gentiles. Do you think she could be persuaded otherwise?"

"Nothing is impossible." I finally dared glance at him. He was staring at me, besotted, and I suddenly wanted to leap out of the open carriage and run. "Though I've heard some rumours about you that would not endear you to her."

With how rapidly Ernest Byron's face was fluctuating between red and white I was starting to worry he'd take a fainting. All that blood rushing in and out of his head couldn't be good for a man.

"Rumours," he echoed haltingly. "Ah. Eloise, I take it?"

"She is a good friend to me." I tried not to think of her lips so close to mine. Tried valiantly. Failed. "She has warned me off you. She tells me you're a scoundrel, sir. A great lover of women and horses."

"*Horses?*"

"Betting, sir."

"Oh."

"Are they true?"

Ernest was stiff in his seat. "I... have not always been the most gentlemanly, it is true." Now *he* was the one wanting to fling himself out of the carriage. "I confess I do have a fondness for vice."

"And women?"

"I'm a man, aren't I?" He caught himself as the words were still leaving his mouth, reaching towards me as though to keep me from, yes, jumping out of the carriage and running away. At this point it was likely we'd both desert the vehicle and it would trundle on through Hyde Park without us. "I mean – I don't – I am committed to change!"

"Really?"

"Yes! Truly! I beg, do not allow my sister's words to colour your opinion of me too harshly. Eloise hates me. She's been a harpy to me since Mother died."

Since Mother died. That was interesting. The way Eloise told it they'd been wrestling for dominance in the cradle. The painting on the wall of the drawing room told a different story, but it was possible for a skilful artist to paint two squabbling children as docile friends, and I'd no reason to doubt Eloise's account. Until now.

"She did mention that the loss was hard for her."

Ernest snorted. "Did she? Well, that's news to me. She's as cold as ice. Even before Mother died she was stepping into her shoes. Literally, she still has a pair of Mother's shoes!"

"I didn't realise."

"Hardly your fault. I'm not surprised she didn't mention it." He crossed his arms over his chest, a little boy uncomfortable in his smart clothes. "I never saw her cry even once, yet she had the audacity to scold me for grieving. And then she got it into that lofty head of hers that I should be grateful to her, because of what happened at the funeral..."

"What happened at the funeral?"

Ernest suddenly remembered who he was talking to, uncrossing his arms and sitting up straight. "It doesn't matter. Forgive me, I did not mean to ramble."

"I don't mind."

"I'm grateful. I confess, I have not had anyone to confide in for a very long time."

The word *confide* was a shiv to the gut. I didn't doubt Ernest Byron had left a string of heartsick women in his wake, but it wasn't my nature to be cruel, and there was definitely something cruel about making a man think he'd found a confidant. And for what? I wanted a better life for Caleb and myself, but could it really be worth this? I'd fought so hard not to turn out like Ma, but here I was, my life revolving around a rich man like he was the sun. Just because I didn't love him didn't make it any better. I still wanted something from him.

And Eloise.

There was a loud patter as a heavy spot of rain landed squarely in my lap. Another fell, and another, and then all at once the heavens opened and dropped a deluge onto Hyde Park, God tipping a bucket over our heads. We both shrieked. Ernest stood, almost launching out of the carriage as the horses halted, and began scrambling desperately to pull up the cover with the help of the groom. His hat tipped clear off him, and I caught it, the rain barrelling down so furiously we'd both be soaked to the skin by the time he succeeded in sheltering us.

"I'm so sorry!" he cried, as if the rain were his doing. His once perfectly styled hair was already plastered to his head, water dripping pathetically from the ends of his moustache.

I erupted into laughter. Ernest paused his frantic mission, goggling at me as if I'd lost my wits.

"Miss de Rothschild?"

"Leave it," I said. "What's the use?"

He hesitated, still holding up the cover, mouth hanging open. I couldn't stop laughing in spite of my conflicted feelings – perhaps even because of them. Everything was hilarious; the sight of him with Acker's Patented Moustache Colourant and Wax running down his chin in streaks. That I wore such an elaborate dress, only to get completely drenched. That all of this was supposed to be a day of genteel courtship. I was laughing so hard my stomach hurt.

"*Il pleut comme vache qui pisse!*" I shouted over the din.

Despite not having a clue what I'd said, Ernest started laughing too.

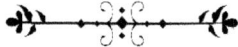

I was still laughing when I bid him goodbye at the door, wet through all my fancy layers of underpinnings and the feathers of my hat drooping miserably. We'd made a hasty retreat after the rain went up, but it had been a remarkably pleasant ride back to Park Street, mostly because the weather dominated our conversation. I hadn't needed to worry so much about being a Rothschild, or navigating the proposal I was terrified was about to come. It had been fun. So much so that beneath the laughter I felt like a monster. I told myself I had no desire to be rich. I'd only entered into this agreement to save Caleb, though he was apparently determined to make me regret it, inviting Gideon Cardoza into his bed. I couldn't deny I enjoyed the pretty dresses, the glittering jewels - but making a man love me to keep them was curdling my conscience like sour milk.

"Would you mind fetchin' me a towel, Tabitha?" I asked, squeezing my hair out in front of the drawing room fire. "You should dry off, too!"

"Yes, Miss," Tabitha said, still unsettlingly subdued. I couldn't bear it any longer.

"What's the matter? Has somethin' happened?"

She paused in the doorway, staring down at her feet. "It's nothing, Miss."

"Tabitha. Please." I stepped towards her, touching her shoulder gently. "You can tell me. I'm not some rich mistress, fixin' to punish you for speakin' up. I know I'm all trussed up like one, but I'm not. What's wrong?"

Tabitha sniffled loudly. She raised her head, eyes big and glistening with tears. A sob broke out of her. I did the only thing I could think to and pulled her into my arms.

"It's Susanna, Miss," she said, between hitching breaths. "Miss Byron gave her the sack."

20

Eloise

I was beginning to believe there was something actually, scientifically wrong with my brother.

He'd arrived back from his ride in Hyde Park with Mirah the day before so wet from the rain that he'd dripped all through the vestibule and up the stairs, earning a harsh chiding from Mrs Sharp, yet hadn't ceased smiling for the rest of the day. He had even joined me for dinner rather than dining at one of his clubs as was his habit, and the entire time he had continued to smile.

It was his behaviour this morning that was the most disturbing. Sophie walked past his open bedchamber door and saw him doing *gymnastics*, of all things. Standing there in his vest and drawers doing knee-bends and stretches, waving his arms like a windmill and boxing an invisible opponent. Plenty of gentlemen swore by a morning gymnastics routine to improve circulation, but Ernest did not rise before noon unless forced, and I'd not seen him exercise since he was a boy.

When I sat across from him at breakfast his pupils didn't suggest opium as the culprit, and so I could only theorise he'd enjoyed his afternoon with Miss Zelikovich greatly. Precisely how much he enjoyed it was a cause for concern, for it was the first time they were truly alone together besides his fleeting visit to her door. Chaperoned, of course, but chaperoned by servants, whom they could send away if desired. How was I to know what happened between them? How could I be certain they had not left their carriage and escorts and stolen away to a thicket of greenery together? My stomach was sick contemplating it.

My worries were only further compounded by the note I received from Mirah following breakfast: *Meet me at Signora Moretti's. It is urgent.*

She was already there when I arrived at *La Moda Italiana,* browsing the rolls of fabric, a colourful mosaic of textiles that filled a whole wall. I recalled how differently she appeared the first time she'd been there, all knotted curls and shabby hems, a hungry shadow of a woman clinging to life out of sheer stubbornness. Now she was dressed every bit as elegantly as the other ladies in the shop, a striking figure in a gown of ochre silk, trimmed with white lace and adorned with blue bows. It was one of my favourites I'd picked out for her. It brought out her eyes. Those clever, piercing eyes, which fell upon me as I entered the boutique.

"Miss Byron."

"Miss de Rothschild."

We went through the motions of greeting each other, Signora Moretti watching discreetly from where she was busy assisting another client.

"Will you join me in the fitting room?" Mirah asked. Tabitha was standing a few feet behind her, hands clasped in front of stomach. "I have a dress being made up that I would value your opinion on."

"Of course," I said, allowing her to lead the way. Tabitha remained behind.

We had barely passed through the curtain into the deserted fitting room before she seized my arm, forcing me up against the nearest wall. I gasped, finding myself staring into her face. She was flushed and focused. Radiantly angry. I wondered if this was how shepherds and farmers of old felt when they were visited by angels. *Be not afraid.* She continued gripping my arm with one hand, the other pressed to the wall behind me to support herself as she leaned over me. I was not afraid. I was something else entirely, taut and thrumming with energy, a devouring heat taking over me from the inside. I fought to maintain my composure, clawing at the last thread of it.

"What is the meaning of –"

"Susanna." She spat the woman's name like poison.

"Susanna?" My confusion was so thorough as to momentarily supersede all other emotions. "What about Susanna? Has she done something?"

"*You've* done somethin'," Mirah said, squeezing my arm to the point of discomfort. "You *dismissed* her!"

That was what this was about? I wanted to laugh, overwhelmed with relief that it was not something more serious. "I had good reason. She was the one who gave Ernest your address."

"Of course she gave it to him, he's her employer!" Mirah released me, moving back. As her shadow lifted from me I wanted to follow it to its source and swallow it up inside of me. Without her warm solidness looming over me I was suddenly cold against the wall.

"Susanna was my friend," I protested. "We've known each other since we were girls. She betrayed me."

"She did what she was paid for. You don't understand, do you?" When I failed to answer, she threw up her hands. "Of course not! God, why would I ever think different? She ain't your friend. She's your maid. You pay her, and it keeps her family warm and puts food in their bellies. The power you have over someone like her – you don't even see it! You can ruin her life. Hell, you have done, sendin' her away for doin' the only thing she could!"

I stammered, scrambling for some kind of retort. Nothing came to me.

"You think she had any other choice when Ernest demanded she give him my address? You think she could've said no?"

"I... well..."

"Of course she couldn't. He'd have sent her away for her disobedience." Mirah shook her head. "You should be flattered. That she was willin' to risk your wrath over his meant she trusted you to be the more understandin' one. Fine job you did of provin' her faith wasted!"

I blinked at her, still speechless. Was it possible she was right? I'd never thought of Susanna as anything but a friend. A confidant who brushed my hair, and fetched my water for my morning wash, and dressed me, and mended my clothes…

"I didn't realise," I whispered.

"I know you didn't!"

"What do you think I should do?"

"You have to offer her her job back," Mirah insisted. "With extra pay for puttin' her through Hell! If you don't you lose me, too. I'll walk, and you can find another woman to seduce your witless brother."

I gawped at her in horror. "No! No, I'll take her back on. I will."

"Good." Mirah's demeanour changed instantly, an awkward, noticeable shift. "Good. That's it, then."

"I'm sorry." I didn't know where the apology sprung from. All I knew was that it felt so necessary and natural that it flowed off my tongue like a tune. "How was the carriage ride with Ernest?" I asked, desperate to move on. I couldn't help that I sounded jealous.

"Fine," was Mirah's huffy reply. She wasn't looking at me now, and I was crushed, wounded by the thought I had upset her. "He was askin' about my family, if they'd approve of him."

"Oh."

Ernest meant his words to me when we'd come home from Mirah's dinner, then. He was in love, or believed so strongly enough that he was preparing to propose. There was no other way to interpret that. Suddenly I didn't know what to think. We were on the cusp of achieving what we'd set out to do, succeeding far easier than I could have ever predicted. And I hated it. The thought of Mirah on my brother's arm, his betrothed, his *beloved,* even if only for a short while, had my heart in a noose. Would there be a wedding night? No, that would be taking it too far. There needn't be any physical consummation of the marriage for it to scandalise Father. The mere public attachment of the two would be enough. Mirah could feign her monthly or a migraine to avoid it.

Regardless, my imagination rushed to fill every crevice of my mind with the image of her in Ernest's bed, his hands in her beautiful hair. Beneath the envy and heartache emerged a flicker of doubt. The sense that I was wronging my brother, in spite of the myriad ways he had wronged me.

"We must continue to keep a watchful eye on Mr Cardoza." I detested that those were the only words to come out of me. That I didn't have the courage to say anything more.

"That won't be too difficult," Mirah muttered.

"Is that all, then?" Why was I speaking this way? Poised and coolly indifferent?

"No. I want you to understand." Her eyes finally sought mine again. They were still burning, but the flames had lowered to a smoulder. "You've dragged me into your world, made me act the part of a lady, and I've done it just as we agreed. But if we're goin' to keep doin' this, I want you to know where I came from, see for yourself what it's like on the other side." She lifted her chin, and the same thrill that rushed through me when she'd pushed me to the wall ran its course again. "You're comin' out with me to Limehouse."

It was a whole week until we were granted the opportunity to visit Limehouse. Privately I'd hoped it would never come at all. I couldn't see the purpose of it. I'd seen Limehouse, and had no desire to examine it any closer. What was there to see but filth and despair? Impressively big rats?

But Mirah insisted, and after the confrontation at *La Moda Italiana* I was loath to refuse her. I hadn't imagined she would be so passionate about Susanna's plight, but the more I thought on it the more worried I was that she was right. How could I call Susanna my friend when the very basis of our relationship was her serving me? I had never considered it a transactional thing before. She had since re-entered my service with higher pay and a gift of one of my own necklaces, but I sensed things were forever changed between us. I could not blame her for that.

What troubled me worse was the notion that I'd done the same to Mirah. I paid her for this role, or promised to. I had made a servant of her too.

There was a shift though, that afternoon in the fitting room. The power changed hands. Now I burned for her, and more importantly, so did Ernest. I would never find another woman to seduce him if she were to walk away, for he was set on her, and I was convinced she knew it. I would be shamed forever if she told the world what I planned. The strangest thing of all was that I didn't mind. When the power slipped from my hands into hers, I hadn't the faintest urge to hold on or attempt to wrangle it back. I'd wanted her to have it. Or perhaps I just felt better about the situation if I told myself I'd allowed it to happen.

The chance to go to Limehouse came on a Thursday evening. For all his newfound devotion to keeping 'good habits', it hadn't taken long for some of Ernest's old ones to creep back, and he set out for one of his clubs following dinner. The second he was gone I sent a note along to Mirah, receiving a reply shortly thereafter. I'd feigned exhaustion in the parlour, declared an intent to retire to bed early to avoid Mrs Sharp relaying my actions to Father, and then slipped out through the street-door wearing a cloak borrowed from Susanna.

I now found myself in the back of a musty, mysteriously damp hansom cab, bounced along on the cobbles so furiously I wouldn't have been surprised if my brain was completely scrambled by the time we stopped.

Mirah had asked that I meet her at the docks, but when the carriage leaned to a halt alongside the Limehouse basin, I began to fear I would never find her. A dense fog crawled in off the surface of the Thames, bizarrely yellowed by the light of a single streetlamp. I popped open the cab window, only to immediately cover my nose with my handkerchief. Though I'd made the journey into Limehouse several times now I was no better prepared for the stench, simultaneously smoky and fishy. Behind the blanket of fog, the water sloshed around the docks, slapping against the hulls of sleeping boats. A lone seagull started up shrieking from one of the rooftops, warning me that I did not belong.

Suddenly I felt dreadfully unsafe. I must have lost my mind to come alone, in the dark, driven by a hansom driver I did not know. I'd been before, yes, but with my own driver, whom I trusted, and the one time I came by cab it had been daylight, with Dr Hartley by my side. How would I even see Mirah, through such a fog? What if I were to approach some hazy figure, only for it to be a stranger? A criminal? I leaned back against the seat, hoping to calm myself. It would be better to return home. I could tell Mirah I tried. Despite this, I made no move to signal the decision to the driver. Underneath the fear lurked a dangerous impulse, the desire to slither into the waiting night and become someone else, *anyone* else. To shake off the mantle of responsibility and the tedium of high society and be free. *What in God's name am I thinking?*

A knock on the window sent me flinging myself into the furthest opposite corner of the cab with a yelp. The single lamp inside the carriage burned so low and dim that it took more than a few seconds for me to realise it was Mirah standing outside, stretched up onto tiptoes to peer through the window at me.

Infuriatingly, my hammering heart didn't settle at this revelation. It only became a different kind of frantic. I leaned over and threw open the door, Mirah having to leap back to avoid it.

"There you are," she said. "You're late!"

"I am?" I'd no way of telling. I'd left my watch safely at home, the tiny gold timepiece a gift from Mother that I didn't fancy having pickpocketed.

"It's fine." Mirah eyed me up and down in such a way that I felt distinctly appraised, like a horse at market. "Open your cloak."

"I beg your pardon?"

"I need to see what you're wearin'."

I was now grateful for the low lighting in the carriage, for it hid how red my face became. I did as she commanded, allowing her a full view of my dress. I'd chosen it carefully, remembering what she'd said of my appearance that night at the music hall. It was my plainest visiting dress, simple lilac silk with very sparing embellishment and beadwork –

"It's too fancy."

"What?" I gawped at her, taken aback. "*How?*"

"It just is. The pale fabric ain't stained by the soot in the air, it's never needed proper mendin', and it's *too* fashionable. Ladies like yourself are leadin' the trends, it takes a bit longer for them to get down to us folk. You can tell these things if you're from 'round here. That thing has 'high tea with the bridge club' all over it." She shook her head. "No fuss. I knew you'd do this, so I bought you a dress." She held up a stuffed canvas bag triumphantly. I stared at it.

"*You* bought *me* a dress?"

"From Spitalfields. Got a good price for it, too."

"It's second-hand?"

"Probably a fair few more hands than that," Mirah laughed. "Most likely some lady like yourself cast it off to a maid who sold it on a couple times. Here." She tossed the bag into the cab, and I scrambled to catch it.

"Where do you expect me to change?" I demanded.

"The carriage has curtains, don't it?"

"In *here?*"

"Why not?"

I couldn't think why not. It was a perfectly sensible suggestion, but I shied away from it all the same. The idea of being anything close to undressed in Limehouse made my skin prickle.

"You can keep your pretty underthings on," Mirah added, quietly. She wasn't looking at me, suddenly fascinated by the split ends of one of her curls. I was glad she wasn't looking at me, and irritated by it, too, simultaneously craving her attention and terrified of receiving it. Something about those words leaving her lips turned that prickle into a pleasant shiver. *Keep your pretty underthings on.*

I opened the bag and pulled out the garment. Mustard-seed yellow, with lace that had once been ivory, now discoloured. I stared at it, heaping fabric in my lap, and then at Mirah, still standing there toying with her hair.

"Will you close the door, then?"

"Oh. 'Course." She cleared her throat and stepped back to do so. I reached across to pull the patchy curtains over the carriage windows, then held the bodice of my newly acquired dress up to the light. It was hideous.

21

Eloise

It was a struggle changing in such tight quarters without the assistance of a maid. Several times I considered asking Mirah for help, but whenever I pictured her hands upon me, even as innocently as fixing the way my skirts fell over my bustle, my imagination let them roam. It was best I didn't involve her in any part of dressing me, lest I be struck with the urge to reverse the whole process, *pretty underthings* included.

When I stepped out of the carriage I was certain I resembled a canary that had been half-mauled by a cat, my creased yellow overskirt my bedraggled feathers. The dress had once been fashionable, but that had been two or three years ago. It was also too big for me, the hem so long that it dragged along the ground. Mirah looked a little better, though she had the opposite problem, her unusual height causing the dress to fall only to her ankles, revealing her black scalloped button boots, wet and shiny from traipsing through puddles. Her gown was a brilliant fuchsia pink, but I could see immediately what distinguished it from those in *La Moda Italiana*; the fabric was dyed unevenly in places, and a subtle but unmistakable mend ran along the seam of one shoulder.

I sent the hansom cab back to my house with my lilac gown, and the two of us set off up the docks side by side. It was cold out, the breeze cutting up the streets off the invisible Thames faintly wet, but Mirah did not take my arm.

"Are we going to an opium den?" I asked.

"An opium den! Bloody hell, you've got a high opinion of me, don't you? 'Course not. We're goin' to the music hall."

"But I've heard Limehouse is riddled with such establishments."

"I bet you have. I've read all about 'Dark England'!" She tossed her long curls back over her shoulder with the imperiousness of a duchess. "The way some of these authors write you'd think every other buildin' was an opium den! Even Dickens had to get his word in. I feel bad for the Chinese folk livin' here, dragged through the gutter as if they don't already live in it. Ain't half as many of them as the papers would have you believe, for one thing, and they're only here 'cause Queenie can't keep her hands in her own pockets."

"So, no opium den?"

"No. No opium den."

It had been eerily quiet on the street where we'd met, but as we walked lights began to appear before us out of the fog, and with them the noise of other people. Music, harsh and jarring, nothing resembling the grand orchestral scores I was familiar with – a fiddle, and a woman belting a jaunty tune. Laughter, shouting. A dog barking, only for a man to yell over it to *hush, you bloody mutt*. The smell in the air changed too, the stink of the river and the gutters softening beneath the heavy, clinging aroma of fried food. The mist cleared, a theatre curtain rolling back to reveal the music hall situated where I remembered it, on the corner by the water's edge. It was livelier than when I'd last been there, rowdy clientele spilling out on the street. I couldn't help the thrill of excitement that passed through me.

The hall itself radiated warmth, amber light shining behind steamed-up windows. The food-smell came from a stall that had taken up residence outside, a heavy cast-iron range upon wheels from which the leather-apron-clad vendor doled out portions of something wrapped in brown paper. The man was near hidden behind the cloud of smoke coughed out by his range, and I struggled to hear what he was shouting over the furious sizzling of the grease pans, but amidst all the noise I made out the words 'penny a piece!'.

"You want somethin' to eat?" Mirah asked.

I shook my head. Whatever it was I wasn't convinced my stomach would keep it down.

"If you don't fancy fried fish there's an eel and pie house down the road."

"I dined before I came out," I said, in lieu of admitting I was frightened of sampling the local cuisine. I sensed Mirah could tell all the same, but generously masked her disapproval. A sharp whistle caught us both by surprise as we made our way to the door. A group of men – labourers or dockworkers, from their appearance – stood by one of the windows outside, rough faces bathed in the warm light from within as they smoked their pipes. One of them, in an overcoat that was too large for him and a waistcoat that was too small, leaned towards us, leering. He reeked of tobacco, his teeth stained as yellow as my dress with it.

"You're a pretty pair of doves," he said. I *knew* I resembled a bird. "How much for a turn with the both of you?"

"More than you can afford," Mirah shot back.

"Ah, c'mon now. I'll buy you both a dram."

"Take a whole barrel to convince me that's a fair deal. Don't reckon you could please two of us, anyway. Best buy your own hand that drink instead."

His friends went off laughing, and the badly-dressed fellow retreated back into the midst of the group to a round of taunts and jeers. Mirah laughed too, and finally, for the first time, reached out to grab my arm. Her hand was firm and hot as an iron brand.

"Come on," she said, flashing me a wolf's grin as she pulled me into the unknown.

It was sweltering inside the music hall, a rush of hot air blasting us both as we opened the door. The lower floor was packed, crammed with bodies from the windows to the stage, stinking of stale sweat and other mysterious odours. It reminded me of playing 'Sardines' as a girl. Whenever we'd played as children I was always the first to find Ernest, who was atrocious at hiding. The two of us gave ourselves away giggling before finding ourselves crushed in by various children of our parents' friends that I scarcely recalled the names of, and even some of the adults when we could entice them to play. Mother never did, of course – she was too sensible for parlour games – but when Uncle Horace was around, he was always willing to play.

The music hall was not just hot and busy, but noisy too. So noisy I could barely hear myself think, music and voices and the clinking of glasses layered on top of each other. A woman hooted like a gibbon as she dangled off the arm of her male companion, and to my right two men argued loudly over either a horse they'd bet on or a woman they both wanted to court. It was impossible to tell which from the way they talked.

My shoes dragged on the sticky floor as we fought our way to the stage, jostling for space. Mirah tugged me aside just in time to avoid something that passed for ale being poured directly onto my head from the gallery above. A man knocked into me, grunting a curse, and did not look twice. That was when I realised the dress Mirah bought me had done its job. To this stranger I was any other patron, invisible in the crowd. Free, for one night, of all my tedious obligations. We squeezed out a path along the back wall, reaching the stage and then passing it down a set of three steps until we came to the same door I'd come through the first time I'd been there. Mirah knocked. The man who answered cut an intimidating figure, tall and portly, with enormous muttonchops and thick, heavy eyebrows to match. "Mirah. Where the bleedin' hell have you been?"

For a heartbeat I feared he was about to yell at her, but then he swept her up in his arms, lifting her clear off her feet and spinning her around. She threw her head back and laughed.

"Bertram! Put me down you oaf!"

"Oh, I'll put you down! In the ground, mind, for disappearin' on us like that! Gave us all a fright!"

"Can't have missed me all that much. This place is heavin'! What happened?"

"Got a new girl, she's a gem."

"Better legs than me?"

"More willin' to get 'em out," he retorted, stepping aside and gesturing with a wide swoop of his arms for us to pass through. "Come on. Everyone'll be pleased to see you. Who's this, a friend of yours?" His eyes flitted briefly to me.

"A friend," Mirah agreed. "Come on, Eloise."

It was odd, being back here under these circumstances. The last time I'd sensed everyone was wary of me, skirting around me as though I were a dangerous animal that might bite without provocation. Now nobody even acknowledged me, a scantily clad dancer bumping me with her shoulder as she hurried past. It was unexpectedly pleasant.

We found Mirah's friends in the same dressing room where I'd first proposed our deal, the lanky Irishman who'd originally greeted me the night Mirah and I met busy fussing over an elaborate sequinned headdress being worn by one of the performers. The woman was striking; Indian, with glossy, oiled hair and big brown eyes that shot straight to Mirah as we entered. She squealed, jumping up from her seat and causing the headdress to go listing wildly to one side. The Irishman swore loudly and made to catch it, but he too forgot his task when he saw us.

"Mirah!"

"Oliver," she said, embracing the woman tightly. "Cora. You look lovely, is that new?"

"Not quite," Cora said. Her accent surprised me, harsh and East End as they came. "Oliver picked it up from some theatre closin' over in Covent Garden. D'you like it? I'm a Hindu priestess. Don't tell anyone that don't exist."

"Wouldn't dream of it. How've you all been? Bertram says you got a new girl."

"Flora," Oliver said, gruffly. "She's American. Well, Mancunian actually, but she puts on the accent like, makes her seem more glamorous. Come from afar an all that."

"Flora and Cora?" Mirah snorted. "You're jokin'!"

"You're one to talk. Where've you been all this time? You vanished off the face of the earth. We thought some fella did you in, or you'd caught whatever your brother had and croaked it."

"Well I haven't croaked it, as you can see," Mirah said, fishing into the front of her dress. I averted my eyes, flushing all the way to the tips of my ears. "Here. To apologise for disappearin'." She held up one of the necklaces I bought her, sapphires twinkling in the gaslight. I nearly protested, barely catching myself. Oliver's eyes grew round as an owl's.

"Hell, how'd *you* come by a trinket like that?"

"I've been put up in an apartment by a fancy rich man," Mirah said, dropping the necklace into his hand with ease. "Pays my way and then some."

"Jammy bitch. He doesn't happen to have a brother who's not the marryin' sort, does he?"

"No. He has a sister, but she's a proper harpy. Eloise here is her lady's maid, ain't you?" She turned to me, and I had no time to be insulted by the insinuation that I was a harpy.

"Oh. Yes. I am indeed her lady's maid."

"Bloomin' heck, you don't half speak fancy," Cora said, tilting her head. The lop-sided headdress clinging to her crown made her resemble a rare parrot. Still prettier than the shabby canary I was. "Where'd you grow up?"

"Covent Garden," Mirah cut in, before I opened my mouth. "And she's gotta speak like that. Can't be servin' a respectable lady soundin' like you, can she?"

Cora laughed, swatting Mirah's ear. "I've missed your smart mouth!"

"Her smart mouth has been busy elsewhere," Oliver said. More laughter.

22

Mirah

The thing was, I'd never expected the bluff to actually *work*.

I hadn't even meant to throw down the ultimatum in Signora Moretti's dress shop, but Tabitha's dismay and poor Susana's predicament had enraged me past the point of good sense, which Caleb would have said I was in short supply of to begin with. When it worked – immediately – I'd nearly been too taken aback to follow through on it. Eloise relented instantly, and in that brief moment I'd realised we were more equal than I first believed. She needed me as much as I needed her.

Not that I needed her anymore, though, did I? Ernest adored me. Was practically eating out of the palm of my hand. If I were to walk away, Eloise wouldn't stand a chance of replacing me.

I had other options, too. I could whisper the truth to Ernest, for one thing; it would shatter his heart, but I could strike a deal to protect him from the public shame of his sister's scheme. I could even use this trip to Limehouse against her, soiling her reputation and rendering anything she said worthless. Or I could bypass all of that entirely. I now possessed a small fortune in dresses and jewels thanks to Eloise's thoroughness. Caleb and I could pack up and vanish in the night, never to be seen again. Eloise couldn't exactly go to the coppers about it - what would she say? The woman she hired to pull off a con with conned her first? Caleb and I had moved around plenty, it wouldn't be a stretch to do it again. I didn't want to do any of that, though. Not least because such dishonesty was not in my nature; pickpocketing to survive was one thing, but swindling the person I'd already agreed to swindle someone else with was a bridge too far. Besides, Caleb would never stand for it. God would invariably enter into his lecture somehow, as if the nosy bastard wasn't already everywhere all at once. More than that, though, I just plain didn't want to. In a way, I understood Eloise's ruthlessness. She wanted what she felt was hers, to live well, and free, not on the leash of a man. It was easy to sympathise with that plight. Any woman would.

I glanced at her, standing beside me in the crowd, our shoulders pressed close. Her eyes were wide and shiny, gazing up at the stage with childlike wonder. She'd been timid and wary when we first arrived, but as the music flowed and the night wound on, I watched the tension gradually leave her. It made my stomach flutter treacherously.

Cora's set was always fun. She played the sitar on a velvet pillow and pandered to an audience of pasty, salivating Englishmen who believed they were living their harem dreams. She sang in her mother tongue, beautifully, and confided to me once that the lyrics were usually insults to the audience - that they were horrible foul-smelling beasts she'd never give the time of day to. They gladly lapped it up, of course, understanding nothing of it. And for the few of her countrymen who came to the music hall it made for a great comedy routine.

"I've never heard music like this," Eloise said, having to put her lips to my ear to make herself heard over the noise. It made me shiver.

"You should get out to Limehouse more often," I joked. "The world is a lot bigger than your drawing room concerts!"

"I know. I've always wanted to see more of it."

Her words rocked me, vibrating against the shell of my ear, but when I leaned away to look at her she was already staring up at the stage again, smiling so wide her teeth gleamed like piano keys. She didn't behave like a woman who wanted to see more of the world. At least not a world like mine. She was fighting tooth and nail to stay in the one she inhabited, after all.

And yet, seeing her now, I believed it. It was as though she'd forgotten to pretend otherwise, caught up in the rushing excitement of the music hall with the rest of the audience.

The next performer was a fiddle player, and the moment the bow hit the strings, the energy in the room changed. I couldn't help myself - I grabbed both of Eloise's hands and pulled her into a small pocket of space in the crowd, swinging us both in a wide circle. Her squeak of surprise became a laugh, loud and musical as the fiddle, and soon we were swinging so energetically we were at risk of flying backwards if our clammy hands slipped apart.

We danced half a dozen dances in the hours that followed, belting along to catch-penny tunes until our throats were sore. She didn't know any of the words, but that didn't stop her from shouting out nonsense lyrics anyway. I didn't imagine our dances resembled any Eloise was familiar with; there was no graceful waltz, no carefully structured march. We did something like a polka, taking turns leading as we pranced around the room, colourful skirts spinning, but most of it was pure movement, without steps, without reason.

The new girl, Flora, was the last set of the night. She sang a burlesque, a travesty full of pastiches and raunchy innuendo, and while I didn't reckon much to speaking ill of someone I didn't know, it was clear she'd been hired to replace me. They'd even stuck a golden wig on the poor girl, and she kept itching at it as she sang. The song imitated a number from Gilbert's *Robert the Devil*, a cheap copy of a parody of a tragedy. Nothing original at all. Her voice was pretty - notwithstanding the poor attempt at a New York accent - but

I couldn't see how her legs were supposedly any better than mine. I complained as much to Eloise as we staggered outside into the cold night, both rasping for air that didn't taste of tobacco and desperate to cool off. Inside Flora continued caterwauling to the crowd. We giggled at every high-gliding vowel and dropped 'r'.

"Did you really dress like that?" Eloise asked, as we crossed the street to lean against the iron railings that looked down into the Thames. The fog that filled the streets when we'd first arrived had dissipated now, and we could see the water sloshing angrily below us, gleaming like oil in the light cast from the music hall.

"Like what?"

"That! The men's clothing, and the tights!"

"Sometimes. Depended on the song. You think it'd suit me?" I made to strike a manly pose, puffing out my chest and raising my chin.

"You'd probably look better than she does," Eloise said, stern with diplomacy. "But she sings well. Although I wasn't aware the song was called *'Animawsity* and villainous *verbawsity'...*" Her voice cracked as she spoke, her serious expression following. We collapsed into another fit of giggles, having to hold ourselves upright on the railings.

"She's not that bad!" I said, having to wheeze it out between laughs.

"She's not," Eloise agreed. "But I think she'd be barred from entering New York if they heard her!"

We laughed again, ignoring the men shouting and whistling at us from the music hall doors.

"Why did you show me this?" Eloise asked, when we'd both recovered. "I'd have thought you wanted me to see how wretched life is here."

I snorted. "What's the use in showin' you that? You already know it's horrible to be poor. You don't need to see it to understand it. I wanted you to see that we're more than that. We're not limpin' dogs you ought to feel pity for.

We're not lessons to move you to charity. We're people, and we find joy and laughter even amongst the shit. Susanna, Tabitha, me – we're just folk like you who didn't get born with as much money."

Eloise glanced down at her feet as I spoke, and I wondered if she was ashamed. I fumbled around in the tattered reticule pocket of my skirt. "Here," I said, offering her a squashed, misshapen cigarette. She looked up again, eyebrows raised.

"Where did you get those?"

"Nabbed 'em from Oliver. You want one?"

"Ladies shouldn't smoke," she said, though her tone was more wary than decisive. "It is a masculine habit."

"You think I should ask Flora if I can borrow her costume?" I joked. "You don't have to do anythin' you don't want to, but don't say no just 'cause of that. You ain't a lady tonight, remember? Just another hardworkin' Limehouse girl like me."

Eloise smirked, taking the cigarette and placing it between her lips. I struck a match, lit my own, then leaned close to put it to hers. Her hand came up unexpectedly to cup and steady mine, our eyes meeting over the dancing flame. I lingered there longer than necessary, nearly setting the whole cigarette alight before I drew back, tossing the match over the railings, an offering to the Thames. I watched it go, lulled by the familiar sounds of Limehouse in the night. The tune drifting from the music hall. Gulls squabbling in the darkness. The retching of a patron vomiting over the side of the railings somewhere down the street. It was funny the things a person found comforting.

"See?" I said. "Your reputation didn't crumble instantly to ash."

"It would if anyone saw me," Eloise argued, though she relaxed, gazing down into the black water. "Sometimes I think I'll be crushed beneath it."

"Beneath what?"

"Reputation." She coughed as she inhaled. "It's enormous. You're fortunate you don't have to concern yourself with it."

I snorted. "Nice of you to say!"

"I'm sorry. I didn't mean..."

"It's all right. I know." I shuffled awkwardly where I stood, watching the embers at the end of my cigarette slowly eating their way up the rolled paper. "Not all your sort care about their reputation that much though. Your brother, for one."

"Don't remind me. Ernest has never cared about anything of importance."

I remembered what he'd told me on our carriage ride, and wondered how much truth her words held. "Are you sure of that? He said things only became difficult between you after your mother's funeral."

"He's confiding in you now, is he?" Eloise murmured. She didn't sound angry – more regretful. "That's not the full truth of it, but he's right that Mother's funeral worsened the matter."

"What happened?"

"I had to do everything. When she became sick I was the only one who cared for her. Ernest disappeared to pubs and gambling dens, and Father was too crushed by his own grief to be of any use." Her eyes glazed over. "Mrs Sharp helped, and Susanna, but most of it fell on me. I sat with her, read to her, brought her meals, made sure she washed. All of it. And when she died I handled all of that, too. Didn't cry. Didn't have time." She bit her lower lip, hard. So hard that when she stopped, it was as red as if she had used rouge. "On the day of the funeral, Ernest was absent, but when it came time to inter her in the family crypt he finally made an appearance. He was drunk. Stinking of it. Staggering off the path. Laughing and crying and everything in between. I intercepted him before he could come too close. If Father had seen the state he was in, making such a public scene, he would have disowned him on the spot. I saved him."

"Why?"

"Because fool that I am, I felt sorry for him." She raised her cigarette to her mouth again at last, an enormous stack of ash falling from the end of it. "Because I love him---*loved* him." She corrected herself seamlessly, but it struck me how she'd used the present tense first. "And do you know how he thanked me for what I did? He took our mother's ring and kept it for himself. It wouldn't even fit on his fingers, but he couldn't abide the thought of me having it."

"That's how the two of you ended up at odds, then?"

"It was the final stroke," she admitted, dropping the spent cigarette into the Thames to join the match. I thought I saw a smear of blood upon the paper before she tossed it. "A lot of it started before then, but I don't think he realised it. When our aunt's dog bit him, I was there, you know? It was hiding behind her armchair, but Ernest didn't understand that it didn't want to play. He carried on bothering it until it snapped. And who was blamed for it, when he went weeping to Mrs Sharp?" She laughed hoarsely. "Me. The younger sister. Because why had I not been more responsible? I'm a girl. I'm bred to be poised and mature and calm. Boys are expected to be rowdy and difficult. I should have watched him more closely." She turned to look at me, and for all she presented herself as a genteel lady, I suddenly saw her for what she really was. A young woman, not much older than I, who'd had the entire weight of her family thrown onto her back like a pack-mule and carried it with dignity anyway. "Why must women be self-sacrificing to be loved?"

I extended my hand to hers, resting on the cold iron railings. The tips of our fingers brushed. Neither of us dared acknowledge it.

"I don't know," I said, thinking of Ma, running herself ragged in pursuit of a man's heart. "I never want to end up like that."

"You already have." Eloise stared down at our hands, then inched her fingers away. "You took on this role to save your brother. I used your love for him against you. I didn't think about that, at the time. Only of myself."

"Might have done you some good to be selfish for once," I allowed. "Seems you spend all the time thinking of your family."

"Someone has to," Eloise said. "Our place in society won't maintain itself."

"You don't like it, though."

Eloise didn't reply. I sensed I'd cut too close to the bone. Perhaps she wasn't even ready to admit it to herself, but I knew what I'd seen in the music hall. For all she was doing to keep it, she seemed to resent her position. She talked so badly of the company she was forced to keep, hated the dinners and recitals. Both of us were pretending to be someone we weren't.

"I have to confess something," she said, after a while. "That night we met, when you asked me how many girls I'd already interviewed."

"Seven," I recalled.

"Yes. And I told you I'd turned them all down?" Eloise swallowed visibly. "I lied. They all refused me."

"So, I was a last resort?"

"No! No. Well, perhaps. I didn't have any other options, but that isn't the only reason I chose you."

"What was?"

Eloise didn't answer, eyes fixed on the dark body of the Thames, and the distant lamps spotted along its bank on the other side. I wondered if our almost-kiss in Park Street had anything to do with it, but I didn't dare ask. Eloise had shown so much of herself to me tonight, opened up like a flower, and I didn't want to see her petals close again. I sighed, hurling my own cigarette over the tails and watching the burning end fade like a falling star. "Don't feel too bad about hirin' me," I said. "I told myself when I accepted that I was only doing it for Caleb, but it wasn't just that, if I'm honest with myself."

She looked at me. "Then why?"

"I wanted to." I smiled wryly. "Deep down, all I've ever really wanted was to be someone. Think it's Ma's fault, puttin' it into my head from a young age. It's why I became an actress. Caleb wanted me to get a job in a match factory, but I wanted to be seen. Good thing, really. I've seen the phossy jaw the match-girls get, it looks like hell. Anyway, all of this has been easier than I expected. I've even liked it, sometimes. If I'm already no one, might as well become a Rothschild."

She didn't know what to say to that. I didn't expect her to.

"May I ask you something personal?" she said, after an agonisingly long time. I nodded. "Why is it that you aren't religious, as your brother is? Did you stop believing in God after your mother died?"

I laughed. "It's nothin' like that. I believe in God, just don't like him very much. Hasn't exactly done me any favours, has he? One of his 'chosen people'. Caleb says there's a philosopher, Spinoza, who said God asked other nations to be his chosen people before the Jews. We were the only ones foolish enough to take him up on it." I shrugged. "For Caleb, it's easy. I think he loves God so much because it's the only thing he's been able to take whenever we go. Me, though? God'll have to offer me somethin' special to get back into my good graces."

"More commonly people think the other way around," Eloise pointed out.

"I'm only common in name," I said, glancing at her. "You sure you don't want to try that fried fish?"

Eloise grinned. "I am getting rather hungry."

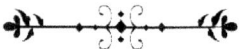

We ate our fish as we walked back up the docks, wheedling out hair-thin bones with our tongues, then waved down a hansom cab on Commercial Road, the driver eyeing us with barely veiled scepticism when we'd asked him to take us to Mayfair. I'd seen Eloise off through the street-door at her house before being dropped on Park Street.

Tabitha had heeded my words about not waiting up for me, a single lamp left burning in the hallway to guide me. I lit a few candles in the drawing room, kicking off my shoes and collapsing onto the divan. I knew I wouldn't be able to retire to bed immediately. My whole body was still trembling with excitement from the music hall, mind alert, turning over my conversation with Eloise as one folds bread dough. My hands fidgeted, fingers curling in towards my palms seeking the memory of a shared touch. There was an unexpected vulnerability in her by the riverside, glimpses of her that had evaded me before. Fear and insecurity, even a thirst for adventure, silently begging to be quenched.

"What on earth are you doing sitting in the dark?"

I shot up off the divan. "Bloody Hell, Caleb!"

He was looming in the open doorway with a single candle, a ghost in his white nightshirt. Though I fancied even ghosts had more shame about flashing their hairy calves at their unsuspecting sisters.

"What do you mean what am I doin' sittin' in the dark?" I muttered, heart still pounding. "What are *you* doing creepin' up on me in the dark?"

"You woke us up," Caleb said. "Even the dead could hear you crashing through the apartment like a bull! Have you been drinking?"

"No!" That was the worst part. I hadn't touched a drop all evening, and couldn't blame my muddled emotional state on anything but Eloise. "Wait. *Us?*" I dearly hoped he meant Tabitha, but even with the candle-flame throwing deep shadow over his features, he looked chagrined.

"No," I said. "Not *him!*"

As though summoned by my dismay, another white-clad figure appeared behind Caleb in the doorway.

"Caleb?" Gideon Cardoza's voice was slurred with sleep, but the instant he saw me he became very stiff, crossing his arms swiftly over his chest. His misplaced modesty might have made me laugh if outrage and anger hadn't so thoroughly supplanted any humour in the situation.

"Do you fuckin' live here now, or what?" I demanded.

Gideon raised his chin. "What do you intend to do, put me out of the house you don't pay for?"

"Listen, you smug son of a –"

"Mirah." Caleb's voice was tight, a violin string wound to its limit. "*Please.*"

I clamped my mouth shut. I was furious, but too tangled up in my own troubles to engage in a shouting match with Mr Cardoza at three in the morning. The way I wanted to yell at him would have woken all of Mayfair.

Gideon yawned. "If all that clamour was just you, I'm returning to bed," he said, and had to absolute raging *audacity* to press a kiss to Caleb's shoulder before he went. I listened to him pad back down the hallway, the bedchamber door creaking shut behind him.

"What the fuck, Caleb?"

"He came over to – discuss Torah," Caleb muttered, addressing his candle rather than me. "He's my *chavrusa*."

"You ain't supposed to bed your study partner."

"Can't you just leave me to my own business?"

"You've never once left me to mine. Why are you doin' this? Can't you find anyone else to – study with? He could ruin us!"

"He won't," Caleb insisted. "I know it's hard to believe, Mirah, but this ain't about your plottin' and schemin'. I'm fond of him. And he's fond of me. It's that easy."

"*Fond?*" My voice pitched upwards. "Fond! You're havin' a lark! You're an imbecile if you're gettin' attached to him."

"I could say the same for you, couldn't I?"

His words brought me up short, like I'd just run head-first into a brick wall. "What?"

"Miss Byron," Caleb said, flatly. "Don't think I don't know what's goin' on with you. I heard more than I said, that night the two of you got into your cups here. I can guess well enough what happened, or almost did."

I stammered. I was determined to spit back something clever and cutting, but my tongue was floppy and useless as a boned fish, and I succeeded only in making an embarrassing sound.

Caleb tipped his head knowingly. "You're actin' out of sorts. It's obvious what you feel for her. You're more a fool than I am, for that. She's so far above us she might as well be in Olympus. You claim you don't want to turn out like Ma, but here you are."

"Stop talkin'," I snapped. "Go back to your bedchamber. Your *chavrusa* is waiting for you."

Caleb shook his head. "Goodnight, Mirah." He turned and swept off down the hallway after Gideon, the light from his candle slowly fading as he went. I sank back down onto the divan in thunderstruck silence, hands shaking in my lap. He was right, God damn him. That was why I so vehemently did not wish to betray Eloise to Ernest, or steal away in the night with all the jewellery and start anew. The realisation was like riding an omnibus that went speeding over a bump in the road; a sickening lurch that pulled my stomach up into my throat before wrenching it back down.

    I didn't want to take any of the smarter, easier options for the simplest, most foolish reason anyone had ever had for anything. A reason that felled empires and started wars. The reason that sent Ma traversing the continent straight into her grave: I was in love.

23

Eloise

The invitations arrived on rose perfumed card, with scalloped edges and our names embossed in gold leaf. While the money was Henry Beauchamp's, it was his wife who put it to good use. Pauline was a renowned hostess, and I had known it would only be a matter of time before Mirah received an invitation to some soiree or masquerade.

The ball was being held by Pauline's dog fancier's club – of which she was the despotic and unchallenged president – to raise funds for The Temporary Home for Lost and Starving Dogs in Battersea.

We had two weeks to prepare for the event, and they were not to be wasted; Mirah did not know how to dance. Well, that was not strictly true. Mirah could dance wonderfully, *had* danced wonderfully that night at the music hall. She exuded natural grace and exuberance, overflowed with it, and I was fortunate enough to catch some of what spilled out. But she did not know how to dance in a ballroom, and that was very different territory. Disciplined, regimented. If she put a foot wrong people would mock her behind her back. If she put more than a foot wrong, they would know she was a stranger to the waltz or two-step. The most generous conclusion people would come to was that the Rothschilds did not care if their daughters could dance, but the least generous might be our undoing. I wished to spare her not only from ruin, but also ridicule.

I had called upon her at her apartment every other day since the invitation arrived, the two of us waltzing languidly around her drawing room as I hummed out a tune. I felt bizarrely as though I was taking turns imposing upon her with my brother, for on the days between my visits she would be out with Ernest. They enjoyed more carriage rides, visited the zoo, and even went ice-skating in Regent's Park, something I personally would not have dared after the disaster in sixty-seven sent forty skaters plunging to their deaths in that very lake. Apparently Mirah harboured no fear in that regard – the depth of the lake had since been reduced, she assured me - and even boasted of her skating prowess. She reported that my brother showed significantly less '*chutzpah*' on the ice, standing frozen and bow-legged as she pulled him slowly along by his scarf.

Part of me wondered if Mirah had taken a dip in the icy waters, for she'd turned abruptly cold on me. I couldn't understand why. We'd parted merrily that night in Limehouse, but since then something had changed. She showed me the sprawling love letters Ernest sent her – sometimes twice daily – and told me everything of their afternoons together, recounting them in the fashion of a detailed inventory: what was said, what they ate, where they walked. But she was not talkative anymore. She did not joke, or even tease. I once told her I found her dry wit exhausting, but now absent from our conversations, I yearned for it.

The dancing was the worst part. Ernest had needed to have a rotten tooth drawn once, and though completely necessary and unavoidable, it had hurt even with the ether. That was how dancing with Mirah felt. The whole time my heart beat erratically, insides coiling and uncoiling, spools of thread in my stomach coming undone and winding themselves into knots. Yet Mirah was stiff. Formal. Marble. I wanted to kiss her like Pygmalion had his statue, feel the blood rush warmly into her lips against my own. I'd have prayed to Aphrodite if I thought it would make any difference. It was torture.

At least when Ernest had his tooth drawn he had had me there to hold his hand. I wouldn't have turned down the ether, either. As we parted from our waltz that afternoon in the drawing room, Mirah didn't even look at me.

"You think I'm ready?" she asked, sitting down in the armchair closest to the fireplace. It grew colder each passing day, the last vestiges of autumn clemency fading with November. Did I think she was ready? I cast my mind to all the young farmhands and goatherds conscripted into armies across the breadth of history, marched off into battle with minimal training and a flimsy pike. Mirah wasn't very likely to be feathered with arrows or knocked down by a cavalry charge, but the ballroom was a battlefield in its own way.

"I don't know," I admitted. "You have made significant improvement."

"Don't try to flatter me, please. I'm sure I'll forget everythin' you've taught me the instant I step into the room."

"You haven't forgotten anything yet," I argued, moving to stand in front of her. The heat of the fire against one side of my body rendered the other markedly colder, and suddenly I craved the warmth, wanted to join Mirah in her plush armchair and curl up like a pair of cats. "If I can sing and smoke in Limehouse for a night, you can dance in a fine ballroom. You are clever, Mirah, and graceful..."

Mirah did not reply, staring into the fireplace as though within the flames she saw visions of Pauline Beauchamp's ball ending in disaster. I outstretched a hand to comfort her, but it did not make it all the way, stopping nervously in the empty space between us until I drew it back, smoothing out the apron of my skirt instead. "Shall I ask Tabitha to fetch us some tea?"

"My stomach won't keep it down," she murmured.

"Very well. Something else, then?"

"I'm fine, Miss Byron."

Miss Byron. I recoiled from my own name as I would a stinging slap to the cheek. I'd not even noticed when she'd slipped from calling me Miss Byron to *Eloise*, but now that she reverted to the former, it was jarring. A shiver ran over the cold side of my body.

"All right," I said, turning away. As I did, I noticed something brown and familiar resting against the foot of the sofa.

"Is that Mr Cardoza's satchel?"

It couldn't be, obviously. That would mean Mirah had entertained Mr Cardoza without my knowledge. In secret. Which she would not do. "Mirah?"

"It ain't as you might think," she said, immediately standing. Now that coldness seized my whole body.

"And what might I think?" I challenged. "What reason could you have for inviting him here and not telling me?"

"I didn't invite him. Trust me, I don't want the bastard here five days a week any more than you do."

"What?" I was positively frantic. "He's here that often? *Why?* Is he blackmailing you?" That was the *best* possibility. The worst was that Mirah intended to betray me. Was that why she had gone so cold? Mr Cardoza was a fine ally to have if one was surveying their legal options, and I could not forget the signed statement I provided her when we'd begun.

"It ain't like that," she said.

"Then what? Mirah, please. You're not planning to –"

"To what? Rat you out? Do you really think that low of me?"

"I don't want to," I said. "But what else am I to think if you won't tell me otherwise?"

"He's not here for me. He's here for my brother."

The silence that followed her words was so dense that the clock ticking on the mantle was suddenly loud enough to make my head ache.

"Your brother?" I echoed. "I don't understand."

Mirah crossed her arms over her chest, her jaw set. "They're... involved."

"You mean –"

"They're *study partners*."

"What –"

"They're lovers, all right? God, I hate even sayin' it! Don't ask me why, I don't understand it."

I stared at her. "When did that happen?"

"That dinner I hosted here."

"But they were at each other's throats!"

"And other body parts, apparently." She shuddered.

"When were you planning to tell me this?"

"Tell *you*? Never."

"Mirah…"

"You ain't usin' it against him." Her tone hardened, and her expression with it. "I know you want to use Cardoza's secret to hush him up, but you ain't using this. And not only 'cause it involves Caleb. I ain't gonna threaten a man with somethin' that doesn't hurt anyone. Especially not this." Her cross-armed posture suddenly looked less cold and stubborn and more as if she was holding herself. "I'm not goin' to make myself a hypocrite like that."

Mirah's words rendered me speechless. I'd begun to think I was imagining it. That my own desires caused me to see something that wasn't there in the looks that passed between us. I knew what it was in myself – the way I shivered under our lingering touches, the short, sharp shock I got when our hands brushed. I'd thought Mirah's willingness the first night we'd met was mere pomp, a woman trying to please a potential patron. Evidently, I was wrong. There was an entire world of differences between Mirah and I, but now I knew a single commonality bound us nonetheless: the shared kinship of loving our own sex. The implications sent me reeling.

"Do you really think I'd blackmail him with *that?*" I asked. That she saw a need to dissuade me dug a strange hurt into my chest. I felt I'd been put on trial for a kind of treason, Mirah both my jury and executioner.

"I don't know," she said, eyeing me warily. "But I do know you'll do whatever you feel you have to. You proved that just by hirin' me."

I couldn't begrudge her for her suspicions. I wanted to, but I'd no right when I was the one who rooted through Mr Cardoza's satchel for damning information. "I wouldn't do that," I said. "Is this why you have been so..." Cold was the only word for it, but I fancied she would not appreciate it. "Distant, since Limehouse?"

"Only as distant as I need to be. This is a business arrangement, remember?"

The words landed like an arrow between the ribs. Nothing of what she'd said was untrue. This *was* a business arrangement. But I had thought there was more to it than that, now. Much more. I fought to mask my devastation. If that was how Mirah felt, then I could not burden her with my foolish heart. It was bad enough that I'd taken advantage of her situation in the first place. To then expect her to spare my feelings, or return them, was outrageous and wholly inappropriate.

"Yes," I said. "It is a business arrangement."

Mirah pursed her lips. "We should return to our dance lessons," she declared, dress train sweeping on the floor behind her as she turned her back on me. "I'm goin' to need a lot of practice."

Since Mirah lacked an appropriate escort, it was decided she would accompany Ernest and me to the Beauchamps' ball in our carriage. It was an ironic twist of fate that made me her chaperone, of sorts. I was the barrier between she and Ernest, the dour, severe sister on the verge of spinsterhood. A high society sentinel, a warrior of moral decorum, duty-bound to walk at Mirah's side and protect her reputation. There was little risk of harm to Ernest's, for men rarely suffered the same consequences as women. There was a reason I was forced to take such extreme measures to implicate him in a scandal, after all. If he had been my sister, I would have had no difficulty – a single too-forward comment or overtly flirtatious look could damn a woman if enough tongues wagged. But no. God cursed me with a brother. Maybe if he'd been a woman he would have been born with more sense, or at least understood me better, and there would be no need for any of this.

It was painfully awkward rattling along towards the Beauchamps' grand Cadogan Place residence with Mirah beside me, our skirts rustling together in the cramped space. We smiled and greeted each other warmly when we met at her front door, but there was a crushing emptiness behind her eyes, a woman made hollow. The sight of her rendered me breathless all the same. The cream satin evening gown I'd had made up for her was beautiful in itself, but I had not yet seen it on her, and wished I'd had prior warning so as to prepare myself. Against the rippling pleats and ruffles of the dress her hair was a brighter, richer gold than ever before. While a crown of it was plaited and coiled on top of her head, most tumbled in tight coils down her back, shimmering in the warm light of the gas-lamps and decorated with wax orange blossom. The flower was popular with brides wanting to take after royalty, and seeing it in Mirah's hair I wondered if she would sport a circlet of it on her fake wedding day. Picturing her as a bride made my heart grow fast, my mind spinning impossible fantasies of marrying her myself, standing at her side as

24

Mirah

When the invitation said the event was being hosted by Pauline's dog fancier's club, I hadn't realised that included the dogs. Stepping into the grand ballroom at the Beauchamp's home, I first thought she had nobly – if unwisely - volunteered to accommodate the entire population of The Temporary Home for Lost and Starving Dogs. The place was overrun, the yapping and squabbling of at least forty small dogs that all appeared to hate each other drowning out the string quartet, who valiantly attempted to play on regardless.

It swiftly became clear that none of these dogs were either lost or starving. All were dressed in increasingly elaborate costumes, smelling faintly of perfumed powder as they ran by, weaving recklessly between men's legs and skidding on the trains of women's dresses. One lady in a spectacular lilac evening gown held a snarling snow-white beast in her arms as one would an infant, feeding the monster hors d'oeuvres from the buffet table as it snapped at her.

"Oh," Ernest said, stiff as marble at my side. The poor man must have believed he was in Hell – that our carriage had careened into the opposite lane of the road and collided with an omnibus, and we were now dead, forced for all eternity to endure Dante's Inferno with dogs.

"I'm sure they'll be contained once the dancing starts," I said. I couldn't be confident of that, but I *was* confident there'd be unimaginable chaos if the animals were left to run amok when everyone took to the floor. People would trip, tails would be squashed beneath silk pumps, and overly precious dog fanatics would be out for blood.

"Mr Byron, Eloise!"

Pauline appeared out of the throng of dresses and dogs as if by magic, sweeping towards us in a gown of rosy pink. She was the only one wearing the colour, and I wondered if there was an unspoken understanding between the dog fanciers that it was hers alone. I pictured her sending a member into exile for daring to show up to the ball in a shade too close to salmon, and had to stifle my amusement.

She embraced Eloise warmly, extending her hand to Ernest for him to kiss.

"How lovely of you both to come," she said, before bestowing me with the same radiant smile. "And Miss de Rothschild. Wonderful to see you again. We were so hoping you'd come."

"I'm delighted to be here," I said. "The food looks lovely."

"Food? Oh, the buffet table is for the dogs!" She waved it off merrily. "Although I did share some of the caviar with Henry."

"The dog or your husband?" I couldn't help asking.

"The dog, of course."

Of course. Eloise hovered close, radiating such nervous energy that I sensed she must have known where my mind was going. The animals at this event were eating better than most families in Limehouse. Better than my brother and I ever had, before this ruse. Better than my mother, too. Caleb had memories of Ma forgoing supper to afford his books when the money started to run out. For all she'd dragged us over the continent, that was something I couldn't fault her for, though Eloise's words about self-sacrificing women rattled around in my head when I thought of it.

Watching the dogs gorging themselves on rich pâté and fine cuts of meat, I felt Ma's hunger as keenly as if it were my own, a curling growl deep in my stomach. Or maybe that was just because I hadn't remembered to eat before coming out. The champagne was going to hit me like a sack of bricks.

I smiled tightly at my hostess. "Well, thank you for the invitation, I wouldn't have missed this for anything."

"A good thing, since you'll never guess who's here!"

"Who?"

"Why, one of your English cousins!"

I stared into Pauline Beauchamp's shining, happy, beaming face, and waited for the punchline.

"That's wonderful," Ernest said, brightly. "I did not realise you knew the English Rothschilds well enough to extend an invitation!"

"Oh, I don't, but it is a charity event, so I suppose they wanted someone in the family to put in an appearance..." Pauline twirled a single long bottle-curl around one finger, trailing off as she looked at me. "Oh my, are you alright? You've come over horribly pale!"

"I'm fine," I choked out. "Only - what a surprise!"

Eloise and I exchanged glances, her wide eyes flashing with a single word: *abort*. We had no agreed protocol for such an encounter, and standing here now I realised how hopelessly naïve that was of us. Why hadn't we planned for this? I began running through every conceivable way to escape the situation. Feigning a sudden illness. Fainting. Upending the buffet table to cause a distraction, and slipping out during the ensuing stampede of tiny dogs. That last one was drastic, but then so were the circumstances.

I didn't have time to deliberate my next move. Pauline was already waving her handkerchief in the air to signal him. It reminded me of a white flag being raised on a battlefield, entirely too fitting for my liking.

"Alfred! Alfred, come over here! Your cousin has arrived!"

As the man turned towards us, Eloise touched her hand to mine, leaning in close to whisper against my ear.

"Alfred Charles de Rothschild," she said, her voice sending a shiver down my spine. "Shares the French particle with you, but very English. Second son, and the director of the Bank of England." I wished she wouldn't brush my hand with hers. It was a dreadful distraction from her words. She dropped it abruptly to instead grab Ernest's sleeve. "Ernest, let's go and greet Mr Beauchamp."

He made to wriggle free like an impatient child. "But I want to meet Mr de Rothschild!"

"Let's leave the cousins to catch up without us, I'm sure there will be time to make an introduction later."

"But –"

"Ernest."

The parting look Eloise threw me was a bewildering mix of encouragement and terror, so perplexing that I doubted even she knew what she was feeling as she led Ernest away towards Henry Beauchamp, who was hiding in a dimly lit corner with a glass of champagne in each hand. My English 'cousin' was briefly waylaid by a dog in a toga attempting to court his leg, and I utilised the distraction to weigh the options again:

Retreat and flee. Instigate a canine stampede.

He stopped a few feet from me, studying me closely. He was neither unattractive nor especially handsome, with thick, dark hair slicked into a neat side-part the same as half the other men in attendance. His eyes were calm and clever, and he sported a well-trimmed beard a few inches shy of the 'intellectual' whiskers Ernest was so intimidated by. And yet, despite being physically unremarkable, the figure he cut was impressive. It was something in his bearing, every bit as lofty and dignified as I'd envisioned a real Rothschild to be, and staring at him like a moonstruck hare I came to the conclusion I'd done a shoddy job of impersonating one. Not to mention there was no resemblance between us whatsoever.

But I was out of time. I had to decide.

"Alfred! How lovely to see you!"

If Alfred Charles de Rothschild meant to challenge my identity when he'd walked over, that intention dissolved as soon as I opened my mouth, suspicion giving way to panicked, poorly concealed confusion.

"Good evening," he said. "Forgive me, I'm not sure I recall your name?"

I met his words with wide-eyed outrage. "You don't? But it's me. Mirah."

"Mirah?"

"I'm Salomon James's daughter! Surely you must recognise me?"

Alfred's cheeks grew very pink. "Salomon? Ah. Yes. He did have a daughter, I recall." I could see his brain working, cogs turning and engines going full steam. "He's dead, is he not? When was that..."

I threw down the only hand I had left to play: I burst into tears.

To say it was some of my best acting would have been a barefaced lie, for they weren't entirely artifice. I was terrified, but it was thankfully rather difficult to tell the difference between sobbing from fear and sobbing from grief.

I'd never seen a man's face change colour so rapidly. As several people in the crowd began craning their necks in our direction, Alfred placed a comforting hand on my shoulder with so much hesitation anyone would have thought he was patting a lioness.

"I am so sorry," he said. "Forgive me, please. I did not mean –"

I shook my head, blowing my nose loudly into the handkerchief he offered. It was embroidered with the Rothschild crest. "Forgive *me*. I did not intend to cause a scene. It is just... still so hard for me to discuss. My poor dear Papa..." I sobbed again.

"Now, now. I understand. I am sorry for my poor manners." He smiled nervously, so embarrassed I thought I might have overdone it, and that he would be joining my supposed father any minute, struck dead by shame. "It is only that we have quite a sprawling family over the continent, and I am very busy. I did not mean to... mis-remember you." Mis-remember was an impressively creative way of saying 'forget'. His gaze dropped to my chest, and I was almost scandalised by how blatantly he ogled my bosom until I realised what drew his attention. "That is a lovely brooch."

"Yes," I said, dabbing my eyes with his handkerchief. "It was a gift from –" I strained to recall the reading Eloise had assigned me. " – my late grandfather."

"It suits you." People kept saying that. Maybe Alfred Charles de Rothschild was already into his cups. "Why was I not informed of your coming to England?"

"My mother is not in society much. She was reluctant to let me go. It took much convincing, and in the end my visit was somewhat spontaneous in nature."

Much convincing and spontaneity were undoubtedly total contradictions of each other, but Alfred nodded sagely, suitably convinced. "Perhaps, Cousin, if your card is not already filled this evening, we might share a dance? I would enjoy an opportunity to make amends for my insensitive behaviour."

"I would enjoy that, too." Over his shoulder I noticed several couples begin taking to the floor for the opening march. "But I have promised dances to several other gentleman, so I must tragically decline. And go. Now. Mr Byron would be bereft if I neglected him."

I was gone before he could speak, all my fears about dancing long forgotten.

Miraculously I managed to avoid Alfred Charles de Rothschild for the next several dances. Even more miraculously, I didn't forget what Eloise taught me, navigating the waltz and two-step as though I'd been born to them. I danced with Leopold Brandt, who was graceful and considerate, and then with Henry Beauchamp, who was not. He stepped on my feet twice during our waltz, distracted by the dogs – which were allowed to continue running unfettered – and bumbled an apology each time. It was a relief when he did; I thought I was the one putting my feet wrong. The dogs, it transpired, had the unexpected benefit of throwing everyone off their rhythm, making any stumble of mine appear the result of kindly concern not to tread on any paws.

Between each set I continued my artful evasion of my dear English 'cousin', weaving through the crowd and never stopping long enough to be set upon in conversation. I passed Helena Hall, wearing yet more cut-glass-diamonds and too busy boasting about having her carriage encrusted with them to notice me. I drank champagne and laughed too loudly at strangers' jokes, and continued moving, moving, always moving. I skilfully succeeded in avoiding Eloise, too. The last thing I wanted was to find myself stuck beside her, forced to sputter out something that passed for idle chitchat. Following my revelation after our night in Limehouse I had made a staunch vow to keep my distance from her. I couldn't succumb to emotion. It would be a disaster for us both. I refused to pine after a rich woman like Ma and her gentleman, especially when we were so close to our goal. If I could suppress these inconvenient desires for a few more months, I would make off like a queen and never have to see Eloise Byron again. I didn't even realise the next waltz was about to begin until Ernest appeared out of the throng, red to the tips of his ears, eyes somewhat haunted and hair tousled. He looked like he'd just come back from war.

"Miss de Rothschild," he said, panting furiously. Had he been chasing after me in the crowd in the hopes of catching me? "Would you – care to – dance?"

"Of course. Are you quite well?"

"Fine! Fine. I simply didn't know where you'd gone to, and last I saw of you, you were with your cousin."

"Is that a problem, Sir?"

"No! No, no... no. Certainly not. No." That was an awful lot of 'no's for what I realised had to be a 'yes'. "I'm positive he's a very affable gentleman. Of course you should wish to spend time with him. You are family, after all."

I remembered what Gideon Cardoza said the night I walked in on him and Caleb – how if I were a real Rothschild I'd have been chaperoned to London, or else to Frankfurt, and told to 'pick a cousin'. That was what made Ernest so frantic, then. He was afraid I was about to declare my intent to become a twofold de Rothschild as Alfred Charles's wife.

"He didn't remember me," I said, simply. Not that that was his fault. It would have been an astonishing feat if he did, considering Mirah de Rothschild didn't exist. "We only met a handful of times when I was a child. Still, it was hurtful."

"Oh, good." Ernest's palpable relief hastily gave way to embarrassment. "I mean – not good. Not at all. Very ungallant of him. You are the most memorable of women, Miss de Rothschild."

"I'm pleased you think so." I hoped for his sake, and my own conscience, that he was merely exaggerating. That when all this ugly business was over and done he'd forget me as soon as another charming young lady entered his line of vision.

"Shall we dance, then?" he asked. His voice trembled. I couldn't tell if it was barely bridled passion for me or fear stemming from being surrounded by so many dogs.

"I'm quite tired from all the dancing I've already done," I said, "Perhaps we should find somewhere quieter to talk, instead?"

Relief flooded Ernest's beet-red face once more, and he sighed, not even attempting to mask it. "Thank God," he said. "The dance floor is..."

"Busy?"

"Very."

And not all the dancers were human.

"We could step out of the house and go across the street to the garden square? The fresh air might restore me." It wasn't only for Ernest's comfort that I suggested it. I was so eager to escape the scrutiny of my 'cousin' that I'd have exited through the nearest window if it was the only way out.

"Alone?" Ernest's eyebrows shot up. "But Eloise is supposed to be accompanying you." I didn't want Eloise accompanying me. I wanted even less the image his words painted in my mind, where it was not Ernest walking beside me in the Cadogan Place garden under a frosty moon, but Eloise, our fingertips touching. I wanted to escape her, and the burdensome feelings she roused within me, just as much as I wanted to escape Alfred and the dogs. I wanted this, all of this, to be over. I wanted to get the job done.

"No one needs to know. And I doubt we'll be the only ones there." There had to be other guests just as desperate to get away. One woman had been furiously sneezing each time I passed her, eyes watering so severely she'd given my tearful performance to Alfred a run for its money.

"But what of your cousin?" Ernest asked.

"I'd rather be with you," I said, gazing up at him from beneath skilfully lowered eyelashes. "Or would you prefer I waltz with Alfred? He did ask."

"No," Ernest said, without hesitation. "No."

We passed an enormous gold-framed mirror as we headed for the doors, and catching sight of us, a handsome pair in all our finery, I could have fooled myself into believing I really was a Rothschild.

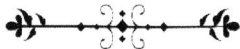

It was freezing cold outside, my breath swirling from my lips as white smoke. It made me long for a cigarette. To my irritation I couldn't even think of those without Eloise making an unwelcome appearance, cupping my hands with her own as I lit the end of her cigarette in Limehouse.

Ernest and I walked side by side up the garden path, gravel crunching beneath our feet. Cadogan Place on a crisp winter's night was not nearly as scenic as I'd envisioned. The trees were bare, the only greenery to be seen that of the grass – frozen solid – and the privet hedges enclosing the garden. The night sky more than made up for Belgravia's deficits, an Impressionist painting daubed with blue and silver cloud. A single clear patch of sky stretched directly above, a window for the moon to peer down nosily upon us.

"I'm aware you must find my fear of dogs somewhat foolish," Ernest said, after we'd been walking in silence for some time. "Or amusing, perhaps."

"Not at all." I'd lied to the man a disgraceful number of times since this act began, but I was not lying now. "If people laugh, it is because they are the foolish ones. Your fear is your body remembering pain. It is completely sensible." Strangely my mind drifted to Ma, and her gentleman, and Eloise, all

25

Eloise

I fought against crying the entire carriage ride home, mourning my victory.

The irony of my grief was not lost on me. I ought to have been popping champagne, toasting my cunning and industriousness. Ernest had proposed. I did not need informing. They disappeared together at the Beauchamp's ball for some time, and upon her return I saw Mother's ring upon Mirah's finger, amethysts sparkling in the lamplight. I'd made a timely exit, abandoning my chaperoning duties.

The most challenging aspect of my plan was complete, and I tantalisingly close to having everything I'd ever wanted. Or thought I'd wanted. I didn't know any more. All I did know was that my heart felt as though it had been crushed into paste in a pestle and mortar. I wasn't popping champagne bottles or toasting anything. Instead, I was battling back tears so furiously that my eyes burned, a thick ribbon of mucus streaming from my nose.

"Are you all right, Miss?" the groom asked as he helped me down from the carriage in Berkeley Square. His voice was gentle, with a subtle Irish lilt. Not as obvious as Mirah's friend Oliver, but nevertheless unmistakable. I realised that somehow I'd never noticed it. Had I ever actually spoken to the man, other than to snap orders? Everything Mirah said about Susanna stirred in my mind once more.

"I will be fine," I said. "Thank you for being so kind as to ask. I'm sorry, what is your name?"

"Noah, Miss."

"Noah. That's nice." And fitting. If I'd let myself weep I would have flooded all of London with my tears – perhaps Noah could live up to his namesake and hastily construct an ark. "You'll have to go back to Cadogan Place, Noah. My brother will wonder where the carriage is."

"Yes, Miss."

Mrs Sharp greeted me when I got in, taking my cloak and hat and fretting over me like a mother hen. I made an excuse for the state I was in – claiming to have sprained my ankle at the ball – and listening to her go on scolding Ernest in absentia for not having the consideration to see me home himself, I found myself thinking that Mother would have approved of the care she took of me. Of us both.

I declined her attempts to nurse my ankle, which she wanted to slather in olive oil and garlic like a lamb shank, and 'limped' off towards the kitchen by myself. I needed hot chocolate, and I was going to make my own. I was fed up to the high heavens of needing to be served. My time with Mirah had made it feel utterly perverse.

I managed to locate a dented copper pot, placed it on the stove, and began searching the pantry for the chocolate. The heavy, gritty block was wrapped in brown paper, sandwiched between the flour and a tin of biscuits. I carried the entire thing out to the table to examine it. Presumably I would have to hack or shave a piece of it off to put in the pot. Where *were* the knives? I would have to light the range, too. How did one do that? There had to be matches. Was there enough coal? Where did we even *keep* the coal?

I sank down onto a chair at the kitchen table, overwhelmed by all the different steps. The urge to cry rose up within me again, fiercer than before. I slapped myself hard across the cheek to halt it in its tracks, the sharp, hot sting shocking my senses straight.

I could not weep for getting what I wanted. I would not. There was no room for weakness, not even an inch. There never had been. The door creaked on its hinges.

"Miss?"

I slapped myself again when the sound of Susanna's voice caused my eyes to burn afresh.

"Miss, what happened?"

Her hand came to rest in the space between my shoulder-blades, devastatingly tender even after all the hurt I caused her. I twisted my neck to look at her, wiping mucus all over my palms like a slug as I went. She was gazing down at me, a gentle crease worrying at her forehead.

"I wanted to make hot chocolate for myself," I said, sounding as though someone had packed my nose with cotton. "I don't know how."

"Is that all?" Her tone was knowing.

"Of course."

"Did something happen at the ball?"

"It worked. Our plan. Ernest proposed. He is to marry Miss Zelikovich and be ruined."

"Then why are you weeping?"

"I'm not."

"You look as though you ought to be."

"Because..." The words caught in my throat, shards of broken glass. I scrunched my eyes shut and buried my face in my hands. *Do not cry. Do not...*

"Miss..."

"I cannot possibly say! You would think me hideously unnatural!"

"I wouldn't."

"Yes, you would."

"Miss, I've always known you – weren't the marrying sort."

My head shot up so fast I nearly dashed my skull against her chin. "What?"

"I'm sorry," Susanna said, stepping back. "I did not mean to offend."

"No. No, you didn't, I just..." I shook my head, mystified. "You *knew?* How long?"

"Years."

"*How?*"

Susanna shrugged. "Small things. Do you remember when we were girls and we played that game, dripping wax into a bowl of cold water? And whatever shape the wax took would be the first initial of your future husband?"

I nodded. It was years ago, but I recalled it vividly. I still had a small patch of shiny white skin on the inside of my right pointer finger from burning it with my candle.

"Well, you must remember how excited I was, when I did mine," Susanna said. "But you went on getting shapeless blobs that did not resemble any letter. I remember thinking I'd have to comfort you, but you looked utterly relieved. I'd never seen anyone so delighted at the prospect of spinsterhood."

"I remember that," I said, chagrined. "What letter was yours, again? I'm afraid I don't recall..."

"The letter 'N'."

"Our groom's name is Noah. Perhaps you will marry him."

"I already have a fiancé, Miss."

"You do?"

"Norbert."

"Norbert?" I exclaimed. "You're marrying a man named *Norbert?*"

Susanna snorted with laughter. I followed, the two of us cackling the way we had when we were girls. I'd missed it.

26

Mirah

Standing in the Byron's cold vestibule waiting to be received, I buried my hands into the silk-lined ermine of my muff and wished I could bury the rest of myself in it too. It was the first week of December, and winter had all of London in her clutches, turning the trees white with frost and the cobbled streets dangerously slippery. Four days had passed since the proposal, and since then I'd begged off indisposed when Eloise and Ernest tried to call on me, not wanting to face either of them. A nasty cough, I said. Something I must have picked up at the ball. Ernest sent me a basket of sweet buns and spicecakes, along with a whole apothecary's worth of tinctures and tonics designed to restore me to immediate health, including Browne's Chlorodyne, which made bold claims of curing everything from coughs and croup to hysteria and diphtheria. It smelled as if it'd knock me flat on my arse, but perhaps that was the desired effect. You couldn't cough if you were unconscious.

I'd played my hand for as long as I could, but now there was no more getting around it. If I'd gone on feigning illness any longer I was positive Ernest would send a whole troop of doctors, and there'd be no fooling the professionals. I'd been forced to make a dramatic recovery.

An invitation to an informal five o'clock tea at the Byron's home followed my happy news, and knowing I couldn't avoid them forever, I donned my warmest wool dress and went. In truth I'd wanted to get out the apartment anyway. We were five nights into Chanukah, and for once Caleb was not hounding me into participating in the usual rituals. Instead Gideon bloody Cardoza joined him to kindle the lights each night, doing so with a sort of awe. His family were apparently too genteel, too *British*, to bother observing the minor festivals, and he was fascinated by it all. It was as if I'd been replaced, my brother finding someone else to be Jewish with. Someone who enjoyed listening to him sing *Ma'oz Tzur*. It was bizarre. I'd never taken any real interest in our faith, but now that I was pushed out of it, I yearned to be included.

It didn't help that the Byrons were hard at work decorating their home for Christmas. Even in the vestibule long reams of ivy snaked up the bannisters of the stairs, decorated with sprigs of holly, their berries blood red against the green.

"Miss de Rothschild!"

Ernest appeared at the top of the stairs, dressed in strikingly bright blue plaid trousers with a matching waistcoat. He hurried down to greet me, clasping both my hands in his to kiss them. His moustache was waxed to the point of immovability, the tips so sharp I fancied they'd prick my fingers if I touched them.

"I thought you were to call me 'Mirah' from now?" I asked.

"I am saving that honour for our wedding day. Come, we're all set for the tea. I must warn you, my sister has suffered some manner of nervous breakdown."

"What do you mean?"

"She has taken up *baking!* I do not know what possessed her. She's prepared much of the refreshment herself, as though we do not have kitchen staff for precisely that!" He shook his head despairingly. "If it is disgusting, please, spit it into your serviette discreetly to spare her feelings. I fear she may need to be sent away to the Mediterranean to recover herself."

Eloise, baking? That was nigh on impossible to picture, the only image my mind provided me being her rushing through the kitchen fanning smoke from the range, multiple pots and pans bubbling over disastrously.

"I won't say a thing."

It was a taxing promise to keep. When we entered the drawing room, where the tea was scattered about on multiple small occasional tables, it became clear Eloise had spent the last week as rough as I'd claimed to be. There were shadows beneath her eyes, big purple blotches like ink stains someone had attempted in vain to scrub out, and one knee bounced restlessly beneath her skirts as she perched on the edge of the divan. She rose when she saw me, her smile brittle as the pretty china tea set.

"Miss de Rothschild. You are looking well in yourself."

"Thank you," I said, eyeing the spread. There was a sugar pot and cream jug, a teapot nestled beneath a quilted cosy to stay warm, and on every other table bar the one holding the tea set, plate after plate of the same ugly fruit cake. They all smelled strongly of brandy – not so much infused as drowned in it – and came in varying degrees of burnt, from 'lightly browned' through to 'is that coal?'. Ernest might not have been far wrong when he suggested Eloise had suffered a nervous break-down.

The three of us carried on in silence for a while, sipping our tea. I braved a tentative bite of one of the cakes, forcing myself to swallow it even when it proved inedible, a stodgy alcoholic brick sliding down my throat. The tension in the room was suffocating, but Ernest was somehow oblivious to it, rambling off his wedding opinions. It was to take place soon – Ernest wanted it to be a splendid affair several months in the making, but I'd succeeded in whittling the wait down to just four weeks, citing a desire to be his wife sooner rather than later. I wanted it over with.

"At some point you will need to meet Father," he said, tacking the incredibly important matter onto the end of a discussion about floral arrangements as if that were a normal thing to do.

"Let's not hurry that part," Eloise said. "Father is so unwell."

"All the more reason to introduce them," Ernest argued. "He will want to know his future daughter-in-law."

"It's a lot of excitement, Ernest. Think of his health."

I knew the real reason Eloise was so reluctant to introduce me to Ambrose. It served us best if he never knew me. The surprise marriage of his only son would scandalise him to begin with, so when it was revealed I wasn't a Rothschild he'd already be primed to react badly. Not to mention his pride; if he met me and was fooled, he'd be embarrassed, too. If he never saw me he could claim it was obvious, and that Ernest should have known better from the start.

"Oh, very well," Ernest said. "Not yet. But soon. Oh!" He turned to me. "I read the Jewish Chronicle yesterday, and I saw that you are having a festival! *Chan*ukah, yes?"

He pronounced it wrong – emphasising the 'ch' as only a Christian Englishman would, rather than the soft Hebrew '*ch*' I was so familiar with. "You read the Jewish Chronicle?"

"I do now," Ernest said. I noticed his teacup was fitted with an odd little porcelain ledge for the protection of his moustache.

"Oh. Well, yes. Chanukah. It celebrates the rededication of the Temple." I thought of Caleb again, kindling the chanukiah, illuminating our apartment with gentle light. I remembered him doing it the year before in our leaky tenement building, remembered holding my hands to the flames to warm my frozen fingers as I listened to him sing. He'd inherited Ma's voice too, lulling me to sleep countless nights as a child when she'd been out chasing down our pa. Last Chanukah he saved for months to buy a roast goose for dinner on the final night, and the smell of it, sizzling with the oil of the latkes, kept me feeling full for days, long after we'd picked the bones clean.

"So, when will your mother arrive?"

Ernest's question brought me back into the present with an alarming jolt. "What?"

"Your mother." He tilted his head. "Surely she is coming to England for the wedding?"

"Oh. Uh..."

"And your English cousins. They'll be present too, I assume?"

My heart began racing. "I don't know. They're all very busy, and it is only to be a small affair, remember?"

"Not so small as to exclude your family!" Ernest laughed, reaching to take my hand. "Especially not your dear mother!"

I glanced at Eloise. She stared back, infuriatingly mute. I wanted her to speak, to slip in some clever comment that would convince me things would turn out fine. On some level I'd thought it would all be easier once I accepted Ernest's proposal. I'd given barely any thought to what came after it. But here, now, discussing the finer details of a fraudulent wedding, it became too much. Far, far too much, a crushing weight pressing me flat. My corset suddenly felt as though it had been laced too tightly. I had to get out. I had to breathe fresh air that did not smell of tea and brandy and *Acker's Patented Moustache*

Colourant and Wax.

"Excuse me," I said, standing. "I think I am still a touch tired from my sickness."

"Oh dear. Would you like some Browne's Chlorodyne?"

"Definitely not. If you wouldn't mind, I think I should return home. We can speak more of the wedding plans tomorrow, once I've rested."

"Of course. Take our carriage, please, rather than sending for a cab."

"I'll escort you," Eloise offered, rising from her seat.

I shook my head. "There's no need."

"You're ill. There is every need."

The last thing I desired was to be confined in a small space alone with Eloise with my heart already dancing out such a fast rhythm, but she took my arm and led me from the drawing room before I could offer any further protest. Ernest ran ahead for the carriage, having the groom bring it around to the front of the house and opening the door for us.

"Go fast," I urged the driver as I climbed up into it.

"No," Eloise said. "Go slowly. The roads are icy." I could have cursed her for her caution.

The door slammed shut behind us, the carriage gave a slight lurch, and we set off at a snail's pace.

"What's wrong?" Eloise asked.

"What's *wrong?* I'm gettin' married to your brother in four weeks, and he's expectin' a whole host of Rothschilds to attend!"

"He can be persuaded otherwise," she said. "Everything will be fine..."

"No, it won't! And who do you think you are, askin' me what's wrong? What's wrong with *you?*"

"I don't know what you're referring to."

"Don't play coy! What's with all the fruitcake? Bakin', Eloise? Really?

Since when did you do 'servant's work'?"

Eloise became redder still, so red that I thought she would explode. "I just wanted to try it. Am I not allowed to take up new hobbies?"

"It's bloody absurd!"

"I need to have control over something, all right?"

Fraught silence followed her admission, broken only by the rumbling of the wheels on the cobbles, the clopping of the horse's hooves. I'd never realised there were types of silence you could *feel,* tangible, smothering. A storm inside a carriage. There were no rain clouds gathering over Berkeley Square, but lightning was about to strike all the same. We stared at each other, a pair of caged tigers.

"Fuck it," I said. "Kiss me, before we both regret this."

Eloise lunged at me from across the carriage. Our mouths met, hard and hungry, and we melted back onto the seat as one, a single fervid entity made up of desperate lips and frantic hands, searching for bare skin wherever they could find it beneath all our layers. Fingers twisted in long bottle curls, teeth knocked against teeth. We broke apart only when we both needed oxygen, Eloise sinking down onto her knees on the floor of the carriage. I spread my legs instinctively for her, gathering my skirts and petticoats up to my waist. Her breath was hot against my legs even through my silk stockings, her hands tracing the seams of my split-drawers, open to receive her.

"Please," I whispered. Her mouth found me, and I was lost.

If Eloise had never done this with a woman before, she had definitely thought about it, at length, often. Her tongue coaxed sounds out of me that I didn't even know I could make, though I muffled all of them in the fur of my ermine muff, the lamp inside the cab swinging back and forth as the carriage moved. I gasped suddenly: there was that lightning I'd predicted, using me as a conductive rod. I seized a fistful of her hair with my free hand, making an anchor of her as I arched up off the seat, hips bucking greedily against her mouth with a whimper that hitched into a cry. My eyes closed, my head tipped back, and God and all the cosmos flashed behind my eyes.

I collapsed back down in a great flump of ruffles and silk as the sensation passed through me, legs shaking uncontrollably in its wake. Eloise rocked back on her heels, resting her cheek on my trembling knee, the bow of my ribbon garter tickling her face. Her skin was hot against mine, her lips parted and red as she gazed up at me, a wild, dark-eyed thing all starving with desire. I'd never wanted anyone more in all my life. I wanted to take the lightning that had struck my soul and run it through hers, too.

"Come here," I begged, reaching down to cup her cheek; she leaned into it like a cat, before climbing up to straddle me on the bench, fighting to raise her own skirts as the carriage jostled her from side to side. I helped, ruching up the fabric so that I could slip my hand between her legs. She was warm there, too, a burning brand on my fingertips, slick and welcoming.

I was almost afraid to touch her, fearful of somehow shattering the moment, so fragile and delicate, at risk of breaking into shards around us, sharp enough to carve my heart clean out of my chest. Eloise dispelled my nerves, reaching down to steady my hand with her own, guiding it to her as she sank down onto my fingers with ease, her breath stuttering, her mouth falling open in silent, blissful fullness. I watched her face as she began to move, shifting her hips slowly and bracing herself against my shoulders. Entranced, I curled my fingers inside her, craning my neck to catch her lips with my own. The taste of myself lingered on her tongue, salt and passion, and beneath that the searing sting of the alcohol from all that awful fruitcake.

We rocked together in time with the carriage, stifling our sounds into each other's mouths, my body aching to be closer to hers, to know the softness of her skin, feel her heartbeat flush with mine. Our embrace did not last more than a handful of clumsy minutes, fleeting, as if we were two rare butterflies destined to die inside a day. Eloise came unspooled with a shudder, a mewl, and then it was over, her head dropping forward heavily to rest against mine.

The two of us stayed that way for a few perfect seconds, our breath mingling into the same cadence, the carriage continuing to rattle along the cobbles. She broke away first, scrambling awkwardly from my lap and slumping onto the seat opposite, her chest heaving, a single stand of ebony hair falling over her face. Our eyes met, overflowing with unspoken words. The carriage stopped abruptly, nearly throwing me across the cab into Eloise's arms. I barely recovered before the door swung open, cold winter air rushing over me and bringing my arms up in gooseflesh. The groom stared at us, so slack-jawed I wondered if he'd heard us coupling like a pair of stray cats.

"Were we... driving too fast?" he asked.

I caught a glimpse of my reflection in the carriage window, hair askew and dress rumpled, and laughed. So much for keeping my distance.

27

Eloise

I blinked awake, squinting against the winter sun shining brightly on the wall opposite and wondering what roused me. I was still delightfully floppy all over, each limb so heavy that I could have sunk through the eiderdown of my mattress to the floor. I couldn't recall the last time I'd slept so deeply, though it took me an age to settle, my stomach vibrating like a wasps' nest. It was still doing it now.

I'd seen Mirah off at Park Street, the two of us parting in quiet politeness despite what happened between us in the carriage. On the way home I'd had to ask the driver to stop twice, leaning as far out of the tiny window as I could, certain I would be ill. Nothing came up, but my insides hadn't stopped threatening to become my outsides for the duration of the journey.

I'd retired to bed immediately upon returning to Berkeley Square, citing that I must have caught the same chill as Mirah. I suspected Susanna knew the truth, or at least guessed at it. She'd offered to bring me up broth and bread on a tray, but tactfully did not push when I declined. Ernest hadn't demonstrated even half the concern he showed his fiancée. That word caused me to wince even now. I kissed my brother's fiancée. Worse, I'd made passionate love to her in a moving carriage. The thrill and dread of it made my heart soar and plummet over and over in endless succession, a bird upon a warm current of air. She felt the same irrefutable pull I did – she had to, else she wouldn't have told me to kiss her. I'd made her mine, tasted the sweetness of her on my tongue. But she was still Ernest's fiancée, even if it was built upon a lie. We plotted together to ruin him, and none of *this* had any place in our plans. Had any place anywhere. There was nowhere in the world where something like that, between women like us, could ever be.

There was a crash from downstairs. The thud of hurried footsteps in the hallway outside.

"Miss!" Susanna called, from the other side of my bedchamber door. She sounded panicked. "Miss, you're needed downstairs urgently!"

I swung my legs off the mattress and stood, pulling on my ruffled dressing gown mid-run and rushing to open the door. Susanna's appearance matched her tone, eyes wide with alarm.

"What's happened?" I asked.

"Your brother, Miss. He's very upset."

I went cold from the tips of my toes to the crown of my head. "Upset. About what?"

He couldn't have found out, could he? Had Noah told him of me and Mirah, so dishevelled in the carriage?

"He received a letter this morning," Susanna said. "From Miss de Rothschild."

"Oh no."

I shot off down the hallway, taking the stairs two at a time and very near tripping on the hem of my nightgown. I'd never run like this before, my open silk robe billowing behind me like a sail, with no clue as to what kind of storm I was heading into. The floor was ice cold on my bare feet, making me think suddenly of the boating lake in Regent's Park where Mirah and Ernest went ice-skating. I wished it would give way beneath me and plunge me into watery darkness.

I found my brother in the drawing room in the most pitiful state imaginable. He was lying flat on his face in the middle of the floor, sobbing. The source of the crash was littered on the carpet around him – a shattered vase and an upturned table. I had no idea what he knew. If he would be angry with me. After what I'd done he could come at me with a shard of broken porcelain, and I would not even begrudge him his rage.

"Ernest?"

He flopped over onto his side like a dying fish.

"Eloise." His face was plum red. "Good morning." Evidently not.

"Susanna told me you received a letter from Miss de Rothschild."

"Yes." He lifted a hand to point to the open envelope resting on Mother's piano. "She has called off the wedding."

"*What?*"

"Her mother wrote to her and refused to allow the match. She said she cannot possibly accept her daughter marrying a Christian. She even included her mother's letter!" He began blubbering again, planting his face on the carpet once more. At this rate poor Sophie would have to scrub Acker's out of the rug.

I stepped carefully over my brother to the piano, inspecting first Mirah's letter, written in her own hand, and then the letter included with it, penned in French. It was not, in fact, a letter declaring a vicious objection to her marriage, but instead a rough draft of a menu. Not that it made any difference to Ernest, who could not read a word of French beyond that on a wine label.

"I do not know what to do," he said, muffled by the Persian rug. "My heart is breaking, Eloise, like a clay pigeon being shattered into a thousand pieces!"

I could not bring myself to tell him the French letter listed a delightful selection of desserts that might improve his mood. There was no ignoring the bone-deep gnawing of my conscience any longer. The buzzing nervousness I had fallen asleep to and awoken with was replaced by shame, thick as cold porridge in my stomach. This was all my fault. I'd set the plan into motion, feeding coal to the engine of a speeding train I'd made no attempt to stop, even when I saw it careening off the tracks. He was like a little boy again, crying at the bottom of the stairs after skinning his knee. What had I done? I'd never expected him to feel this strongly. I'd thought he would desire her, chase her, wed her on a foolish whim – not this. This was more than he deserved, cruelty that I scarcely recognised myself the architect of. But I was.

I knelt down beside him, resting one hand on his head. His hair was so much like mine, the same colour, the same texture, silken between my fingers. "I'm sorry," I whispered. I wish he knew precisely all that I was apologising for. I was too cowardly to enlighten him.

"I want to talk to her," he mumbled, addressing the pattern on the carpet as much as me. "Will you come with me? She is your friend. She will listen to you."

I doubted that, but I knew what I had to do.

There was no answer at her door when we arrived at Park Street, but that did not prevent Ernest from making a scene. He continued hammering on it, calling up to her windows, his moustache bent in two completely different directions from its intimate encounter with the drawing room rug.

"Miss de Rothschild, please! I must speak with you!"

One of the windows squeaked open, and a figure appeared above us, leaning over the railing of the balconette to peer down. I recognised the unruly curls of her brother instantly.

"Miss de Rothschild is indisposed," Caleb yelled. "She doesn't want to see you, sir!"

"But I have so much I need to say!" Ernest protested. "Miss de Rothschild, I know you're in there! Charlotte Leonora Hannah Constance – uh –"

"Mayer," Caleb put in, most unhelpfully.

"Whatever! Mirah – speak to me!"

"She asks that you go away," Caleb said, flatly. "And refer to her letter as to why."

"I understand about her mother, truly! But I will do anything to make things work, I – I'll convert!"

"Ernest!" I hissed. "Don't be ridiculous!"

"I'm not! I mean it! Do you hear me up there, Mirah? I'll convert! Yes, it will… take some time, adjusting to life without my member, but…"

"Is *that* what you think circumcision is?!" Mirah shrieked, dragging her brother back by the scruff of the neck so she could lean out of the window instead. Apparently she was listening after all. "You are a *fool*, Ernest Byron! Go away! Go home!"

"Is that not what –?"

"No! How do you think we make children?!"

"Ah."

"Ernest," I gripped his arm tightly, "perhaps I should go in and speak with her, instead?"

"Oh. Yes. If you think that would be wiser."

"I do." I glanced up at Mirah, our eyes locking before she retreated inside. Briefly I thought she was to refuse me too, but then the front door opened, Caleb watching Ernest intently as he motioned for me to enter.

"Your brother must wait out here," he said.

Mirah was pacing the drawing room, a frenzy of colourful silk that swept the polished parquet floor with each agitated turn. Her hair was loose, a glorious mane in the sun. I wanted to run my hands through it. She stopped in her tracks when she noticed me in the doorway.

"What are you doin' here?"

"I wanted to talk to you. Ernest is very distressed."

"And whose fault is that?" Mirah said, lifting her chin. "I'm not the one who started all of this!"

"I know. It's my fault and mine alone. I wish I could take everything back."

"But you can't." She crossed her arms over her chest. "You have to send him away. Caleb wanted to tell him I was dead."

"Probably for the best you didn't let him."

"I can't go through with this anymore, Eloise. Not after..." She trailed off, wetting her dry lips with her tongue. *After.* The mere memory sent my stomach rolling like the wheels of the carriage. Had it only been yesterday? The sounds she'd made, and tried not to make, were etched into my bones. I felt as if I'd been in love with her for forever.

"I'm sorry," she muttered. "I know bowing out of this means givin' up the apartment, the dresses, everythin'. It's fine. It's what I'd prefer. I'll go back to Limehouse and find a way to get by."

"No," I said, closing the distance between us. I wanted to touch her, lay my hands on her arms. I was scared she would pull away. I would never recover if she did.

She stepped back. "I won't do it anymore, you hear me? He's a fool, but that's all, and I don't want to break his heart."

"I'm not asking you to."

"Then what —"

"Marry him." I had to push the words out of myself, labouring with them like a squalling, horrible, exceedingly ugly babe. "Marry him for true."

Mirah rocked back, shock and confusion mingled in her expression. "What do you mean?"

"I mean *marry him*. If you believe you could find comfort with him, even a little, then become his wife, and we will not reveal you."

She laughed. "And how do you expect me to keep up this Rothschild act for the rest of my days?"

"You and he can go away somewhere. To America, or Canada. The Rothschilds are not as established there, there will be fewer questions. Take your brother, too. You can say you have no contact with your family because they have disowned you for marrying him. You'll be secure, wealthy, happy..." I drew in a deep breath. "Both of you."

I did not want this, to see her go away with Ernest, be his bride, live a life without me. But it was all I could do. We could not be together, and at least this way I might atone for the hurt I'd caused my brother with my scheming. Marriages were rarely made for love anyway, and Mirah could find contentment of a sort with Ernest. He adored her, and under his protection she would always be comfortable and provided for, if he had truly changed enough not to squander his inheritance. Even if he hadn't, Mirah was shrewd, and would keep all her jewels and dresses to insure against his idiocy. She could live as a Rothschild in a foreign land, Ernest blissful with his wife, never knowing the level his sister lowered herself to in the name of envy. And I... well. I would inherit whatever Father set aside for me, and live alone and poor in London. I pinched my arm furiously to stop myself bursting into tears.

It was what I deserved. Perhaps I could live off fruitcake.

"Happy," Mirah echoed. She turned away, staring out of the window at the bright winter sky, the light tracing her profile, illuminating her noble still holding my pose even now, seated on the sofa in the Byron's home in a lilac satin gown, the brooch Ernest gifted me pinned shining to my breast. I reasoned I'd best get used to it, since I'd be holding the pose for the rest of my life if I went through with marrying him and crossing the Atlantic.

I didn't have to do it - it was hardly transportation for life. I still had all the other options I'd considered at my disposal. Telling him the truth. Running away into the night with my dresses and jewels. But there was sense to Eloise's words, however much I hated them. In America I could be someone more than a Limehouse actress admired for her good legs. It was a fresh start, and the notion upping and leaving to a new country was so familiar to me that it bordered on comforting.

The engagement reception was split by the sexes, an observation which amused me. It reminded me of the Great Synagogue at Duke's Place, where on the rare occasion Caleb wheedled me into accompanying him I would be exiled to the gallery to watch from above. All the women crowded into Eloise's private parlour with me to partake in tea and cake, while Ernest entertained the gentlemen in the drawing room with brandy and cigars. Judging from the booming laughter occasionally echoing up the hall, they were having much more fun than we were. Probably because they all actually knew Ernest, friends from his various clubs. I was a stranger, and yet the centre of attention, orbited by prune-faced old aunts and distant cousins of my soon-to-be husband, who fluttered with excitement at the prospect of having a Rothschild in the family. More than once I was asked (with no lack of disappointment) why my cousins were not in attendance, having to repeat over and over that marrying 'out' was frowned upon, but that I was positive they'd come to accept the match once they saw what a shining example of manhood Ernest was. I was a mechanical toy, wound up to repeat the same action over and over.

The only women I did know, save Susanna and Tabitha – who'd begged to be brought along – were Mrs Beauchamp and Helena Hall. And

Cleopatra the dog, I supposed, since she'd come with Pauline, accompanied by two others I hadn't met. I recognised one as the dog in the toga who'd made passionate advances on Alfred de Rothschild's leg at the ball. Hadrian, Pauline introduced him as.

The whole reception was prepared so beautifully that I could only assume Eloise, for all she'd opted not to be present, had some part in its arrangement. Even when she'd removed herself from the picture she was aiding me in playing my role. The fire was roaring, warming the whole room, and a prettily decorated table was placed in front of it, boasting a vase of pansies. Scattered around this centrepiece was a ring of delicate china plates of finger sandwiches, crystallized fruits and assorted nuts, along with an elegant, painted Russian samovar out of which the boiling water for the tea was being dispensed with a deft hand by Susanna.

"I cannot wait for the wedding," Helena said. She'd joined me on the sofa, Pauline at my other side, Cleopatra straining in her arms to climb into my lap. "You will be such a beautiful bride. You could borrow my diamond necklace if you'd like." She lifted her chin in an unsubtle effort to display said necklace, a sparkling constellation of stars adorning her neck. Glass stars, I remembered, biting back a laugh.

"I thank you for the generous offer, but I have my own jewels to wear. They have more sentimental value." More *actual* value too, though the remark about sentiment wasn't a lie. Eloise had bought them for me. If I was to never see her again, at least I would have some tangible memory of her to carry forever, a piece of her to wear no matter where I went or who I pretended to be.

Helena's smile was pinched. "Oh. Naturally." She brought her teacup to her lips.

"Are you going to have to convert to marry Ernest?" Pauline asked.

"No, we are having a civil marriage. He would never ask such a thing of me. Although he did offer to convert to my faith instead."

Helena inhaled some of her tea, spluttering loudly.

"Oh dear, is the tea too hot?" I asked, feigning ignorance as I offered her my handkerchief.

"I'm fine," Helena muttered, using it to dab her mouth.

"That is sweet of him, though bold." Pauline tilted her head dreamily. "I do so adore a real love match, being part of one myself."

I felt my eyebrows come together in a frown, but mercifully did not have a chance to say anything. Pauline suddenly covered her mouth with one hand, the colour leaching from her cheeks.

"Oh," she said. "Please excuse me." She set Cleopatra down and rose to leave the room. I seized the opportunity to do so myself, snatching my handkerchief out of Helena Hall's claws to follow Pauline into the hallway. She made it to a vase by the staircase before her stomach emptied itself of all the tea and impossibly tiny oval-cut sandwiches she'd eaten.

"Fuck," I said, before catching myself. "I mean – oh dear. Do you wish me to send for a doctor?"

Pauline shook her head, straightening herself up and taking my handkerchief with a word of thanks. "Do not trouble yourself," she said. "I am perfectly well. My stomach is merely delicate at present, on account of expecting."

"You're having a baby?" I dearly hoped so, because the alternative was that she was experiencing physical symptoms in sympathy with one of her dogs. Pauline nodded.

"*How?*" I wanted to clap my hand over my mouth and force the word back down my throat the second said it. Pauline blinked at me, and then, to my utter surprise, laughed.

"Oh, your face! You are so alarmed! Do not fear, I'm more than aware of my husband's proclivities."

I was dumbstruck. There was no other word for it.

"You know? But you're *married*. You said it was a love match!"

"It is, in a way. I do love Henry. I've known him since he was a boy." Pauline carefully folded my handkerchief into a small square. "We've been friends all our lives. When we grew up, we agreed to be married. He needed a wife to divert suspicion from his preferences, and I decided I would enjoy being a wife without the chore of marital duties. Married, I can go wherever I like unchaperoned, and Henry is happy to let me spend his fortune as I see fit." She shrugged, handing the handkerchief back to me with an easy smile. "It benefits us both. And I do adore Leopold, he is so witty and fun. Far more cultured conversation than my husband, and he doesn't step on my toes when we dance. The three of us get along swimmingly."

Her burst of candour was so unexpected and shocking I thought I'd have to collect my jaw off the floor. Pauline giggled. "Don't be so shocked. Everyone in society plays parts not their own. Even you." She arched one eyebrow. "Your secret is safe with me, Miss de Rothschild. It really doesn't concern me who you are."

"Thank you?"

"You're welcome. I hope there's no ill blood between us, regarding that little test with Alfred at the ball. I couldn't help myself, I was so curious, but I did not intend to cause you distress."

"No. No ill blood."

"Good. Now, shall we return to your engagement reception? It is a lovely event, you must thank Eloise for putting it on. She has such a talent for these things."

I nodded, still reeling. "If you know how Henry is, then how..." I pointed wordlessly to her stomach. Pauline laughed again.

"I would never ask him to perform in a way that is so incompatible with his nature," she assured me, gliding back up the hall. "The child is my lover's."

I good as leapt out of my own skin, spinning on one foot like a ballerina to see Gideon Cardoza leaning against the wall of the house.

"For fuck's sake," I hissed. "How's it you show up bloody everywhere?"

"Good luck on your part, perhaps," Gideon supplied. "Well?"

I'd a mind to refuse, but he looked as fed up as I was with all of this, and if I gave the other cigarette away maybe I'd cease thinking of Eloise. I handed him the packet and matches. He lit up, tipping his head back against the cold stone as he exhaled.

"Thank you. You've escaped too, then?"

"For now," I said. "I expect they'll miss me sooner than you."

"I expect the same. I pity you for that."

"What are the men talkin' about?"

"I lost track a few subjects ago. Something about a racehorse, I believe. It really is the dullest room I've ever been in, and I practice law."

I fought back the smirk that threatened my face. "Unfortunate."

"It is," Gideon said. "We may have our differences, but we at least know the gulf between us is less than between us and half the ridiculous snobs in there."

I made a vague sound of assent. I didn't wish to commit too fully to agreeing with Gideon Cardoza. "Why are you among this lot, anyway?" I asked. "People don't ordinarily adopt their solicitor into their circle of friends. From a genteel background like yours I'd have thought you'd be part of some suffocatingly insular Jewish set, payin' lip-service at the synagogue on Upper Berkeley Street on the high holy days only."

"My family are not in London."

"Where are they?"

"Portsmouth, mostly."

"Then why are you here?"

"It's easier for me this way," he said. "I am not in a position to be around my family."

"Ah." I took a long drag off my cigarette. "Because you bed men. Forgive me, I was nearly lucky enough to forget what's goin' on with you and my brother. Who blackmailed you?"

Gideon laughed roughly. "You think my love of men is the reason I was blackmailed? Oh, no. You're mistaken there."

"Then what?"

"It's a complicated matter." He pulled his cigarette from his lips, holding it at arm's length to watch the smoke drifting from it, its end a glowing firefly in the twilit courtyard. "You see, where most men are born sons, sometimes, occasionally – rarely, I'd expect – they are born daughters, instead."

I stared at him, certain I'd misheard. "You're a –"

"Not a woman," he cut in, firmly. "There are aspects of my anatomy that might align more traditionally with yours, but I am not a woman. I am no more a woman than your betrothed. Although I don't know what goes on in that head of his. I suspect not particularly much."

I shook my head, awed. "I don't understand it," I admitted. "But I've known other people like you, around Covent Garden and Soho, in some of the gin shops and music halls."

"I thought as much. Identities are funny things, aren't they? Some of us pretend to be things we are not, like Rothschilds, and some of us run away from home at eighteen so they are not forced to do the same."

"Why are you tellin' me this?"

"Because I need you to realise I mean no ill intent towards your brother," Gideon said. "I know that with only a handful of words I could ruin your life. Well, now you could ruin mine. We are equals, at last."

I respected his honesty nearly as much as his courage. "All right," I muttered. "We're equal. And I'm sorry someone blackmailed you with... that. It's wrong."

"Do not pity me. I mean to return to the bar soon. The fellow responsible died recently, as it happens."

"God works in mysterious ways," I said, coming to join him in resting against the wall.

"Evidently so. Apparently, the fool got himself stinking drunk and stood up on the top deck of an omnibus. Collided with a pub sign that was hanging further into the street than it ought to."

"I'll bet that makes for a colourful obituary."

"Indeed. I paid a visit to his widow," Gideon added. "It felt only right to ensure she did not need any help with his estate. I found her drinking champagne with his handsome valet, so I think it's safe to assume she'll recover from her loss."

The bastard finally broke me: I laughed. So did he. I didn't want to find him funny, but I couldn't help it.

"What is it you want from my brother?" I asked, when I stopped.

"I don't think you want to know all the things I want from your brother," Gideon said.

"Not like that. I mean – do you truly care for him?"

"I do. Caleb is helping me connect with our shared peoplehood in ways I haven't had the joy of before. Granted, we have our differences, on account of me being of Portuguese extraction and you and he being of... whatever."

"You're very charmin', you know."

"My point is, I get along with him grandly. Though if I have to hear him pronounce *challah* as *cholla* one more time we may yet come to blows."

I snickered, hurrying to bring my cigarette back to my lips to chase the last ghost of it, having neglected it over the course of our conversation. The light in the sky continued fading, a hint of blue dusk visible through the layers of cloud, where stars would soon appear.

"What's your plan now, then?" he asked. "With this whole Rothschild thing?"

"Eloise has changed her mind about revealin' me. She feels bad for her brother. Instead she's suggested I marry Ernest and the two of us go off to America together. I can pretend to be a Rothschild in exile there for the rest of my life."

Gideon grimaced. "That's disappointing. What of Caleb?"

"I'd like him to come with me," I said. "But if he chooses to remain here with you, I won't begrudge him that." Just because I was to be miserable and unfulfilled did not mean I wanted the same for my brother. Even if that meant a life with Gideon Cardoza.

"Thank you," he said. "But I'm sure he'll go with you. I am only a recent pastime, and he cares about you more than you could imagine. Worry for you consumes him." He rolled his eyes. "He worries so much for you it is beginning to rub off on me. You must be careful."

"I will." I scowled. "Wait. Your – thing."

"You're also very charming."

"Caleb knows?"

Gideon flicked away the remnants of his own cigarette with a snort. "Of course he bloody well knows. What in God's name do you think we've been doing in his bedchamber, actually studying? I'm going inside now. Marvellous little *tête-à-tête,* Miss de Rothschild. Have a good evening, and many congratulations." He bowed as if I were a real lady. "I wish you long life."

29

Eloise

It was a queer form of self-flagellation, sitting alone in my bedchamber listening to the merriment of the reception downstairs. I'd fooled myself into believing I'd make use of the time reading or embroidering, perhaps pressing more flowers for my parlour wall. Instead, I spent most of the afternoon curled up in bed, straining to pick out Mirah's muffled voice among a sea of others. My ears and mind conspired in cruel trickery, at times convincing me that I heard her animatedly relaying her excitement about the wedding. It was bitterly unfair. Here I was, sacrificing once again, only now I was not to be loved for it. Very much the opposite.

Eventually I succumbed to sleep, where my mind continued to taunt me. I dreamed of Mirah in a gown of white shot silk, a wedding veil covering her face. Whenever I tenderly moved to pull it back another appeared miraculously beneath it. I grew more agitated, more desperate, until I was throwing back veil after veil as she laughed and laughed. I dreamed of receiving a letter postmarked with an American stamp, accompanied by a charming family carte de visite that showed Mirah seated dotingly beside Ernest, with a chubby, golden-haired baby smiling in her lap. Granted, the baby turned purple and began to meow like a cat, but still. I awoke furious with my own brain.

A week had elapsed since then. If wedding plans were underway, I was unaware, for I passed the majority of the time in my bedchamber penning abysmal poetry like a heartsick schoolgirl. I ate only broth and water-biscuits, and stubbornly resisted sleep. I failed, naturally, and my dreams grew more bizarre still, for they were not always of Mirah. Sometimes it was Mother playing at her piano, sweet music flowing from her fingertips. Sometimes they were less dreams than memories: hiding behind a sheet flapping on the washing line to scare Ernest when we were children. He'd shrieked so loud it hurt my ears, running back into the house and tripping on the back step. I'd been scolded terribly for it. Then it would be Mother again, playing her piano, more sweet music. Glimpses of a childhood sandwiched awkwardly between musical notes.

After eight days I emerged from my chamber, grudgingly admitting that I couldn't hide any longer without being presumed dead.

Rather than venture downstairs and listen to Ernest making wedding arrangements, I occupied myself with filial piety, visiting Father's room with the first volume of *Middlemarch* in tow. I'd read *Adam Bede* to Mother on her sickbed. She dubbed it a miserable story, and I was moved to agree – why was it that the character of Dinah was forced to give up her preaching to wed boring Adam and bear his boring children? I understood why Mother hadn't liked it.

Father was awake when I entered, sitting upright in bed in one of his moments of lucidity. The curtains were drawn as usual, the air in the room close and hot from the fire and the gas blazing from the wall sconces.

"Eloise," he said, as I took a seat on the end of the bed. "Are you all right, my dear?"

"Yes."

"You look sallow."

I opened the book pointedly to somewhere in the middle, which was not at all helpful for reading. "The room is dark. How would you tell?"

"It is clear," Father said. "And Mrs Sharp tells me you have not left your bedchamber all week."

"That isn't true. I went downstairs to make hot chocolate and fruitcake."

"Something is troubling you."

I expelled a deep breath through my nose. It was just my luck that he chose now to develop a sense of fatherly concern, after having never paid me the barest attention as a child. I turned one of the pages mindlessly. "I've had a chill, but I'm well again now."

"No, it is a different kind of unwellness. I recognise it. Your mother looked that way, when she was in low spirits." His voice was lined with such regret that I forgot my efforts to be petulant, glancing at him. His eyes had adopted a misty, far-off quality. I feared he was about to lapse back into a state of confusion, but when he spoke, it was with utter clarity. "I would have liked to see her smile again, before the end."

I could not tell whether he meant her end or his own. I supposed it did not matter.

"I would like to see you happy, too. Safely settled and content."

"Are you to suggest a husband to me again, Father?" I murmured.

"Not unless you want one." His gaze shifted to me, and he smiled. "You are heartsick, aren't you?"

I froze in place, *Middlemarch* still open in my lap so wide the spine was strained. "Father..."

"I shan't press for details. You are sad, though, so I presume you and your sweetheart must be at odds."

My mouth was dry as parchment paper. "Yes," I whispered. "We are at odds."

"What happened?"

"It doesn't bear talking of. It's over."

"Nonsense. Tell me."

I hesitated, then closed the book. "I did something awful, and yet – he will take the blame for it, if it comes out. And our... affection, would break another's heart."

"You've not taken up with a married man, have you?"

"No. But he has another suitor, towards whom I pushed him, like a fool. I would be heartless and selfish to want him back after that."

"Does he love you also?"

I drew the book close to me, a shield held tight to my chest. "I believe so."

"Then it would be more heartless and selfish to allow him to marry another, if he does not love her. More heartless and selfish to her, too, poor thing. She would know if his love was not honest. Perhaps not immediately, but over time. Spare everyone the pain and be true to yourself."

My fingers gripped the edges of the book until they hurt.

"What happened between you and Mother?" I asked, quietly. "You never told me. Mrs Sharp says you were happy together once."

Father lay his head back upon his pillow with a sigh. "We were."

"What changed?"

"I made a dreadful mistake. A dreadful choice, and it tore your mother and I apart. I regret it bitterly. Even more so, I regret that I was not brave enough to make amends with her and admit that I was wrong. I was prideful and cowardly, and Edith never forgave me."

"What was it?" I begged. "What did you do that was so unforgivable?"

He gave a hollow chuckle. "Your Uncle Horace did something. Something that I knew to be cruel and immoral. Instead of confronting him, or doing what I knew in my heart to be right, I helped him to hide his sin."

"That isn't what I mean," Susanna said, taking up sewing again. "Only that it is good to see you allowing yourself to be unhappy. You never cried when your mother died. It is better for you this way."

It was an assessment that made me feel as though I had just been stripped to my underpinnings in the middle of Trafalgar Square, but worst of all, it was not untrue. I thought of Mother at her piano, Ernest, gap-toothed and floppy-haired, running into the house in floods of tears. I began to suspect my week of wallowing and water-biscuits was not solely because of Mirah. She was the catalyst, yes, but maybe not the cause. Mirah was merely the radiant, maddening, curly-haired trigger of a pistol that was already primed. Just as Doctor Hartley worked to ease Mother's symptoms, the source of them was not so easily cut out. Grief had a way of growing back.

"I need to speak with Ernest," I said, suddenly remembering the urgency of my cause. "I am done with this ruse. I must tell him everything before he learns it some other way."

Susanna stopped her task. "He's gone, Miss. He left a while ago."

"Gone? Gone where?"

"To Marlborough House."

My head jerked back with such immediate force my neck twinged. "*What?* Since when does Ernest get invited to Marlborough House?"

"Mr Byron isn't the one who was invited," Susanna said. "It was Miss Zelikovich. That 'cousin' of hers from the Beauchamps' ball secured her an invitation. He's going to introduce them to the prince. Your brother has been talking about it all week. I didn't want to tell you because you seemed so upset."

There was a resounding thud, my copy of *Middlemarch* hitting the floor. I was positive Mirah would have gleefully taken credit for introducing to my vocabulary the only two words that came to me:

"Oh *fuck*."

30

Mirah

I may not have had a fancy tutor like Caleb did, but I'd still learned a few valuable lessons when I was a child. One in particular had served me well my whole life.

We'd been living in another warm country, in a room that overlooked the sea. The view was breathtaking, a sweeping expanse of sky and sea both so blue that on some days they blurred together. I often knelt on the bed I shared with Caleb, directly beneath the window, watching the sailboats moving sluggishly over the sparkling cerulean water, tiny white dots crawling ant-like in the distance. The view was the only pleasant thing. The room stunk, badly. Salted fish and rotten seaweed. It was loud too, a family of seagulls nesting on the roof forever embroiled in a noisy domestic dispute. Caleb collected some of the feathers, crafting them into a fan he'd then given to me, which I'd broken in an hour.

My lesson came the day we went to the beach. Ma went off somewhere in her prettiest bonnet, leaving Caleb to watch me. I'd gotten sick of sitting in the baking hot sand while his nose was buried in a book, and wandered along the beach to a cluster of rock-pools, all slippery and black, dressed with ribbons of shiny green kelp. I joined a troupe of other children, mostly boys, fishing for sea-life and mermaid's purses, which Caleb told me were actually shark eggs. I wanted to find one and sit on it like a mother bird to see if it would hatch. I reckoned no one would give us any grief if I'd a shark for a pet. One ruddy-faced boy plucked a hermit crab out of the water, pulling the poor creature from its shell. We'd gotten into blows over his cruelty, our scrap ending in me pushing him straight off a rock into a pool. He'd been fine, suffering only wounded pride and a wet arse, but he'd yelled bloody murder as his friends went tearing off. All the noise brought Caleb over to drag me away by the collar, but in the chaos of it all everyone forgot the hermit crab, scrambling for cover. As Caleb led me away a cloud of gulls descended upon it in a feathery frenzy. That was when I'd learned what happened to creatures without shells.

So I'd grown my own, hard and impenetrable, and it served me well for years. And then Eloise Byron dragged me from it as that boy had the crab, before leaving me to fend for myself, exposed and without armour.

Marlborough House was stunning. Several stories high, with two tall wings either end and grey balustrades running the length of the flat roof. It was red brick, turned mauve by the darkness, with corners made out in white stone, glowing orange in the lamplight.

We'd entered down the driveway, through grand, wide-open gates ordinarily closed to people like myself. I'd thought the queue to enter the Beauchamps' ball was long, but it was paltry compared to this, dozens upon dozens of carriages much finer than ours waiting to be admitted. They were draped in tasselled cloth of blue, green, gold, equipped with liveried grooms and drivers in tricorn hats, and the people that streamed out of them were something otherworldly. A flock of colourful birds, all trussed up in miles of satin and silk of every shade, rippling in the flickering torchlight. Every woman sported a dazzling piece of jewellery intended to stir envy among the others, from glinting gold opera chains to enamelled butterfly brooches, and his love of beautiful women.

Without any false modesty, I was more than up to snuff.

Ernest brought us to a stop outside the doors, moving aside to allow others to pass as he pulled something from inside his tailcoat, raising it to his lips and tipping it back with a flash of silver.

"What are you doing?" I hissed, attempting to snatch the flask from his hand. "There are drinks inside!" No doubt a literal fountain of champagne, bubbling over like the Trevi for the prince's pompous friends to lap from.

"Come off," Ernest grumbled, surrendering it at once. "I need something for courage. I'm bloody terrified." I'd never heard him so short or honest with me, and I wondered if my own anxiety translated to him somehow, like a nervous horse absorbing the fears of its rider.

"Fuck," I said. He had a point. I knocked it back myself, not caring how wide Ernest's eyes grew. Why bother breaking my neck to maintain airs of social grace, at this point? Might as well be pleasantly lushy when the truth came out. I'd be less conscious of the rats chewing on my toes in my cell in Newgate.

"Here." I pressed the empty flask back into Ernest's waiting hand. He tested the weight of it, eyebrows raised so high I thought they'd migrate into his hairline.

"Dear God. Whenever did you learn to drink like that? You'd put a sailor to shame!"

I wiped my mouth with the back of my hand, making my delicate satin glove stink of port. "You don't learn. You just do. Come on."

We moved through the doors unchallenged. Ernest presented our invitation, and it wasn't torn to pieces in front of us as I'd imagined. No guards rushed us, no accusations were made as we were swept down the elegant hallway and through the tall doors into the drawing room, caught in a stream of other guests like salmon. My last chance to flee had passed.

A dense haze of tobacco smoke curled in the air, burning so hotly in my nose with each breath that I thought it would singe my nostril hairs. It was so thick anyone would be forgiven for believing the London pea-soup fog had rolled into Marlborough House through an open window, and it took several minutes for the smoke to clear before the veil was lifted and the features of the drawing room revealed themselves.

When they were I was hard pressed not to react.

The ceiling sweeping above our heads was fitted with squared, tiered moulding, gilt and glorious with a hexagon at its centre, and in the middle of the room four towering pillars hugged the walls, etched with markings that made them resemble the trunks of enormous palm trees. Various chairs were scattered about, most already taken. A *confidante* sofa, designed to seat three or more engaged in gripping conversation, was placed squarely in the middle of a vast Persian rug that looked as though it could have wrapped around the world twice-over. The entire room was decked out for the festive season, windows and tables festooned with banners of holly and ivy, a lofty pine tree standing in one corner adorned with stringed orange slices and beads. Candles were clipped to its branches, and between that and the suffocating heat of the gas-lamps, the whole tree appeared to be wilting tragically, in danger of going up in flames at any second. A fire-risk to rival Havdalah candles.

The prince was standing by the fireplace – or so a woman near us whispered to her companion. I couldn't see him myself, my view obstructed by an elegant folding screen, but with a tight cluster of men and women gathering there en masse I was inclined to believe her.

I leaned close to Ernest to relay this knowledge, but he was distracted, head turned towards a group of jovial, rosy-cheeked young women. It was a relief. I might have been the only woman in the world wishing for her intended to stray. At least if he was embroiled in some scandalous liaison breaking off our engagement would be easy.

Still, I tugged his sleeve. "Ernest."

He swivelled to face me at once, red creeping up the back of his neck like a rash. "Yes?"

"The prince is over there," I said, gesturing with my chin.

"God almighty," he murmured. Save for his neck he'd come over awfully pale. "I cannot believe we are here. I don't belong among people like this."

I laughed. "Don't be ridiculous!"

He had to be joking. The Byrons were wealthy and glamorous beyond comprehension, with their Berkeley Square town-house and modern carriage. They had a fleet of staff, and fashionable clothes, and Ernest attended Oxford, though Eloise informed me he left without a degree, sent down for skipping classes.

"Do not laugh at me," Ernest said, suddenly bristling in a way I'd never seen. "It's true. My family are not worthy of this company. We're wealthy, but we're mere merchant class. Purveyors of – of moustache wax, for God's sake! They wouldn't even let me join the Savile Club!"

I frowned. "Eloise said you are a member."

"I lied." Ernest was beginning to resemble an extremely worried beetroot. "I tried thrice to be admitted, but they wouldn't have me. As if they would let someone like myself into the same room as literary greats and baronets! I am an imposter!"

Truly, I wanted to laugh again, harder. So that was the way of it. For all their money and pomp, Ernest placed himself beneath the set at Marlborough House. He, too, felt the keen sting of fear and shame that came from pretending to be something he was not. Perhaps everyone in this room felt the same. A baronet might consider himself inadequate before a duke, who'd in turn gaze in awe upon the prince.

Maybe, in another world – one where I'd never met Eloise, and where

I was deaf, mute, and blind to his wandering eyes – Ernest and I would have been a good match after all.

"Cousin!"

I recognised the voice behind us from the Beauchamps' ball immediately. Alfred Charles de Rothschild fought his way through the eager throng to greet us, kissing my hand politely before shaking Ernest's.

"Wonderful to see you here," he said, his smile impossible to read. Either the letter was sincere, or the Rothschilds had a strong talent for acting, in which case perhaps I was related to them after all. "It is particularly good to meet you, Mr Byron. I must confess some surprise at the match. Certain family members have been heard to say they would sooner see their children dead than married out." That smile grew less friendly, and I had the distinct sense we were being snubbed. "But I'm positive you are a respectable fellow. What is it that you do, again?"

Ernest hesitated, emitting an awkward spluttering like a blocked engine.

"His family are in the cosmetics industry," I said. "Have you heard of Acker's Patented Moustache Colourant and Wax?"

"I daresay I've probably used it myself, on occasion. That is the family business, then? Moustache wax? That is..."

"Industrious, I know." I smiled the way I'd learned from watching Pauline Beauchamp. "All mighty dynasties must begin somewhere, mustn't they? Sometimes even a ghetto in Frankfurt!"

Alfred nodded, but I sensed he wasn't convinced, still exuding the imperious air of someone with no living memory of the hardship his empire was founded upon. Had he unknowingly passed his ancestors in the street he'd have considered himself a cut above them.

"Come, then, allow me to introduce you to the prince." He swept his arm towards the other end of the room. "We have known each other since our days at Trinity College."

I smiled tightly, allowing Alfred to guide us both over in the prince's direction. Nearing him, in all his stately glory, I briefly contemplated penning a memoir, when all of this was over. It wouldn't be published, and not even because I was a woman, or possibly about to become a convicted fraudster – fraudstress? No, it would never be published because no one would ever believe I'd gone from eating bow-wow-mutton in a tenement in Limehouse to meeting the Prince of Wales. But I was about to. Imminently.

I got all the way to the fireplace before I lost my nerve. Or rather, experienced a piercing moment of clarity in which I abruptly realised lying to the future king of England was a bad idea. This ruse had gone decidedly too far. I needed to get out, and I feared the only way I could politely excuse myself from this room was under a doctor's care. Unable to tear my gaze from the prince, I took a deep breath and employed my best stage fall, allowing my legs to crumple beneath me. Ernest didn't even try to catch me, busy ogling Prince Edward, and I went down like a sack of bricks, hitting the polished parquet floor to a chorus of horrified gasps and cries. It hadn't even occurred to me until I was already down that the prince would try to help me. Of course he would - he was royalty, and there was a roomful of people watching. He could hardly shove a fainted woman aside with his shoe and carry on his conversation. A dashing, chivalrous effort was required to save face.

Before I knew it, I was scooped up off the floor like an injured dove and carried gallantly to the nearest sofa, placed there as if I were made of porcelain. The Prince of Wales himself waved a small silver bottle of smelling salts beneath my nose, sending a footman for iced water with lemon and mint.

"Are you all right, Miss?" he asked, while a crowd of other gentlemen flocked to waft me with fans taken from their wives.

I blinked, dazed. The prince looked exactly like all the *carte de visites* and illustrations of him. Not astonishingly handsome, but with an undeniable magnetism nonetheless. I wondered if that magnetism would be there if he wasn't royalty. A man's proximity to power could be a heady aphrodisiac.

"I am well, Your Highness, thank you," I said. It was a miracle the words weren't completely garbled by panic. "I merely came over lightheaded."

To the casual observer my fall might have appeared intentional, a clever move to snatch the prince's attention, and laying there on the plush velvet *confidante* feigning a recovery I noticed several other young women watching through narrowed eyes, cursing that they hadn't thought of it themselves.

"Not on my account, I hope." The prince took the glass of iced water from his footman and held it to my lips personally. I forced down a few tentative sips and smiled, face burning up.

"It is all quite overwhelming, Your Highness. I think I should step outside for some air."

"Would you like me to accompany you?"

I shook my head, praying to God he did not think me rude. "I could not be such an imposition on your time, Your Highness."

"It would be no such thing, Miss...?"

"De Rothschild," Afred put in, hovering behind the sofa. I'd forgotten about him completely. "She is a distant cousin of mine." He did not sound impressed by my display. I noted I'd been demoted from 'cousin' to 'distant cousin'.

The prince was amazed. "Is that so? How it is that we've never met? I would remember a face like yours, Miss de Rothschild."

"I'm visiting from France," I squeaked out, swinging upright on the sofa. "Please, Your Highness, I am thoroughly embarrassed by my comportment. Allow me leave to step outside. My fiancé will accompany me..."

"Fiancé?" The prince's eyes flashed to Ernest, perhaps trying to devise a way to remove him from the situation. "Ah."

"Yes." I smiled again, so sick with nerves I was almost positive the port I'd downed on my way inside would make a reappearance. "Make I be excused, Your Highness?"

The prince only appeared ruffled for a second before he nodded. "Of course, Miss de Rothschild."

"Thank you." I stood with impressive confidence given my supposed frailty, grabbing Ernest's arm and pulling him towards the nearest door. He had been positively useless as I lay there, gawking at the prince the entire time with his mouth hanging open. As we made our escape the entire drawing room whispered in our wake.

Safely outside Marlborough House, drinking in the crisp night air instead of choking on tobacco smoke, I could finally breathe again.

"I do hope you'll be all right," Ernest said. He was pacing back and forth beneath the portico, wringing his hands. "Though I am relieved to be out of there."

"It's very busy," I agreed, knowing full well that wasn't what unsettled him. I was cautious of speaking too frankly in front of the guards still stationed at the door, impassive, immovable statues. Only the gentle fluttering of the tiny feather atop their hats belied that they weren't carved from stone. "Maybe we should send for the carriage and retire early?"

Ernest nodded. "That would be wise." He ceased his pacing abruptly. "Mirah. I must thank you. From the bottom of my heart."

"For what?"

"For not thinking less of me, on account of the business. You are the daughter of a mighty dynasty, as you said. I am not worthy of marrying into the Rothschild family, but you make me believe I could be, one day."

It was as though he'd punched me square in the gut. The sincerity in his eyes, the vulnerable, pained edge to his voice. I couldn't keep this up any longer. It was destroying me. I forgot about the guards at the door, the party still going on inside. All that existed in the world was me, Ernest, and a thousand-ton weight of guilt.

"Ernest," I began. "I'm not –"

I didn't get to finish, cut short by someone shrieking my name. I recognised the voice immediately. What was Eloise doing here? My first instinct was that our plot had been uncovered, that she had been arrested and I was next. It was hard to think anything else, what with her being frogmarched across the courtyard by two armed guards. She looked like she'd been dragged backwards by her ankles through a hedge, her hair half loose and leafy, her dress rumpled and moss stained.

"What in God's name –" Ernest went jogging over, waving them down with both hands. I followed. "Stop! That is my sister!"

"She's hysterical," one of the guards said. "Caught her trying to climb over the garden wall!"

"She *climbed over the wall?*"

"No, I said she was *trying* to. Got herself stuck, didn't she?"

"I was not stuck," Eloise protested. "I was merely taking a moment to collect myself before alighting."

"Stuck," the guard said.

Ernest shook his head in disbelief. "Eloise, what happened?"

"That's really something we ought to discuss somewhere private," Eloise said, twisting in the guard's grip. "I told you my brother was here! I need to speak with him!"

"I don't care. No one is granted entry without an invitation. We get this all the time," the guard added breezily to Ernest and me. "Women wanting to throw themselves at the prince. Completely unbecoming."

Eloise squeaked indignantly. "That is definitely *not* what I was intending to do!"

"Please, there must be an emergency for her to have attempted something so brash," Ernest begged. "Allow me to handle her."

The guard scoffed, glancing at his companion before shoving Eloise roughly in Ernest's direction. "Fine," he said. "She's for you to deal with. But you'd best leave."

My eyes met Eloise's. A twig was sticking up out of her hair, and she was missing an earring. If I wasn't so certain why she'd tried to scale the garden wall of Marlborough House I'd have found the whole situation hilarious.

"Don't worry," I said. "We were already planning on it."

31

Eloise

I didn't tell him in the carriage. It wouldn't have been right, or wise, for it risked him ordering the driver to stop so that he could disappear into the streets to drown his sorrows in a dingy, smoke-stale pub, where he'd only get himself into trouble. He bombarded me with questions, though – what happened? Was it about Father? Was he – *oh god, was he*...? I assured him that it did not relate to Father at all, but that I would only elaborate further once we were safely ensconced somewhere private. Even more questions followed. What were you doing climbing a garden wall? Don't you know there's a privet hedge on the other side of it? Are those bird droppings on your dress? No, I hadn't known there was a privet hedge on the other side of it, obviously, but I was acutely aware of it now. And yes. It probably was.

Mirah stared at me from the seat opposite the whole ride, an unspoken conversation passed in meaningful looks.

When we arrived back at Berkeley Square a hansom cab was parked outside, and as we stepped into the vestibule Susanna came running out of the drawing room in a great flap. "Miss! I'm sorry, I shouldn't have admitted him, but he was adamant - what happened to you?" She swerved mid-explanation. "Is that bird –"

"Perhaps it would be best if you leave," Ernest muttered to Mirah and Caleb, avoiding Mirah's gaze as one would Medusa's. "For now, at least. Father is ill."

Mirah nodded, seizing her indignant brother by the arm to lead him off. She paused mid-turn, wiggling Mother's ring off her finger and returning it to Ernest.

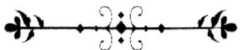

For a man who never knew when to guard his tongue, my brother's silence was impressively intimidating. It was the same silence that accompanied us in the carriage from Park Street the night of Mirah's dinner. The silence of tense, uncharacteristically profound thought.

We sat on opposing sides of the bed, Father tucked under the blankets and quilts between us, already snoring again. It was easy getting him back to bed, working together. I plumped up his pillow as Ernest fetched a jug of water from the kitchen, and then we made to stoke the fire in the hearth, which looked to be failing, the two of us making such a bad go of it that in the end I'd sent sheepishly for Susanna.

Now we were alone, plunged back into that awful quiet, chipped away only by the whooshing of the fire as wind rushed down the chimney, the whole room breathing in time with Father.

"I'm sorry," I said finally, the words feeling indescribably fragile. Ernest clasped his hands tightly in his lap, gaze fixed past me.

"No," he whispered. "I'm sorry, Eloise. I did not realise you'd come to hate me so fervently."

"I don't hate you. I was desperate. You wouldn't see sense when I tried to talk to you of the future. I know that none of this makes what I did acceptable, but I don't hate you. Even if I thought I did, for a while."

Ernest laughed – or something resembling it, a rough imitation of the sound. "You want to talk of the future? You won't even talk of the past."

"I don't..."

"I know my behaviour at Mother's funeral was wrong," he said, shortly, spinning her ring around the tip of his finger. "Do you think I was not sick to my stomach with shame the next morning? I was. And every morning after. But I did not know what else to do. It was as if my world had fallen apart and I was the only one grieving! I kept her ring because it was *hers*, not to spite you!"

"You think that I didn't grieve?" I said, horrified. "Ernest, it devastated me!"

"You did not show it!"

"I couldn't! Don't you understand? I couldn't. Father was beside himself, and you were gone to your clubs and gambling dens. Someone had to pick up the pieces. Someone had to ensure we carried on. She wasn't going to bury herself, Ernest." I only noticed I was weeping when I felt something wet roll down my cheek. It was an unfamiliar sensation, so foreign to me after all these years that I didn't know what to do about it. I knew well now how to stop the tears from coming – a sharp slap, a hard pinch, but with them already flowing, I was helpless. Withdrawing my handkerchief rapidly to wipe away the evidence, I was struck by how much it resembled a white flag.

Ernest's breath hitched, his head dropping so that his chin was resting against his chest.

"You're right. I know you're right. I didn't do what I should have, as a son. As a brother. I wasn't there to help you with all of that. But you weren't there for me, either. I only wish you'd talked to me."

"And I only wish you'd talked to me, too."

That was the crux of it, the rotting root of a sore tooth. I mourned, and he mourned, but we did everything differently. Even as children, when we'd been playing the piano with Mother, we'd been positioned at opposite ends of the instrument. It was only right we'd do our grieving in different keys as well. Ernest's demeanour following her death perplexed me. How he was able to carry on with such levity and piquancy, playing cards and smoking cigars. On some level I had envied him, coveting for myself his ongoing ardour for life, the freedoms allowed to him as a man. I wanted to smoke and shoot and kiss pretty women myself, but instead I was relegated to spoon-feeding Father clear broth and entertaining vapid society ladies like Helena Hall.

Conversely, I could see why Ernest thought me callous. Weren't women made to weep and wail? Clutch posies and embroider memorial samplers? Heaven forbid any one of us appear cold. It was ironic. My sex were forever doing the unsung, unseen work, yet we were expected to be expressly emotional creatures. My question was where we supposed to fit in the time to cry into our handkerchiefs between being nurses and mothers and wives. I'd become callous in the end, though. I couldn't ignore that.

"What you did was... dreadful," Ernest said, giving voice to my conscience. "But you were right that I have also been cruel and careless. Taunting you with threats of marrying you off, dismissing your perfectly reasonable concerns. We have been awful to each other, Sister."

"Can you ever forgive me?"

Ernest's moustache twitched as his lips moved. "I think so. With time." He straightened himself up, pulling back his shoulders and frowning suddenly. "This woman, then. Miss... not de-Rothschild. Who *is* she?"

"Her name is Mirah Zelikovich. She's a Jewess from Limehouse who earns her keep in a music hall." *And the fiercest, most bewildering, most beautiful woman I have ever known.*

"What were you paying her?"

"Ten percent of whatever I inherited. She was desperate, Ernest, and I took advantage of that. I beg you not to take it to the authorities. She is a wonderful, intelligent woman who deserves far better than a prison sentence for my wrongdoing."

Ernest tilted his chin, eyeing me peculiarly. "You're fond of her, aren't you?"

"Yes. She has become a dear friend."

"No," he wagged his finger at me. "No, it's more than that, isn't it? I've a powerful sense for these things."

I scrunched my handkerchief up into a ball. "Ernest..."

"It's all right. I've always known why you were gunning for spinsterhood. You used to pad after Susanna like a lost pup, and you begged to go to boarding school. Most girls of that age do not want to be torn away from their home and families to lodge with a roomful of other young ladies."

I squirmed listening to him, wanting to sink through the floor and disappear. To be seen for what I was by Susanna was one thing. To be seen by my brother was another entirely.

"Do you love her, then?" Ernest asked, with a light, unexpected curiousness. "Miss – uh..."

"Zelikovich," I said, picking at the dry white skin of my cuticles with poorly feigned nonchalance.

"That's it. Do you?"

I hesitated. Nodded.

"I'll marry her still, then," Ernest declared. "Rothschild or no. If I do that, she can come to live with us, and the two of you can be together, can't you? I won't expect a real marriage."

"You'd make a cuckold of yourself for me?"

"I'd sooner not use *quite* those words, but yes. Why not."

"That's what Uncle Horace did," I said. "He was involved with an unsuitable woman." Unsuitable was a word I'd taken to questioning heavily of late. If what I suspected was true, it was Horace who'd proven the unsuitable one. It was no surprise. Uncle Horace was unsuitable in a myriad of ways. The only surprise was the sheer, horrible coincidence of it.

Father nodded. "A French Jewess. He wrote of it to me in letters. I kept them all." His watery eyes scoured the room, settling on his inlaid bureau. So that was what he was hiding in the locked drawer I'd tried to force. I left the bed.

"We need to see them," I demanded, glancing at Ernest and hoping he would unite with me on this matter. He blinked, apparently a few steps behind in understanding, but scrambled off the mattress anyway.

"Yes," he said, clearing his throat. "We need to."

Father sat up slowly. "Wait..."

I held up a hand to silence his protest. "No, Father. I'm sorry, but we simply must do this. Ernest, fetch the poker from the fireside."

For once in his life Ernest did precisely as he was told. I took it from him, wedging the tip into the groove of the bureau drawer.

"For the love of God, stop!" Father yelled.

"It is in the interest of justice!" I cried, gritting my teeth as I wrenched back the iron poker. Ernest came to help me, adding his weight to it, both of us straining to prise the drawer open. The fancy polished wood gave a low groan, then split with a deafening crack, the bureau surrendering its secrets. I dropped the poker. It landed with a metallic clang at my feet.

"I'm sorry, Father," I said, panting from my efforts. "It needs to be done."

"I bloody know that! I was telling you to stop because Mrs Sharp has the key on her chatelaine!"

I formed a soundless 'o' with my lips, burning to the tips of my ears.

"Reckless children," Father sighed, sinking back down onto his throne of pillows. "I swear you want to put me in the grave faster!"

32

Mirah

The apartment on Park Street never felt like home, but that wasn't a feeling exclusive to Mayfair. Nowhere I'd lived ever felt like home. Occasionally it started to, but I'd invariably be torn from it before any real familiarity set in. Life had been a foggy rotation of different lodgings. The room on the water that stunk of fish, the sunny apartment where oranges grew, a shabby loft in Vienna where we'd had a violinist for a neighbour, who I'd pressed my ear against the damp, mildewy wall to listen to. Each place took up a small part of me, but none significant enough for me to miss.

It made packing up the Park Street lodgings much easier, though it was easy to begin with, for Caleb and I had few possessions of our own, and I wasn't going to steal the silverware or attempt to cram a whole credenza into my trunk.

I hadn't a clue what came next. All I knew was that we couldn't stay in Mayfair. Caleb and I both agreed we wouldn't take Eloise's charity even if she offered it. I was sick to the teeth of relying on the goodness of wealthy folk, even one I loved. I'd haggle for adequate payment for my services – to hold onto a few of the dresses, maybe, and some of the jewellery, which would be destined for a jerryshop to keep us in a good way for a while. Maybe we'd take rooms somewhere a touch nicer than Limehouse.

All of this was dependent upon me not winding up in Newgate, of course.

I watched Caleb meticulously sorting through the bookcase for what belonged to us, his brows puckered in concentration – or irritation.

"I know you think I'm a fool for all of this," I muttered.

"I don't think you're a fool," Caleb said. "Not really. It was unwise, but I can't blame you for wantin' more for us. I do too. Who wouldn't want the means to be comfortable, and help other people?"

"I'm sorry it didn't work out."

"Don't be. I've got you. That's what matters."

A furious hammering at the front door went up before I could respond. I jumped to Caleb's side, expecting a whole pack of coppers to tear into the drawing room and apprehend me. For some reason I grabbed one of the books on the table and raised it above my head, as if I'd be able to fight them off with a dog-eared copy of *Caleb Asher*. Tabitha entered followed closely by Gideon Cardoza – and Eloise.

"What are you planning to do with that?" Gideon asked dryly. "Educate me to death? Put it down. Nothing bad is happening."

I lowered the book, cheeks hot. "What are you doin' here?"

"I've come to inform you that you have a strong claim to a fortune," Gideon stated, eyes darting meaningfully to Caleb. "Or rather, your brother does."

Caleb spluttered. "What? What on earth are you talkin' about?"

"Your mother was Leah Zelikovich, correct?"

"Yes."

"Wrong. Your mother was Mrs Horace Hughes, as she'd long claimed to be." Gideon slammed his leather satchel down on the table, whipping it open to take out a bundle of letters, tied with twine, and holding them aloft. "Mr said. "It's a shock."

"Of course," Eloise said. She was intensely awkward, flexing her hands in front of her to grasp something intangible and uncertain. "You are in no hurry to leave. The rent is paid until the end of the month. I understand you will have much to arrange, so do not concern yourself with lodgings. You could even take over the lease, now..."

I said nothing. My future was unfurling before my eyes in absurd splendour – the dresses, the carriages, the tedious afternoon teas and dinner parties organised with military precision. Was that to be my life now? I'd spent all this time pretending at it, I didn't know if I'd ever be able to feel like I wasn't a fraud. I didn't think I even wanted it. Eloise made it seem like torture.

"I will begin writing to some contacts in Paris," Gideon said, collecting his case.

"Don't leave," Caleb murmured, reaching out to catch Gideon's sleeve. "Gideon…"

Gideon's hand drifted from his case, fingers curling around Caleb's. "I may be inclined to stay a while."

Eloise nodded. "Very well. I, however, will take my leave. Feel free to keep the letters. They are most illuminating." I bet they were. Part of me writhed with curiosity, a desire to learn of the man my mother had dragged me all over Europe in pursuit of, to make sense of what had gone on in his head. Would he and Caleb write in a similar fashion? Would I see traces of my brother in a stranger's hand? In the end I set them down on the table, unopened.

There was nothing that man could write that held any value to me.

When the invitation came, with its ominous black border, I'd been uncertain of accepting. I hadn't known Ambrose Byron – he was a stranger to me, a figure I saw but once at the top of a staircase, a man who I should have perhaps even harboured bitterness towards, for his part in making us poor. And yet I was completely ambivalent.

I'd donned my darkest dress and gone to the funeral anyway. Not for myself or for Ambrose, but for Eloise. We hadn't seen each other or spoken since she'd come to my house with the letters from Horace Hughes, but I thought of her every day, longing to call upon her. Caleb advised me against it, at least until we were settled in our new lodgings, and I was able to think clearly about the future. For once I'd agreed. I'd had a thousand complicated feelings to reckon with, and twice as many complicated thoughts to untangle and make sense of. Now, though, I knew what I wanted.

It was a good thing Mr Byron was to be interred in the family crypt, for the earth in Brompton Cemetery was frozen so solid I wagered the gravediggers would have been working forever to break ground. It was the end of February, and the bleakest depths of winter refused to be shaken off, but behind the thick covering of grey cloud the sky was blue and bright, tiny slivers of sapphire peeking through when the wind made room for them.

The cemetery was large, and it took a while to find the funeral party. I felt a fool when I did, for it was impossible to miss. A glass-sided hearse was parked in the middle of the wide gravel path, the horses stamping impatiently, heads adorned with plumes of ebony feathers. A short distance away, congregated around a large stone mausoleum that looked as though it could house a small family, stood a group of mourners all shrouded in black. A shivering, miserable murder of crows.

It didn't appear to be particularly heavy grief rendering those in attendance so melancholy, so much as the weather conditions. One of the fifth-cousins-twenty-times-removed I'd met at the engagement reception stuffed her entire forearms into her fur muff to keep warm, the teeth of the man next to her chattering so hard I thought they were about to fall out. A small child in an itchy wool dress seated herself on an adjacent tomb, pouting as she shredded dandelion leaves into a fine confetti and sprinkled them on herself. I was surprised to see Dr Hartley there too, the two of us sharing a conspiratorial nod when our eyes met.

I joined Gideon Cardoza on the fringes of the crowd. We'd come from the same address at different times via different routes. The last thing either of us wanted was to be seen together in a way that might stir rumours of involvement, or cause anyone to inspect why Mr Cardoza was spending quite so much time at my lodgings. With my brother.

"You're late," he said, flashing me his silver watch. His breath was like smoke on the cold air, and it made me want a cigarette. "They're closing the mausoleum now."

"I got lost." I wasn't paying much attention to him, busy searching the crowd for that figure so familiar to me. When I found her I nearly failed to recognise her. Not because of the veil covering her face – no, I could identify Eloise from her posture alone – but because she was leaning heavily against Ernest Byron. The two of them sagged towards each other like bowing willow trees, clinging to each other's sides. Eloise was weeping. I couldn't hear her, but I saw her dabbing at her eyes with a black-trimmed handkerchief beneath her veil.

Ernest squeezed her hand. Their mother's ring glittered on her finger.

Most of the guests were relieved to get out of the cold. They didn't bother disguising it, groaning with gratitude when Ernest dutifully thanked everyone for their attendance and suggested they make their way back to Berkeley Square. People trickled off down winding paths towards the nearest gate, blowing into their frozen hands and muttering that it 'looked like rain'. I lingered behind, waiting until Gideon and I were the last two standing there, feeling the chill more acutely now that I was not packed in among two dozen mourners.

Ernest and Eloise walked over to greet me as one, Ernest's shiny leather shoes squeaking on the damp grass. I was surprised when he smiled at me, after everything.

"Miss Zelikovich. Thank you for coming."

"I regret that I didn't know your father more," I said. It was half true. Maybe if I'd known the man I'd have gotten the truth about Caleb's pa out of him sooner, and a lot could have been avoided.

There was a beat of uncomfortable silence, crows cawing overhead, and then Ernest clapped his hands together. "Well. I'm going to ensure everyone gets back to the house safely. Eloise, feel free to stay awhile and take a walk. You are always espousing the merits of fresh air to me, after all."

I didn't know what expression Eloise made thanks to her veil, but she went very stiff. "Oh... yes. I'd like a walk." Her dark, featureless face turned towards me. "Would you care to join me, Miss Zelikovich?"

"A walk would be nice."

"Excellent." Ernest cleared his throat. He looked exceedingly pleased with himself. "I will leave you to it, then." He bowed his head, then set his silk topper back on. "Ladies. Come, Mr Cardoza, you can ride back with me."

"How blessed I am," was Gideon's deadpan response.

Even with the two men retreating, Eloise and I waited until they were

Eloise hummed. "And what of you? I expect you're enjoying life in Bayswater? I'd imagine you're spending a lot of time and money at Whiteley's!"

"The department store? I've been once. Caleb found it overwhelmin'. I didn't enjoy it much."

"Oh. You'll grow accustomed to it, I'm sure. You're a lady now, after all..."

I smiled wryly. "No I ain't. I'm a gentleman's sister, at best. Mr Hughes wasn't my pa. I'm glad of it," I added, before she chimed in with words of consolation. "I don't want to be a lady, turns out. I've seen high society now, and it ain't for me. We're givin' a sizeable chunk of the money to charity. Best to do some good with it."

"But it's his birthright."

"And he doesn't want it. Neither do I. Ain't got any interest in Mr Horace Hughes. Why would I? I'm proud of my ma, and all she tried to do for us. I'd rather be her daughter than his. Besides, Caleb finally cracked and told me who my pa really was."

"Who?"

"Well, he didn't say it explicitly," I said. "But he did say he'd neglected to mention his tutor had lovely golden hair." I flashed her a grin. She laughed again.

"I cannot fault your mother for that, even if I do not personally see the appeal."

"Not a fan of golden hair, then?"

"Don't be silly."

"So you *do* like it?"

Eloise flushed so brightly I half expected her to throw her veil over her face again to hide it. "I should have told you something sooner," she said. "When you told me you wanted to be someone? I should have told you then that you already were, instead of telling you to go away to America and pretend to be. That wasn't your chance. You're already someone. To me, you're everything."

I stopped on the path to face her, the wind blowing a few errant curls into my face. "We're equals, finally," I said. "Neither high nor low."

Eloise smiled nervously. "So, what happens now?"

I smirked, catching her hand with my own, and leaned close, watching her cheeks grow even redder. It was delightful. "You've spent a whole lot of time doin' what you thought you needed to do," I said. "But what do you *want* to do?"

Epilogue

The gulls bickering outside was a grating lullaby to our afternoon nap, but we didn't mind. We hadn't ended up doing much sleeping anyway, escaping the heat of the midday sun only to generate more of it ourselves in private.

I rolled over on the mattress with the letter in hand. "Caleb says school is goin' well," I reported, "and that Gideon is still as dry and relentless as ever. He writes that he hopes we're behavin' ourselves."

Eloise giggled, her bare foot searching for mine beneath the sheets. "He would probably be delighted to hear what it is you've been doing."

"I don't think he'd want to know what I've been doin'!"

"You know that's not what I mean." Eloise propped herself up on her elbow to beat me across the face with her pillow. "I'm referring to the candles."

She was right about that. Caleb would be delighted to hear that I'd taken to kindling the Shabbos candles each Friday night, muttering the blessings in my ill-practised Hebrew. More than delighted, he'd be bordering on dangerously euphoric. I wasn't going to mention it in my letters just yet. There was something about keeping that little ritual between myself and God for now that pleased me.

We'd taken the rooms on the Bay of Naples a month ago, and would be leaving again in two weeks, on to the next leg of our journey. Eloise had

Florence on her list, where she wanted to see the red dome of the Cathedral at sunset, and ride in a gondola in Venice before we crossed the border into Austria.

We'd decided on a year of travel. Even with all her family's riches she'd only ever seen the corner of the world to which she'd been born, an outrage, in my mind, when she'd been equipped with all the means to do so. It was a constipated Englishness on the part of her father that kept her feet planted on British soil. Now, unencumbered, she longed to taste different food and bathe in foreign waters. In short, to adventure.

At the end of that year, though, we would return to London and take up permanent lodgings somewhere. A small apartment that we'd furnish to our liking, where we'd put family photos on the mantle-piece, hang sprays of pressed flowers on the wall. A home for us both, two humble spinsters keeping each other company. It was an elegant compromise. Besides, I wasn't going to turn down holidaying across the continent with the woman I loved, staying in modest rooms and feeding each other delicacies I remembered from childhood.

"What did your letter say?" I asked, resting my head against Eloise's. "Any news?"

"Nothing of importance," she said, burrowing herself into my side, a warm, comforting solidness. "We've been invited to visit the Beauchamps when we return to London, to meet their son. He is a bonny thing I'm told but bears an uncanny resemblance to one of their grooms."

"Mysterious."

"Indeed. Henry and Leopold are said to be doting fathers, though. I expect it's much easier with three pairs of hands."

"And a whole fleet of staff."

Eloise grinned. "Ernest writes that he's vowed only to involve himself with women who know his nature fully. I suspect he has met a girl just as much of a scoundrel as he is. Perhaps he'll end up wedding an actress after all.

Wouldn't that be poetic?"

I laughed, slinging one arm around her to draw her even closer, her skin hot and silky against mine. Leaning in to steal a kiss, I nudged my knees between her thighs, still trembling from our earlier efforts. She squeaked with surprise, smiling against my lips. "You are a scoundrel yourself, it appears."

As the sun trickled into the room through the slats of the shutters, and Eloise pulled me on top of her with an eager, keening moan, I decided I was perfectly happy being myself. The Rothschilds would have envied me.

I was wealthier than them by far.

THE END

Printed in Great Britain
by Amazon